Praise for *The House Gun*

"One of the great living writers. Her authority, stamped on every paragraph, makes most contemporary novels seem the pale, diluted products of insufficient insight and imagination as she shifts effortlessly from microcosmic intimacy to a vision of an entire country undergoing transformation."
—*San Francisco Chronicle*

"Gordimer is a major literary figure, working at the peak of her craft. . . . *The House Gun* is an awe-inspiring work."
—*Cincinnati News and Observer*

"*The House Gun* is like a well-cut diamond. Its many angles and planes catch the light and illuminate understanding, laying bare the emotions of a people caught in the transition from one world to another."
—*The Orlando Sentinel*

"An intellectual thriller with a soap opera engine. . . . Nothing short of epic."
—*The Baltimore Sun*

"As complex, compelling and memorable an account of race and class as any of her earlier works. . . . A brilliant, beautifully crafted novel of betrayal."
—*Dallas Morning News*

"Exquisitely drawn . . . passionately intelligent, it's more complicated than any detective story. Complicated not so much by plot, it's about the mystery of the human heart."
—*USA Today*

"[Gordimer] has an eye for detail, a feeling for subtle nuance, the ability to convey volumes of information with a few deft strokes that place her firmly in the company of the great novelists."
—*The Houston Chronicle*

"A tense postapartheid family drama as vital as anything she has ever written."   —*Time*

"Fascinating. . . . Gordimer never loses her focus on the dramatic nuances of human character, and her narrative, though related in cool prose, resonates with compassion. . . . The message of this powerful novel rings true."   —*Publishers Weekly*

"[Gordimer] seamlessly, beautifully combines the domestic, the moral and the political . . . a potent mix."
                              —*The Washington Times*

"An empathetic and provocative tale offering much to think about."   —*The Philadelphia Inquirer*

"Intelligent, compassionate and compelling, and it has a lot to say. It touches on politics, prejudice, history, social ills, mental illness. But, at its center is the mystery of the human heart, and for this, it will be read and re-read."
                              —*Memphis Commercial Appeal*

PENGUIN BOOKS

THE HOUSE GUN

Nadine Gordimer, winner of the Nobel Prize in literature in 1991, was born and lives in South Africa. She has written twelve novels, including *My Son's Story*, *A Sport of Nature*, *Burger's Daughter*, *The Conservationist* (cowinner of the Booker Prize in England), and *None to Accompany Me*. Her short stories have been collected in nine volumes, and her nonfiction pieces were published together as *The Essential Gesture*. Gordimer has received numerous international prizes, including, in the United States, the Modern Literature Association Award, and, in 1987, the Bennett Award. Her fiction has appeared in many American magazines, including *The New Yorker*, and her essays have appeared in *The New York Times* and *The New York Review of Books*. She has been given honorary degrees by Yale, Harvard, and other universities and has been honored by the French government with the decoration Officier de l'Ordre des Art et des Lettres. She is a vice president of PEN International and an executive member of the Congress of South African Writers.

ALSO BY NADINE GORDIMER

NOVELS

The Lying Days
A World of Strangers
Occasion for Loving
The Late Bourgeois World
A Guest of Honor
The Conservationist
Burger's Daughter
July's People
A Sport of Nature
My Son's Story
None to Accompany Me

STORIES

The Soft Voice of the Serpent
Six Feet of the Country
Friday's Footprint
Not for Publication
Livingstone's Companions
A Soldier's Embrace
Selected Stories
Something Out There
Jump and Other Stories

ESSAYS

The Black Interpreters
The Essential Gesture—Writing, Politics and Places
(edited by Stephen Clingman)
Writing and Being

OTHER WORKS

On the Mines (with David Goldblatt)
Lifetimes Under Apartheid (with David Goldblatt)

THE
HOUSE
GUN

·

NADINE

GORDIMER

PENGUIN BOOKS

PENGUIN BOOKS

Published by the Penguin Group

Penguin Putnam Inc., 375 Hudson Street, New York, New York 10014, U.S.A.

Penguin Books Ltd, 27 Wrights Lane, London W8 5TZ, England

Penguin Books Australia Ltd, Ringwood, Victoria, Australia

Penguin Books Canada Ltd, 10 Alcorn Avenue, Toronto, Ontario, Canada M4V 3B2

Penguin Books (N.Z.) Ltd, 182–190 Wairau Road, Auckland 10, New Zealand

Penguin India, 210 Chiranjiv Tower, 43 Nehru Place, New Delhi 11009, India

Penguin Books Ltd, Registered Offices: Harmondsworth, Middlesex, England

First published in the United States of America by Farrar, Straus & Giroux, Inc. 1998
Reprinted by arrangement with Farrar, Straus & Giroux, Inc.
Published in Penguin Books 1999

10 9 8 7 6 5 4 3 2 1

The excerpt from Constance Garnett's translation of Fyodor Dostoevsky's *The Idiot* on
page 47 and the excerpt from H. T. Lowe-Porter's translation of Thomas Mann's *The
Magic Mountain* on pages 71–72 are used with permission of Random House, London.
The quotation on page 71 is from Richard Howard's translation of André Pieyre de Man-
diarque's *The Margin*, and is used with permission of Calder Publications, London. The
excerpt from Willa and Edwin Muir's translation of Hermann Broch's *The Sleepwalkers*
that appears on page 142 is used with permission of Pantheon Books, New York. The
passage from Robert Fagles's translation of Homer's *The Odyssey* which appears on page
293 is used with permission of Viking Penguin, New York.

THE LIBRARY OF CONGRESS HAS CATALOGUED THE HARDCOVER AS FOLLOWS:
Gordimer, Nadine.
The house gun / Nadine Gordimer. — 1st ed.
p.   cm.
ISBN 0-374-17307-9 (hc.)
ISBN 0 14 02.7820 6 (pbk.)
I. Title.
PR9369.3.G6H69   1998
823—dc21   97-28787

Printed in the United States of America
Set in Goudy
Designed by Abby Kagan

FOR ORIANE AND HUGO

THE CRIME IS THE PUNISHMENT.

—Amos Oz, *Fima*

PART ONE

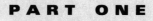

Something terrible happened.

They are watching it on the screen with their after-dinner coffee cups beside them. It is Bosnia or Somalia or the earthquake shaking a Japanese island between apocalyptic teeth like a dog; whatever were the disasters of that time. When the intercom buzzes each looks to the other with a friendly reluctance; you go, your turn. It's part of the covenant of living together. They made the decision to give up the house and move into this townhouse complex with grounds maintained and security-monitored entrance only recently and they are not yet accustomed, or rather are inclined momentarily to forget that it's not the barking of Robbie and the old-fangled ring of the front door bell that summons them, now. No pets allowed in the complex, but luckily there was the solution that theirs could go to their son who has a garden cottage.

He, she—twitch of a smile, he got himself up with languor directed at her and went to lift the nearest receiver. Who, she half-heard him say, half-listening to the commentary following the images, Who. It could be someone wanting to convert to some religious sect, or the delivery of a summons for a parking offence, casual workers did this, moon-lighting. He said something else she didn't catch but she heard the purr of the electronic release button.

What he said then was, Do you know who a Julian-somebody might be? Friend of Duncan?

He, she—they didn't, either of them. Nothing unusual about that, Duncan, twenty-seven years old, had his own circle just as his parents had theirs, and these intersected only occasionally where interests, inculcated in him as a child by his parents, met.

What does he want?

Just said to speak to us.

Both at the same instant were touched by a live voltage of alarm. What is there to fear, defined in the known context of a twenty-seven-year-old in this city—a car crash, a street mugging, a violent break-in at the cottage. Both stood at the door, confronting these, confronting the footsteps they heard approaching their private paved path beneath the crossed swords of Strelitzia leaves, the signal of the second buzzer, and this young man, come from? for? Duncan. He stared at the floor as he came in, so they couldn't read him. He sat down without a word.

He, she—whose turn.

There's been an accident?

She's a doctor, she sees what the ambulances bring in to Intensive Care. If something's broken she can gauge whether it ever can be put together again.

This Julian draws in his lips over his teeth and clamps his mouth, a moment.

A kind of . . . Not Duncan, no no! Someone's been shot. He's arrested. Duncan.

They both stand up.

For God's sake—what are you talking about—what is all this —how arrested, arrested for what—

The messenger is attacked, he becomes almost sullen, unable to bear what he has to tell. The obscene word comes ashamedly from him. Murder.

Everything has come to a stop. What can be understood is a car crash, a street mugging, a violent break-in.

He/she. He strides over and switches off the television. And expels a violent breath. So long as nobody moved, nobody uttered, the word and the act within the word could not enter here. Now with the touch of a switch and the gush of a breath a new calendar is opened. The old Gregorian cannot register this day. It does not exist in that means of measure.

This Julian now tells them that a magistrate was called 'after hours' (he gives the detail with the weight of its urgent gravity) to lay a charge at the police station and bail was refused. That is the practical purpose of his visit: Duncan says, Duncan says, Duncan's message is that there's no point in their coming, there's no point in trying for bail, he will appear in court on Monday morning. He has his own lawyer.

He/she. She has marked the date on patients' prescriptions a dozen times since morning but she turns to find a question that will bring some kind of answer to that word pronounced by the messenger. She cries out.

What day is it today?

Friday.

It was on a Friday.

It is probable that neither of the Lindgards had ever been in a court before. During the forty-eight hours of the weekend of waiting they had gone over every explanation possible in the absence of being able to talk to him, their son, himself. Because of the preposterousness of the charge they felt they had to respect his instruction that they not visit him; this must indicate that the whole business was ridiculous, that's it, horribly ridiculous, his own ridiculous affair, soon to be resolved, better not given the confirmation of being taken in alarm by mother and father arriving at a prison accompanied by their lawyer, states of high emotion etc. That was the way they brought themselves to read his injunction; a mixture between consideration for them—no need to be mixed up in the business—and the independence of the young he had been granted and asserted in mutual understanding since he was an adolescent.

But dread attends the unknown. Dread was a drug that came to them both not out of something administered from her pharmacopoeia; they calmly walked without anything to say to one another along the corridors of the courts, Harald standing back for his wife Claudia with the politeness of a stranger as they found the right door, entered and shuffled awkwardly sideways to be seated on the benches.

The very smell of the place was that of a foreign country to which they were deported. The odour of polished wooden barriers and waxed floor. The windows above head height, sloping down searchlights. The uniforms occupied by men with the impersonality of cult members, all interchangeable. The presence of a few figures seated somewhere near, the kind who stare from park benches or lie face-down in public gardens. The mind dashes from what confronts it, as a bird that has flown into a confined space does, there must be an opening. Harald collided against the awareness of school, too far back to be consciously remembered; institutional smell and hard wood under his buttocks. Even the name of a master was blundered into; nothing from the past could be more remote than this present. In a flick of attention he saw Claudia rouse from her immobility to disconnect the beeper that kept her in touch with her surgery. She felt the distraction and turned her head to read his oblique glance: nothing. She gave the stiff smile with which one greets somebody one isn't sure one knows.

He comes up from the well of a stairway between two policemen. Duncan. Can it be? He has to be recognized in a persona that doesn't belong to him, as they know him, have always known him—and who could identify him better? He is wearing black jeans and a black cotton T-shirt. The kind of clothes he customarily wears, but the neat collar of a white shirt is turned down outside the neck of the T-shirt. They both notice this, it's an unspoken focus of attention between them; this is the detail, token submission to the conventions expected by a court, that makes the connection of reality between the one they knew, *him*, and this other, flanked by policemen.

A blast of heat came over Harald, confusion like anxiety or anger, but neither. Some reaction that never before has had occasion to be called up.

Duncan, yes. He looked at them, acknowledging himself.

Claudia smiled at him with lifted head, for everyone to see. And he inclined his head to her. But he did not look at his parents directly again during the proceedings that followed, except as his controlled, almost musing glance swept over them as it went round the public gallery across the two young black men with their legs sprawled relaxedly before them, the old white man sitting forward with his head in his hands, and the family group, probably wandered in bewildered to pass the time before a case that concerned them came up, who were whispering among themselves of their own affairs.

The magistrate made his stage entrance, all fidgeted to their feet, sank again. He was tall or short, bald or not—doesn't matter, there was the hitch of shoulders under the voluminous gown and, his hunch lowered over papers presented to him, he made a few brief comments in the tone of questions addressed to the tables in the well of the court where the backs of what presumably were the prosecutor and defence lawyer presented themselves to the gallery. Under the ladders of light tilted down, policemen on errands came in and out conferring in hoarse whispers, the rote of proceedings concluded. Duncan Peter Lindgard was committed for trial on a charge of murder. A second application for bail was refused.

Over. But beginning. The parents approached the barrier between the gallery and the well of the court and were not prevented from contact with the son. Each embraced him while he kept his head turned from their faces.

Do you need anything?

It's just not on, the young lawyer was saying, I'm serving notice to contest the refusal, right now, Duncan. I won't let the prosecutor get away with it. Don't worry.

This last said to her, the doctor, in exactly the tone of reassurance she herself would use with patients of whose prognosis she herself was not sure.

The son had an air of impatience, the shifting gaze of one who wished the well-meaning to leave; an urgent need of some preoccupation, business with himself. They could read it to mean confidence; of his innocence—of course; or it could be a cover for dread, akin to the dread they had felt, concealing his dread out of pride, not wanting to be associated with theirs. He was now officially an accused, on record as such. The accused has a status of dread that is his own, hasn't he!

Nothing?

I'll see to everything Duncan needs—the lawyer squeezed his client's shoulder as he swung a briefcase and was off.

If there was nothing, then . . .

Nothing. Nothing they could ask, not *what is it all about,* what is it you did, you are supposed to have done?

His father took courage: Is he really a competent lawyer? We could get someone else. Anyone.

A good friend.

I'll get in touch with him later, find out what happened when he saw the prosecutor.

The son will know that his father means money, he'll be ready to supply surety for the contingency that it is impossible to believe has arisen between them, money for bail.

He turns away—the prisoner, that's what he is now—in anticipation of the policemen's move to order him to, he doesn't want them to touch him, he has his own volition, and his mother's clasp just catches the ends of his fingers as he goes.

They see him led down the stairwell to whatever is there beneath the court. As they make to leave Court B17 they become aware that the other friend, the messenger Julian, has been standing just behind them to assure Duncan of his presence but not wanting to intrude upon those with the closest claims. They greet him and walk out together with him but do not speak. He feels guilty about his mission, that night, and hurries ahead.

As the couple emerge into the foyer of the courts, vast and lofty cathedral echoing with the susurration of its different kind of suppliants gathered there, Claudia suddenly breaks away, disappearing towards the sign indicating toilets. Harald waits for her among these people patient in trouble, no choice to be otherwise, for them, he is one of them, the wives, husbands, fathers, lovers, children of forgers, thieves and murderers. He looks at his watch. The whole process has taken exactly one hour and seven minutes.

She returns and they quit the place.

Let's have a coffee somewhere.

Oh . . . there are patients at the surgery, expecting me.

Let them wait.

She did not have time to get to the lavatory and vomited in the washroom basin. There was no warning; trooping out with all those other people in trouble, part of the anxious and stunned gait, she suddenly felt the clenching of her insides and knew what was going to come. She did not tell him, when she rejoined him, and he must have assumed she had gone to the place for the usual purpose. Medically, there was an explanation for such an attack coming on without nausea. Extreme tension could trigger the seizure of muscles. 'Vomited her heart out': that was the expression some of her patients used when describing the symptom. She had always received it, drily, as dramatically inaccurate.

Let them wait.

What he was saying was to hell with them, the patients, how can their pains and aches and pregnancies compare with this? Everything came to a stop, that night; everything has come to a stop. In the coffee bar an androgynous waiter with long curly hair tied back and tennis-ball biceps hummed his pleasure along with piped music. In the mortuary there was lying the body of a man. They ordered a filter coffee (Harald) and a cappuccino (Claudia). The man who was shot in the head, found dead. Why should it be unexpected that it was a man? Was not that a kind of admittance, already, credence that it could have been done at all? To assume the body would represent a woman, the most common form of the act, *crime passionnel* from the sensational pages of the Sunday papers, was to accept the possibility that it was committed, entered at all into a life's context. *His*. The random violence of night streets they had expected to read in the stranger's face of the messenger, this was the hazard that belongs there, along with the given eternals, the risks of illness, failure of ambition, loss of love. These are what those responsible for an existence recognize they expose it to. To kill a woman out of jealous passion; for it to come to mind—shamefully, in acceptance of newspaper banality—was to allow even that the very nature of such acts could breach the prescribed limits of that life's context.

We're not much the wiser.

She didn't answer. Her eyebrows lifted as she reached for the packets of sugar. Her hand was trembling slightly, privately, from the recent violent convulsion of her body. If he noticed he did not remark upon it.

They now understood what they had expected from *him*: outrage at the preposterous—thing—accusation, laid upon him. Against his presence there between two policemen before a magistrate. They had expected to have him burst forth at the sight of them—that was what they were ready for, to tell them—what? Whatever he could, within the restriction of that room with the policemen hovering and the clerks scratching papers together and the gallery hangers-on dawdling past. That his being there was crazy, they must get him out immediately, importune officials, protest—what? Tell them. Tell them. Some explanation. How could it be thought that this situation was possible.

A good friend.

The lawyer a good friend. And that was all. His back as he went down the stairs, a policeman on either side. Now, while Harald stretched a leg so that he could reach coins in his pocket, *he* was in a confine they had never seen, a cell. The body of a man was in a mortuary. Harald left a tip for the young man who was humming. The petty rituals of living are a daze of continuity over what has come to a stop.

I'll insist on getting to the bottom of it this afternoon.

They were walking to their car through the continuum of the

city, separated and brought side by side again by the narrowing and widening of the pavements in relation to other people going about their lives, the vendors' spread stock of small pyramids of vegetables, chewing gum, sunglasses and second-hand clothes, the gas burners on which sausages like curls of human gut were frying.

In the afternoon she couldn't let them wait. It was the day come round for her weekly stint at a clinic. Doctors like herself, in private practice, were expected to meet the need in areas of the city and the once genteel white suburbs of the old time where in recent years there was an influx, a great rise in and variety of the population. She had regularly fulfilled this obligation; now conscientiousness goaded her, over what had come to a stop; she went to her clinic instead of accompanying Harald to the lawyer. Perhaps this also was to keep herself to the conviction that what had happened could not be? It was not a day to examine motives; just follow the sequence set out in an appointments register. She put on her white coat (she is a functionary, as the magistrate is hunched in his gown) and entered the institutional domain familiar to her, the steaming sterilizer with its battery of precise instruments for every task, the dancing show of efficiency of the young District Nurse with her doll's white starched crown pinned atop her dreadlocks. Some of the patients did not have words, in English, to express what they felt disordered within them. The nurse translated when necessary, relaying the doctor's questions, switching easily from one mother tongue to another she shared with these patients, and relaying their answers.

The procession of flesh was laid before the doctor. It was her medium in which she worked, the abundant black thighs reluctantly parted in modesty (the nurse chaffed the women, Mama, doctor's a woman just like you), the white hairy paps of old men under auscultation. The babies' tender bellies slid under her palms; tears of terrible reproach bulged from their eyes when she had to thrust the needle into the soft padding of their upper arms, where muscle had not yet developed. She did it as she performed any necessary procedure, with all her skill to avoid pain.

Isn't that the purpose?

There is plenty of pain that arises from within; this woman with a tumour growing in her neck, plain to feel it under experienced fingers, and then the usual weekly procession of pensioners hobbled by arthritis.

But the pain that comes from without—the violation of the flesh, a child is burned by an overturned pot of boiling water, or a knife is thrust. A bullet. This piercing of the flesh, the force, ram of a bullet deep into it, steel alloy that breaks bone as if shattering a teacup—she is not a surgeon but in this violent city she has watched those nuggets delved for and prised out on operating tables, they retain the streamline shape of velocity itself, there is no element in the human body that can withstand, even dent, a bullet—those who survive recall the pain differently but all accounts agree: an assault. The pain that is the product of the body itself; its malfunction is part of the self: somewhere, a mystery medical science cannot explain, the self is responsible. But this— the bullet: the pure assault of pain.

The purpose of a doctor's life is to defend the body against the violence of pain. She stands on the other side of the divide from those who cause it. The divide of the ultimate, between death and life.

This body whose interior she is exploring with a plastic-gloved hand like a diviner's instinctively led to a hidden water-source, has a foetus, three months of life inside it.

I'm telling you true. I was never so sick with the others. Every morning, sick as a dog.

Vomit your heart out.

D'you think that means it's a boy, doctor? The patient has the mock coyness women often affect towards a doctor, the consulting room is their stage with a rare chance for a little performance. Ag, my husband'd be over the moon. But I tell him, if we don't come through with it right this time, I don't know about you, I'm giving up.

The doctor obliges by laughing with her.

We could do a simple test if you want to know the sex.

Oh no, it's God's will.

Next come a succession of the usual heart ailments and bronchial infections. Life staggers along powered by worn bellows of old people's lungs and softly pulses visibly between the ribs of a skinny small boy. Some who turn up this week as every week have eyes narrowed by the gross fatty tissue of their faces and others continue to present the skin infections characteristic of malnutrition. They eat too much or they have too little to eat. It's comparatively easy to prescribe for the first because they have the remedy in themselves. For the second, what is prescribed is denied them by circumstances outside their control. Green vegetables and fresh fruit—they are too poor for the luxury of these remedies, what they have come to the clinic for is a bottle of medicine. The doctor knows this but she has ready a supply of diet sheets which propose meals made with various pulses as some sort of substitute for what they should be able to eat. She hands a sheet encouragingly to the woman who has brought her two grandchildren to the doctor. Their scarred grey-filmed legs are bare but despite the heat they watch the doctor from under thick woollen caps that cover the sores on their heads and come down right to the eyebrows. The woman doesn't need the nurse to interpret, she can read the sheet and studies it slowly at arm's length in the manner of ageing people becoming far-sighted. She folds it carefully. Her time is up. She shepherds the children to the door. She thanks the doctor. I don't know what I can get. Maybe I can try buy some these things. The father, he's still in jail. My son.

Charge sheet. Indictment. Harald kept himself at a remove of cold attention in order to separate what was evidence against interpretation of that evidence. Circumstantial: that day, that night, Friday, 19th January, 1996, a man was found dead in a house he shared with two other men. David Baker and Nkululeko 'Khulu' Dladla came home at 7.15 p.m. and found the body of their friend Carl Jespersen in the living-room. He had a bullet wound in the head. He was lying half-on, half-off the sofa, as if (interpretation) he had been taken by surprise when shot and had tried to rise. He was wearing thonged sandals, one of which was twisted, hanging off his foot, and beneath a towelling dressing-gown he was naked. There were glasses on an African drum beside the sofa. One held the dregs of what appeared to have been a mixture known as a Bloody Mary—an empty tin of tomato juice and a bottle of vodka were on top of the television set. The other glasses were apparently unused; there was an unopened bottle of whisky and a bucket of half-melted ice on a tray on the floor beside the drum. (Evidence combined with interpretation.) There was no unusual disorder in the room; this is a casual bachelor household. (Interpretation.) The room was in darkness except for the pin-point light of the CD player that had come to the end of a disc and not been switched off. The front door was locked but glass doors which led from the living-room to the garden were open, as they generally would be in summer, even after dark.

The garden is one in which a cottage is sited. The cottage is occupied by Duncan Lindgard, a mutual friend of the dead man and the two men who discovered him, and they ran to him after they had discovered Jespersen's body. Lindgard's dog was asleep outside the cottage and apparently there was no-one at home. The police came about twenty minutes later. A man, a plumber's assistant, Petrus Ntuli, who occupied an outhouse on the property in exchange for work in the garden, was questioned and said he had seen Lindgard come out on the verandah of the house drop something as he crossed the garden to the cottage thought he would retrieve whatever it was, for Lindgard, not find anything. He called out to Lindgard but Lindgard already entered the cottage. Ntuli did not have a watch not say what time this was, but the sun was down. The police searched the garden and found a gun in a clump of fern. Baker and Dladla immediately identified it as the gun kept in the house as mutual protection against burglars; neither could recall in which of their three names it was licensed. The police proceeded to the cottage. There was no response to knocking on the door, but Ntuli insisted that Lindgard was inside. The police then effected entry by forcing the kitchen door and found that Lindgard was in the bedroom. He seemed dazed. He said he had been asleep. Asked whether he knew his friend Carl Jespersen had been attacked, he went white in the face (interpretation) and demanded, Is he dead?

He then protested about the police invasion of his cottage and insisted that he be allowed to make several telephone calls, one of which was to his lawyer. The lawyer evidently advised him not to resist arrest and met him at the police station where fingerprint tests were inconclusive because the clump of fern had been watered recently and the fingerprints on the gun were largely obliterated by mud.

This is not a detective story.

Harald has to believe that the mode of events that genre represents is actuality.

This is the sequence of actions by which a charge of murder is arrived. When he recounts to Claudia what he heard from the lawyer she moves her head from side to side at each stage of detail and does not interrupt. He has the impression she is hearing him out; yet when he has finished, she says nothing. He sees, from her silence, he has said nothing; brought back nothing that would explain. Duncan came out of that man's house and dropped something in the garden on his way back to his cottage. A gun was found. Duncan said he was asleep and did not hear either his friends or the police when they knocked at the door. None of this tells anything more, gives any more explanation than there was in the confrontation across the barrier in court. His brief embrace with head turned away. His reply to any need: nothing. Harald sees, informed by Claudia's presence, that what he has related, to himself and her, is indeed a crude whodunnit.

Bail application by the good friend cocksure lawyer had been again refused.

But why? Why? All she can call to mind is some unquestioned accepted reasoning that one who is likely to commit another crime cannot be let loose on the mere security of money. Duncan, a danger to society! For god's sake, why?

The prosecutor's got wind of some idea that he might disappear—leave.

The country?

Now they are in the category of those who buy themselves out of retribution because they can afford to put up bail and then estreat. He did not know whether she understood this implication of refusal, for their son and themselves.

Where does the idea come from?

The girl's been called for questioning, apparently she said he's been threatening to take up a position he's been offered with a practice in Singapore. I don't know—to get away from her, it sounds like. Something she let slip, maybe intentionally. Who can fathom what was going on between them.

If Claudia is dissatisfied with what little Harald has learned in explanation, could she have been more successful? Well, let her try, then.

An awaiting-trial prisoner has the right to visits. Her turn: I'd like to talk to that Julian whatever-his-name, before we go.

Harald knows that both have an irrational revulsion against contact with the young man: don't kill the messenger, the threat is the message.

Claudia is not the only woman with a son in prison. Since this afternoon she has understood that. She is no longer the one who doles out comfort or its placebos for others' disasters, herself safe, untouchable, in another class. And it's not the just laws that have brought about this form of equality; something quite other. There's no sentimentality in this, either, which is why she will not speak of it to anyone, not even to the one who is the father of a son in prison; it might be misinterpreted.

She telephoned the lawyer to obtain the number of the messenger who had presented himself at the townhouse security gate and entered at the hour of after-dinner coffee. She was adamant, Harald could hear as she reached the messenger, that he should come back that evening. Not tomorrow. Now.

This time when he opened the door to the messenger, Harald offered his hand to him: Julian Verster. Claudia had noted down the name.

How did they seem to him? The occasion had no precedent to go by; a social occasion, an inquisition, an appeal—what kind of hospitality is this, what signifying arrangements are appropriate, as the provision of tea or drinks set out, the placing of ashtrays and arrangement of a comfortable chair signify the nature of other occasions. Everything in its customary place in the room; that in itself inappropriate, even bizarre.

Their attitude towards him had changed, overcome by need. They saw in this young man the possibility of some answers, they might read even in his appearance something of the context in which what had happened could happen. Everyone wears the uniform of how he sees himself or how he disguises himself. Bulky running shoes with intricate embellishments, high tongues and thick soles, that cabinet ministers as well as clerks and students wear now, and Harald himself, at leisure, wears; pitted skin on the cheeks, the tribal marks of adolescent acne, wide-spaced dog's-

brown eyes darkened by heavy eyebrows authoritatively contra-
dicting the uncertainties of a mouth that moves, shaping and
reshaping itself before he speaks. A face that suggests a personality
subservient and loyal: an ideal component of a coterie. In business,
Harald is accustomed to being observant of such things when
meeting prospective associates.

—I'm sorry to have interrupted your plans for the evening, like
this, but when you came that night we were all . . . I don't know
. . . we couldn't say much. It was difficult to take in anything. As
Duncan's friend, you must have felt something the same—it must
have been hard for you to have to come to us. We know that.—

The young man acknowledges with an understanding down-
turn of the lips that this is, in turn, her way of extending a hand
to him.

—I felt awful—that I did it so badly—I couldn't think of any
other way. Awful. And he'd asked me, he left it to me.—

They sat in a close group now. Claudia was turned to him,
sharing the sofa, and Harald drew up a chair, to speak.

—Why didn't he call us himself.—

But it was a judgment rather than a question.

—Oh Harald . . . that's obvious.—

—He was terribly shocked, you can't imagine.—

—That was at the police station?—

—No, the house, he reached me on my cell phone and I just
turned round in the middle of the road, where I was . . . he was
still with the police at the house, the cottage.—

Claudia's knees and hands matched, tight together, hands on
knees. —You went to the house.—

—Yes. I saw. I couldn't believe it.—

To them, what was seen is the man in the mortuary (Claudia
knows the post-mortem procedure; the body may be kept for days
before the process is performed). But—there in his face—to this
Julian Verster what was seen was his friend, as Duncan is his friend.
This realization makes it possible to begin to say what it is they
want of him. Out of some instinctive agreement, neither has any

right above the other, they question him alternately; they've found a formula, at least some structure they have put together for themselves in the absence of any precedent.

—Could you give us an idea of how, at all, Duncan could have been mixed up in this, how his—what shall I say?—his position as some sort of tenant, his relationship to the men in the house —these friends—could have led to the *circumstantial* evidence there seems to be against him? I was at the lawyer's today. You belong to that group of friends, don't you? We don't know any of them, really—

Claudia turned to Harald, but with eyes distantly lowered for the interjection. —Except the girl, his girl-friend, he's brought her with him once or twice, here. But apparently she wasn't there on Friday. She's not been mentioned.—

—Could you tell us something about the friendship, they all more or less share the property, they must have got on well with one another, to decide to do that, live in such close proximity— what could lead to Duncan being accused of such a horror? You must understand we've lived, my wife and I, parents and son, as three independent adults, we're close but we don't expect to be privy to everything in his life. Different relationships. We have ours with him, he has his with others. It's been fine. But when something like this falls on your head—we understand what this —respect, I suppose, for one another, can mean. Just that we don't know anything we need to know. Who was this man? What did Duncan have to do with him? You must know! We can't go to see Duncan tomorrow and ask him, can we? In a prison visitors' room? Warders there, who else—

—We've all been friends quite a long time, well certainly Dave, he studied architecture along with Duncan, and so did I—I'm with Duncan in the same firm. But I didn't join them when they took the house and the cottage together. Khulu's a journalist, I think Duncan got to know him first, when Khulu wanted to move into town from Tembisa. Carl, Carl Jespersen— (it is difficult to speak of, or hear spoken of, in the tone of ordinary information, a man lying in a mortuary) Jespersen came I think about two years ago with a Danish—or maybe it was Norwegian—film crew and somehow he didn't go back. He works—was working with an advertising agency. The three of them took the main house and Duncan took the cottage. But they more or less run the whole place together. I mean, I'm often there, it's pretty much open house, some good times.—

There are his inhibitions to be overcome; his loyalty, the prized confidentiality bestowed upon the messenger by the privilege of friendship with one he admires or who is, perhaps, professionally cleverer than he. What is emerging is an aside: the nature of his relationship with their son. It is difficult not to become impatient.

—So everyone got on well together, all right. There were no real tensions you know of? How serious they would have to be if we are to believe that Duncan, *Duncan* . . . ! Never mind the gun, never mind what the man in the garden says he saw! Isn't there someone else who really did have what he thought was a reason to attack Jespersen? Why Duncan? Anyone you know of?—

Harald's line of thought scored across hers.

—Where was the girl. Where was she on Friday? Has the affair broken up, were she and Duncan no longer lovers?—

The young man has to adjust himself to communication with a father who does not require the euphemism 'girl-friend' as suitable in communication with parents.

—They're still together. Of course you know—she was there. The day before, Thursday night. We all ate at the house. Carl and David cooked for everyone.—

Was there nothing more to say? To be got from him; he is the messenger, he must not know more than the text he has been entrusted with.

Claudia drops her hands at her sides; the fingers stir. —Please tell us.—

Harald stands up.

The young man looked from one to the other as if for mercy, and then began in the only way he could manage, the dull defused tone of one relating the circumstances of a traffic accident in which no-one was hurt: the matter-of-factness that defends cornered emotion.

—Last year, in June, Carl got her a job at the advertising agency and they began to go to work in her car every day. Or sometimes in his. I don't know the arrangement. So they'd often have lunch somewhere together, too. But it was all right.—

—What do you mean?— Harald is looking down at him.

—Duncan didn't mind. Didn't have anything to worry about.—

—Didn't mind that his lover was spending all day with another man?—

—Well, Carl and David were lovers. The three of them in the house are gay, Khulu too. Gay men are often very good friends to women, and they're no threat to women's lovers, you know that, of course. Carl and Duncan and Natalie are great friends. Special friends, in the group around the house. They were.—

—I see.—

But Harald, conscious that this is the reaction of himself as a heterosexual man, does not see how Duncan could not resent his woman spending her days with another male, no matter what sex was attractive to that male. His monosyllabic response opens the way, to him and to Claudia, for the return of dread, the dread that came with the pronouncement of the first message, that night; that Friday.

—Please tell us.—

It's a knell that Claudia sounds.

—On Thursday we all stayed quite late up at the house. There were some other people there, a couple of Khulu's friends as well. When we left, and Khulu'd gone off with his crowd, I walked with Duncan back to the cottage. Natalie had volunteered to help Carl with the washing-up, David had had a few drinks too many and went to bed. But apparently when everything was tidied up in the kitchen, Natalie didn't go to the cottage. Duncan woke up around two o'clock and saw she wasn't there with him. He was worried something might have happened to her, crossing the garden in the dark, and he went over to the house. Yes. Carl was making love to her in the living-room. Duncan didn't arrive at work on Friday morning and he called me at the office. He told me. He said he found them on the sofa—that sofa, you know. What can I say. It wasn't the first time Natalie had had some sort of thing going on the side with someone else—I know, we all knew, of one, at least. It's in her nature, but I think she loves him—Duncan. In her way. And he—he's absolutely faithful to her, completely possessive, other women don't exist for Duncan. Recriminations and tears— the usual thing—and then she comes back to him. But this time —Carl. A man who doesn't love women, but goes for Natalie. To put it crudely. Makes Natalie the exception, leaves his lover asleep in the bedroom and makes love to Natalie on that sofa. Duncan was—I can't describe it, a terrible state. She wouldn't come back to the cottage, I suppose she was afraid of him. She left. Got in her car and left in the middle of the night, and she didn't come back on Friday, either. She wasn't there. When whatever happened, happened. So that is all I know, and I'm not saying Duncan must have done what he's supposed to have done, I'm not implying anything, I won't have you thinking that what I've told you is conclusive, I wasn't there, I didn't see, although I know Duncan well, your son, I don't know what went on inside him—

They are all three on their feet now, it's as if again something for which there is no preparation is going to happen, the atmospheric pressure of that house where Duncan enters, the other man alone on that sofa drinking a Bloody Mary, is produced by them, overcomes them, as anxiety can produce an outbreak of sweat on the body. But it cannot be admitted; it has to be transformed into something understandable, that can be dealt with under control. The messenger is about to wheel his steed around and leave: that's it. He cannot withstand, he has had enough of, their need.

—Don't go.— Claudia appeals, although he has made no move. So it's accepted; all that was going to happen was that he was going to walk out on them. She opens her hands in a gesture towards where they were seated, and takes her place.

In order to keep him with them they turn to discussion of practical matters. The possibility of yet another application for bail, once the case comes up for a first hearing; the conditions under which an awaiting-trial prisoner is kept. There is much, he and they know, they could continue to ask and he could tell about that house with the sofa, and the cottage, and the tracing of their son's life there, but the young man is clearly in conflict between what is, they feel, an obligation to them, and a betrayal of the codes of friendship. The closest way they can come to this area is to ask whether lately Duncan seemed under any particular strain, say, at work (which is not a context of intimacy). Did it show, there? This was as far as Harald could go in approaching any long-term distraught state of mind that might have existed in the cottage.

—Duncan's a strong person.—

That might satisfy Harald but Claudia jerked her head away from the two men. —You work with him in the same office, d'you mean it's simply that he conceals his moods, his feelings? Even from you? He called you, talked to you on the phone, on Friday.—

—If we feel like discussing something, we do; if one of us doesn't want it, we don't. We let it go.—

—He's always been a reserved person. It might have been better if he had talked before.—

—Reserved, how can you say that, Harald—he's always been affectionate and open—you didn't expect him to discuss his love affairs with you?—

They were talking of their son, Julian Verster's friend, as if he were dead. To be in prison is to be dead to connection with consciousness outside, to exist there only in the past tense. Appalled silence interrupted them. Harald gave Claudia the look that in familiar signals between them, suggested they should give the young man a drink. She seemed uncomprehending, not to be approached. He fetched glasses and bottles, cans of soda and fruit juice, the usual habit of hospitality. The filled glasses gave them something to do with their hands; if they could not speak they could swallow.

—I don't remember ever seeing him drink whisky.— They followed her: to the bottle of whisky, the unused glass, and the bucket of ice beside that sofa.

Before he left, it was safe to ask whether as a friend (close as he evidently is) Julian Verster can suggest anything in particular that they might take with them on the visit the next day.

Nothing, of course. Nothing.

Awake in the night, there is enactment of what might take place. Instead of the landscapes of dreams, darkness forms the prison, steel grilles, keys (maybe now there is electronically controlled security, like the green or red eyes that signal or bar right of entry or egress through bank doors). If they had never been in court before, it is certain that neither had ever been inside a prison. The structure comes from the narrowing perspective of corridors in scenes from television films, the eyes through Judas apertures, with a sound-track of heavy echoes, since of all the sough of ordinary life, the conversation of birds, humans, traffic, only shouts and the cymbal of boots striking concrete floors remain. The wearers of the boots don't have to be dreamed; they already have been encountered in Court B17; young men with open-air faces who stand by in stolid inattention with the expression of contented preoccupation with their own private lives while crime and punishment are decreed. The cell—but prison visitors won't see the cells, there will be a visitors' room, the cells will be like whatever it is to which the prisoner went down under the well of the court: unknown. There is no privacy more inviolable than that of the prisoner. To visualize that cell in which he is thinking, to reach what he alone knows; that is a blank in the dark.

You can't sleep, either.

Beside her, he doesn't answer. But she hears from his breathing—it does not have the familiar rhythm—that Harald is not asleep. In the dark, his attention is too concentrated to respond. That is all. He, too, has an inviolable privacy: he is praying. Harald is what is known as a great reader, which means a searcher after something that is ambitiously called the truth; both conditional concepts he would be the first, amusedly, to concede. He has tried, over years, through different formulations he has come upon, to explain prayer to her in a way that would be understandable to someone without religious faith, and the nearest he has come to this was to offer Simone Weil's definition of prayer as a heightened form of intelligent concentration. When she questioned the proviso 'intelligent'—what else could concentration be?—he satisfied her uncertainty by pointing out that there exists the possibility of a bug-eyed concentration on something trivial, which does not imply intelligence in the religious and philosophical sense. Prayer as a form of intelligent concentration is secularized in a way Claudia has had to accept. She has done this by separating the intelligent concentration from to whom or what it is addressed; then it is not a communication with a supposedly existing God, but a heightened means of communicating with one's own resources in solution of guidance through fears, failures and sorrows.

Harald is praying. His prayer enters the enactment of what will take place tomorrow. She lies in the dark beside him. What is he praying for? Is he praying that their son did not do what he is accused of? If Harald needs to pray for this, does that mean he believes what he cannot say, that his son killed a man?

They got up earlier than they would do routinely on a working day. There was time to fill before the opening hours of admittance. They passed pages of the newspaper back and forth between them, reading the continuation of crises whose earlier episodes they had been watching when the messenger came. For him, the photograph of a child clinging to the body of its dead mother and the report of a night of mortar fire sending nameless people randomly to the shelter of broken walls and collapsing cellars was suddenly part of his own life no longer outside but within the parameters of disaster. The news was his news. For her, these events were removed, even farther than they had been by distance, further than they had been in relevance to her life, by the message that had interrupted them: private disaster means to drop out of the rest of the world.

He went and hung about in the small garden allotted, walled and maintained, within the landscaping of the townhouse complex; the intricately paved path under the Strelitzias was covered in a few steps, back and forth. Nowhere to go. Where he stood, the angle of the sun struck into flame orange and blue wings of blooms perched like birds. She was in the kitchen, occupying herself with something. When it was time, she appeared with a plastic bowl covered with tinfoil which she placed on the floor of the passenger seat. While he drove she steadied the bowl between her sandalled feet.

I suppose they'll allow this.

He rocked his head uncertainly. Awaiting trial, maybe.

It's just a salad and some cheese.

Of course. Women, only women, have this sort of resource. They think of how to ameliorate. He was subliminally aware of tenderness and scorn, not for her so much as for them all, poor things; to be envious of.

At that place, the prison, to which they were inescapably headed, they were received with the kind of courtesy that is learnt in public relations training of a new police force intended to obliterate the tradition of the racist and brutal authority of the past. Anyway, the officer in charge is an Afrikaner, himself a middle-aged man with all that implies of adult children, parental burdens, family sentiments etc. he would assume in common with a white couple. Go ahead, he indicates the bowl of food. —But not to worry, he's getting a good diet, everything. And you can take his washing and so on, nê.—

Prison is a normal place. That is what they don't know; the officer has a computer and several kinds of telephones, regular and cellular, in his bureau and there is a basket of flowering indoor plants with its bunch of plastic ribbons that has no doubt marked an anniversary or other celebration. The echoing corridors from the night's darkness are there but these are ways they will not go down; they are led by the strong buttocks of a young black policeman to a nearby room. It is right that there is nothing to characterize that room; if there is, they don't see it. It's the space, closed off from all that is recognizable in life, where they sit on two chairs facing a table on the other side of which is their son. Duncan. It's Duncan come from the echoing corridors, come from the cell, come from what he contemplates, in himself, there. His spread hands hit the table as they enter, as if striking chords on a piano and he's smiling in a warning, there is to be no emotionalism. Signals fly like bats about the room. Don't ask me. We only want to know what to do. I need to see you. If you don't tell us. I don't want to see you. Whatever: have to know. You can't know. At least how did it. You don't have to get mixed up. You can't keep us out. Don't ask for what you won't be able to take. Come. I want to see you. Don't come.

Even here—this place that surely cannot exist for these three —there has to be a premise on which spoken communication can take place. The bats must be fought back to the dark from which they come, the cell, the wakeful night. There can be only one premise, one set by the parents: he did not do it. He is, in the vocabulary of the law, innocent, even though they are prepared to believe, they now must know, he is not innocent in the sense of the context of the awful event, the kind of milieu in which it could take place. For it *to have come about* implies that they have to rearrange life in that house and cottage of young friends as they had pictured it, rearrange the furniture of human relations there, Duncan among compatible friends, just a stretch of pleasant garden away, living with a girl in what might or might not become a permanent liaison.

Duncan is not innocent, but he cannot be guilty. The crucial matter, then, is the lawyer; again there must be the best lawyer. That decision they are not prepared to leave to him, they will be adamant about this, mother and father.

The lawyer, the good friend, they met in Court B17 has briefed a top Senior Counsel, someone, he says, in the class of Bizos and Chaskalson—Hamilton Motsamai.

That is all their son says, he does not give reassurance; only the assurance that he will be defended by what they wanted, the most capable individual available. He does not tell them; he does not tell that he will be safe because he is not guilty of the death of the man on the sofa. This has become a delicate matter that cannot be brought up, as if it were some prying question into a son's sex life. And indeed—about the girl, of course the subject of the girl can't be mentioned, although surely she may be needed to give valuable evidence of some sort, she must know she was not worth killing for, that kind of act isn't in the range of emotional control in which their son's character was formed, or the contemporary ethic that men don't own women. Therefore the act could not have been committed. A gun in the mud. Someone else throws it there. A gardener thinks Duncan has dropped something, perhaps it was a cigarette butt discarded, and the police come upon a gun. What they burn to ask their son is: does he know why the man was killed? But that, too, is not possible, for different reasons: the warder, the policeman, is there as the three chairs and table are, but one must remember that the warder hears although his face is composed in the sulky distance of incomprehension: what the answer might be could be used in damaging evidence, the nature of some circle—how could they know—in which the son moves. Once grouped around an act of violence, anything and everything becomes suspicious.

At least, as a doctor, she has something to say.

—How much exercise are you getting? Do you manage to sleep all right?—

Either to satisfy them or in defiance, he makes light of this concern. —Well, it's not the five-star accommodation I'd recommend.— He laughs. This room is not used to laughter; it comes back at them from the walls as a cry. —There's some sort of yard I walk around twice a day. Oh—about the dog. I suppose Khulu or someone is feeding him, but—

—Because I can speak to the medical officer and prescribe a mild sleeping pill. And better exercise facilities.—

—No. Don't. It's not necessary. What about the dog?—

This is something for his father; these parents are appealing for tasks.

—I'll find a solution; I'll fetch him. And books?—

—Philip has brought me a few and I can buy newspapers. But you could get some of mine. From the cottage—and clothes.—

—What about a key?—

—Khulu.—

Time must be nearly up, this produces a new height of awkwardness in the awareness of each of the three: the dread of his going back down the corridors of concrete and steel and their driving away to leave him abandoned there; and the shameful impatience to have the visit come to an end.

The warder signals. The parents don't know whether to linger or quickly leave; what the protocol is for this kind of parting, what makes it endurable. They embrace him and his father feels a hand press three times on his shoulder-blade. As their son is led away, there's an aside, delaying for a moment the warder who accompanies him. —Don't bring anything I was in the middle of reading.—

What he must think of us!

Think of us?

Well, what did we say to him? So cold, matter-of-fact.

He glanced aside from the road ahead and saw her hands in her lap, the thumbnail of one twisting beneath the short fingernails of the other.

What could be said?

The warder standing there. We'll have to see if we can't meet him alone with the lawyer, lawyers have privileges of consulting privately with the person they represent.

That's not it.

The capsule in which they were contained moving between the irreconcilables, prison and life, was suddenly filled with their voices let loose. The fact is, we don't know what it is we ought to be discussing.

We don't know what his entanglement is in this whole terrible—thing—he doesn't give any sign. He says he's going to have a first-class advocate but we don't have any idea of what he's going to give *him*; what line of defence the advocate's going to be able to follow, what he's going to prove, when he pleads.

What about the advocate.

They had heard it at once, in the shock of the name; the choice of a black man. She's not one of those doctors who touch black skin indiscriminately along with white, in their work, but retain liberal prejudices against the intellectual capacities of blacks. Yet she *is* questioning, and he is; in the muck in which they are stewing now, where murder is done, old prejudices still writhe to the surface. Looking at the appointment of someone called Motsamai that way, he can find an answer within its context.

Could be an advantage. If there's one of the black judges on the bench.

His voice is dry: that he should be thinking like this. Ashamed. And why should such a calculation come to mind—a black judge inclined to think better of an accused because he has chosen a black advocate—when we are not talking here of a criminal, a murderer, appearing before him. Where does such a thought come from, for God's sake!

But do you know anything about him? Maybe he's just another good friend.

We can make some enquiries. I'll talk to someone at the top, I've met him a few times, he'll understand although it's not usual to expect one advocate to pass an opinion on another, I suppose.

Damn what's usual. I'm trying to think. What else should we be doing, Harald? Just sat there—chatting. Chatting. You might at least have assured him we'll pay for the lawyers, anything. How do we know whether fees didn't come into the choice? These senior counsel cost a fortune a day. If he thinks he'll have to find the money himself, it might affect everything.

He knows it's not a question of money. He knows he can depend on us. Not the time or the place to make some kind of magnanimous announcement.

I just thought you'd say . . . his father . . . oh all right, not about money, something—

All you could think of was to prescribe a sleeping pill.

I know. Well at least it was some sort of message that if he wasn't being well treated I'd have pull with whoever the medical officer is. But *something*—

You tell me what we should have said to him.

She hit her thighs with her fists.

That we believe him.

When he says what? He has said nothing. We know nothing. I read the record of circumstantial evidence. The man is dead. A gun in the mud. What does that mean?

While he is speaking she is hammering across his words. That we believe in him! That we believe in him! That there's no possibility, ever, in this world, that we would not! That's what wasn't there, wasn't said—

He was checked in obedience to a traffic light. His hand went down to shift the gear to neutral and she moved slightly to avoid contact with the hand. He waited, with the red light, then spoke.

Believe?

You know.

There was no response.

That we believe he could never do such a thing and we're right about that.

He was carried along with the traffic as if the car drove itself. His head was stirring, almost weaving, in some unshareable conflict, intolerable reluctance.

Claudia—he knew he should qualify the formal use of her name with some intimacy, but the old epithets, the darlings and dearests were out of place in what had to be stated, hard. Begin again.

We don't even know if he accepts that we believe in him.

Accept? Why should he not? What's accepting got to do with it!

He cannot allow it to become real to them both by pronouncing it, the father's voice enunciating it to the mother, but it is there, secreted in the car between them as he arrives at the security gates of the townhouse complex: Because he knows he did what was done. That is why nothing was said in that half-hour in the prison visiting room; the premise we were there on does not exist. That is what our son was conveying to us. That is what there is to believe.

He presses the electronic gadget which lets them into their home but provides no refuge.

The Board of his company has its own prominent firm of legal advisers, one of whom sits on the Board. Harald approaches him for his opinion on all legal matters.

In ordinary circumstances. But he can do now what he would not find proper in ordinary circumstances. He can use the slight acquaintance at public dinners to importune one of the prestigious figures in the legal profession for a confidential opinion of the capability, reputation and status of the advocate Motsamai. He has no compunction in being presumptuous. Such conventions of his life—what do they matter.

Of course the man knows, everyone knows, the story has been a gift to the Sunday papers. But what is he thinking as he listens to the reiteration of facts, my son is accused of murder, there's been a decision to place the case in the hands of Senior Counsel Hamilton Motsamai. My wife and I do not know this person, we have no personal feelings for or against him, we are concerned only with whether he is the best possible professional to act for our son.

Is he interpreting, beneath one of the familiar silences of lawyers, translating the private language of what is not being said: this Senior Counsel is black. Is that it?

But for the moment the question should not be addressed between them; first, to protect the speaker from remarks inimical to the ethics of the profession, there must come a disclaimer: —There would be a number of 'best possible' defence counsel. You understand. I would not place one above the other. But Motsamai is known as eminently capable. And experienced. In his four years back in the country he's appeared successfully in a number of challenging cases. Political, yes—but also of other natures. He has the kind of aggressive spirit—controlled, mind you, by strong intelligence—that puts him on a high level of competence in cross examination. Very clever—some would say exceptional.—

Harald does not need a general opinion, which may be given in the caution of all fairness; he must know what this man himself really thinks. There is no time, no space between cell walls for the dangerous reservations of 'all fairness'. —And you? What would you say?—

It must be impossible to be confronted by Harald Lindgard at this time and not to be shocked—and shock is always within a breath's distance of fear—by what it is that could happen to a man like him; like oneself. The last time they met they were standing around drinks in hand discussing with the Deputy Minister of Finance the pros and cons of lifting foreign exchange controls! Although the man did not know Lindgard more intimately than this, he had to put aside professionalism as if he doffed the black robe he wore in court. —Look, I don't sprinkle exaggerated epithets around, but I can tell you the fellow's remarkable. You don't know anything about his background? I can't remember exactly what part of the country he grew up in, usual thing, a poor lad from uneducated parents, and he managed to get into Fort Hare for his law degree in the late Sixties. Then he was involved in Youth Group political activity, detained. When he was released he fled to England and somehow—scholarships—continued law studies there. Before he came back in '90, he'd been accepted at Gray's Inn and appeared for the defence at the Old Bailey. So there could hardly be any difficulties raised against his getting admitted to the Bar, here. Frankly—you can well imagine, after years when blacks were discounted as brains in the legal profession, now there's considerable eagerness to show credit given where credit is due—in fact, Motsamai is providential . . . a star was needed and he appeared in our constellation . . . He's what the popular press would term much sought-after. Fortunately this isn't just an affirmative action display. No no.—

That may be the concluding statement to be carried away; but Harald senses a weight that keeps him from making to leave.

—You've had doubts about your son's defence being conducted by a black man.—

There it is. Laid out before them, Harald and his distinguished mentor. But it is presented as what might be expected, a simple regression, belched up from the shared dinners of the past.

—We don't have to attribute that doubt to racial prejudice, because it is a fact, incontrovertible fact, that due to racial prejudice in the old regimes, black lawyers have had far less experience than white lawyers, and experience is what counts. They've had fewer chances to prove themselves; it's their disadvantage, and you would not be showing racial prejudice in seeing that disadvantage as yours, if entrusting defence to most of them. If you were to say to me, now, that you still would prefer to have a white counsel— that's a different matter. I should have no comment. You are the one who has the grave burden. I can simply say: with Motsamai you are in good hands. If there's anything else I can do—

Harald feels as he sometimes does when he walks out into the street, the world, after taking communion; a meditative quiet, some sort of certainty, at least, before he takes up to what it must be applied.

It was possible in these early days to get through them with attention fixed ahead in very short span on some action. There was the appointment to meet the Senior Counsel who had been briefed, Hamilton Motsamai.

They came independently to Advocates' Chambers, she from her surgery, he excusing himself from a board meeting of the insurance company where he was a director. They greeted each other absently; only when they were seated side by side across from the broad and deep expanse of the advocate's grand desk did they become the couple, the mother and father, the ominous bond. Motsamai was like his chambers, well-appointed. There was immense self-confidence in his combining the signs of success in a prestigious profession—the intercom instruction to his secretary to hold calls, the group photographs with distinguished Gray's Inn colleagues in London, the library of law books with slips of paper standing up from their pages, marking frequent reference, the presentation plaque on the tray of desk-top accoutrements—with the wisp of beard just under the point of his chin that asserted a specific traditional African style, another order of dignity and distinction. His staccato and fluent English was strongly accented, he retained the drawn-out rounded vowels of African languages and established the right of the reverberating bass murmurs customary to their discourse, in dismissal of those other wordless conjunctions, the ums and ahs of white speakers. A new form of national sophistication. In his elegant grey suit, here is a man who has mastered everything, all contradictions that were imposed upon him by the past. Turning over papers (apparently his notes taken on the brief he has accepted) he glances up now and then at the man and woman before him, the whites of his eyes (he even removes his glasses for a moment, dangles them) strikingly clearcut in his small mahogany face as the glass eyes set in ancient statues. His is a face made by disciplines of the mind, the features drawn closed by concentration, even the mouth, hovering slightly as he responds inwardly to his text, has somewhat tightened its generosity. They study him; whatever is there is what they are dependent on as neither has ever before been dependent on anyone.

His intermittent attention to them was a kind of rehearsal of how to approach what he has to tell them. He had been briefed —in the lay sense, as well—about these clients by the good friend Philip, so knew they were not nobodies—one of the directors of a large insurance firm with a pragmatically enlightened policy towards blacks, and the wife, evidently, a doctor. Educated people to whom he could speak plainly so that they would understand his position: that is, the limitation of his possibilities in undertaking the brief.

—I have talked to your son. Of course I'll be seeing him again, many times. Ah-hêh . . . He is not an easy young man to understand. But I am sure you know that.—

The father was about to speak but the mother preceded him. —No. We've always had a good relationship.—

—What you're saying is now—he's not easy to understand now? Is that it?—

The advocate was nodding, tapping extended fingertips in a

little tattoo of agreement with the father. —Exactly, that is so. But it's only the beginning. There is often—always—difficulty when an individual is in trouble, is in shock. You know (to her) it's like when someone comes to you after an accident, in trauma, just like that.—

—To be told your friend's dead and to be accused of it. Yes.—

The advocate knows the accused's mother is accusing *him*: of being too measured. He's accustomed to this kind of reaction, fear turned to resentment. In her case no doubt exacerbated by the fact that she is accustomed, as he has reminded her, to being the professional adviser instead of the victim. He looks away, flicking aside the shred of irrelevancy.

—Unfortunately. Unfortunately—I have to tell you, when he (a wide gesture) when he opens up, when he begins to co-operate with me—at this moment in time he's somewhat hostile, you know—that is when he and I will have to tackle what there is to face.— He paused, to gauge if they were ready. —I have to tell you that the evidence is overwhelming. Conclusive. With just the exception of the weapon, the question of the dirt, you know, the mud—the fingerprints. But the final report still has to come in, and there are tests that might be able to find matching traces. He's left-handed, that's so? If traces should be found and they match, that will be very serious for us. Very, very. You understand? It would wrap up the prosecution's case. We have to proceed on the assumption that this is going to happen. His hostility is not a good sign. In our experience, it means there is something—everything —to hide. The person doesn't want to co-operate with the lawyer because he doesn't believe the lawyer can do anything for him.—

—He's guilty.—

Counsel received the father's interjection with the approval of an instructor for a pupil.

—The person believes or knows he's guilty, that's right.—

This man with his glib use of the grandiloquent nonsense 'this moment in time' when he means *now*, and his generalized evasions;

Harald does not accept the impersonal version of his words: 'the person' is his son. —He's guilty. Duncan. That's what you're saying, Mr Motsamai.—

—Wait a moment, sir. That's not at all what I am considering. It is for the court to decide whether or not an accused is guilty, not his lawyers, not even his parents. What I am asking you to understand is that I—we—the attorney and I—have to prepare our argument for such a contingency. In the light of this, all the circumstances—from childhood, even, the background, the temperament, the character and so on, of the young man, are vitally important. Any detail may be of use to us; that's why, if you can —just calmly—get through the hostility that he shows to me, I mean—I'm sure it doesn't apply with you—if you can influence him to tell his lawyers everything he knows about himself, his friends, the lot—that is essential. He must understand that there is nothing he cannot tell us.—

—Hostility—I don't know whether you could say he has no hostility towards us. What it is that he shows . . . But how can his father or I approach him in our usual, the old way if anything went wrong, when we see him in that room with a warder hearing everything that might be told. He didn't even say how crazy it was. For him to be there. No protest. He only made some kind of joke, almost, about where he's shut away. We sat there as if our tongues were cut out. There was no possibility he'd say what happened. I can't see how we could do what you ask while we see him under those circumstances.—

I fully appreciate, I fully understand, the advocate repeated in different formulations, developing what lawyers call their arguments. *Ah-hêh.* But it was not possible for them to talk to their son in complete privacy; that was the regulation. No possible harm could result, however, from them indicating to him, openly, in the presence of warders, that they were convinced, in his best interests *at this moment in time,* that he should trust his lawyers absolutely, that he tell his lawyers everything there was to tell. The glass-marble glance flashing again, as if it should hardly be necessary to pronounce the obvious: —The warder would be most unlikely to comprehend anything you talk about, anyway. Most of those chaps are still a hangover from the old days. Sheltered employment for retarded sons of the *Boere*.— He tosses an indiscretion he knows won't go amiss with these people. —Our government finds you can't change the prison system overnight—or many nights. Ah-hêh.—

During these early days they seem to repeat an inescapable ritual of departure from the same kind of compulsory encounter which leaves each waiting for the other to speak. And each is wary of the kind of interpretation that may be revealed by the other; that would set the encounter up or down on some scale of use, of hope, for them. So long as the silence lasts, this time, they do not have to face in one another what the advocate, Senior Counsel Motsamai, has said has to be faced. It is best to break the silence obliquely, as near to gently, within devastation, as you can get.

What d'you think of him?

She drops her chin towards her breasts a moment; lifts her head to speak under the still-falling avalanche of the meeting. Full of himself. Somehow arrogant. We're in a mess that he wearily is expected to get us out of. I don't know.

Probably what looks like arrogance is the kind of decisive presence that's impressive in court. Judges themselves are reputed to have that kind of presence. I didn't like him much, either. But that's irrelevant, he's not there to ingratiate himself with us—I respect that, he's there to do his job.

And he's decided what that is.

That's what he's briefed for, isn't he. His expertise.

And he's decided that Duncan killed. I can't, can't even hear myself say it. I can't say to myself, Duncan killed, Duncan performed a pathological act. Duncan is not a psychopath, I know enough about pathological states, grant me that, to say so. And I'm not bringing us into it, I'm not basing my disbelief on any proud idea that this can't be because he's *our son*, this isn't what a son of *ours* would do. It's Duncan, not *our son*, I'm talking about. There must be some explanation of how this 'circumstantial evidence' came about. The man doesn't know, but he's preparing what?—his defence, on the premise that this 'circumstantial evidence' means that Duncan killed. Duncan killed because that little bitch who shacked up with him, who wasn't too particular who attracted her fancy, and he'd tolerated this before, had a tumble on a sofa with one of the other friends. I'm sure she wasn't the first girl in Duncan's life, don't you remember the others—Alyse or whatever-her-name-was, happened to be a medical student who came to assist me, for the experience, two years ago—she was the favourite for a while.

Why doesn't Duncan speak.

I can't tell you, can I? I don't know. Perhaps because the lawyers keep battering him with 'circumstantial evidence' so that he can't have any faith that the truth will count, you can't win against circumstantial evidence, a gardener sees you crossing the grass and later the police pick up a gun. A man who doesn't even have a watch, can't say what time all this was. If you can't prove your innocence, you are guilty, isn't that what Duncan's come to.

Why doesn't he speak.

Well, that's the only positive thing the man said, so far as I'm concerned. We have to try and get him to confide in the lawyer even if he won't in you or me. And don't ask me why he won't.

She and he.

But what are they to do, if in his dire need, he does not need them? He, Harald, has to keep his eyes on the road, away from her, because they suddenly are deluged with tears, as if a sphincter has been pressured to bursting point. These drives. These drives back from disaster.

Harald was in the cottage. He had gone first to the room at the end of the garden where the plumber's assistant and part-time gardener lived. A padlock on a stable door; the property was old, the man occupied what once must have housed a horse.

Harald had avoided the house, expecting to send the man to fetch the cottage key for him, although there was a car in the driveway, indicating someone was at home. When he knocked, a half-recognized face appeared at a window, and Khulu Dladla came to the door. He had met Dladla a few times—Duncan now and then had his parents over for drinks in the garden, they didn't expect him to bother with providing a meal, and usually one or other of the friends on the property would join them. Harald had the key from Khulu; the heavy young man thumped off barefoot to fetch it; the word-processor at which he was interrupted shone an acid green eye on that living-room; that sofa. Harald was left standing alone with it. The young man's feelings as he handed over the key to the cottage drew his features into the kind of painful frowning of one who is tightening a screw.

—I can come with you, if you want.—

No, Harald was touched by the awkward kindness that suddenly brought him together with this man but there should be no witness to the implications of Duncan's absence from the cottage.

Harald was in the room where Duncan slept. And the girl. There was a pot of face-cream among the cigarette packs on the left bedside table. He turned away respectfully from the appearance of the room, took shirts and underpants and socks from a wall-cupboard while ignoring anything else, none of his business, stacked there.

Don't bring anything I was reading.

The books weighing a rickety bamboo table to the right of the bed; but he went over, he picked them up, read the titles familiar or unfamiliar to him, with an awareness of being watched by the empty room itself. The table had a lower shelf from which architectural journals and newspapers were sprawled to the floor. To him they had the look of having been dropped there, that day, when the occupant of the bed lay listening to battering on his door. He knelt on one knee and straightened them into place but the shelf sagged and they spilled again, and mixed up with them was a notebook of the cheap kind schoolchildren use. He balanced it on top of the pile—what for? So that Duncan would be able to put his hand on it when he came back to sleep in that bed? As if the delusion existed that he was about to do so.

He took up the notebook and opened it. He felt settle on the nape of his neck the meanness of what he was doing as he turned the pages, the betrayal of what the father had taught the son, you respect people's privacy, you don't read other people's letters, you don't read any personal matter that isn't meant for your eyes. It was all ordinary, harmless—date when the car was last serviced, calculations of money amounts for some purpose or other, an address scored across, note of the back number of some architectural digest, not a diary but a jotter for preoccupations come to mind at odd hours. Then scrawled on the last page to have been used there was a passage copied from somewhere—Harald's love of reading had been passed on when the boy was still a child. Harald recognized with the first few words, Dostoevsky, yes, Rogozhin speaking of Nastasya Filippovna. 'She would have drowned herself long ago if she had not had me; that's the truth. She doesn't do that because, perhaps, I am more dreadful than the water.'

During the period of awaiting trial there are no proceedings in a criminal case with which the papers may feed sensations to the public. When the first reports of the Lindgard son accused of killing a man were published, there was a tacit hush formed around the arrival of the member of the Board of Directors at his office. Newspapers were turned face-down on the headlines or removed from where his eyes and those of others might meet above them. The chairman did not know whether, in the privacy of the Board Room, there should be a formal expression of sympathy and concern for the colleague held in high regard, and his wife, in their time of trouble—that was the phrasing he would have used—or whether it was more tactful and helpful to evade any official attention, the sort of thing that would be remembered although not recorded in the minutes, a kind of conviction-once-removed, going on record against Lindgard, the biological father, at least, of a crime. It was decided to make no statement from the Board. Individual members found appropriate moments when they condoled with him briefly, to limit embarrassment on both sides. The general attitude to be adopted was to show him that of course, the whole thing was preposterous, some ghastly mistake. He thanked them, without concurring; they took this to mean simply that he did not want to talk about the ghastly mistake. Most of them had sons and daughters of their own for whom such an act would be equally impossible.

The period was dealt with on the only model within Lindgard's and his colleagues' experience: a remission in an illness about whose prognosis it is best not to enquire. In the men's room one day a colleague with whom he had been a junior together and who had more concern for frankness of human feeling than about maintaining some convention of his dignity, spoke while peeing. As if it were a double relief: —When there's ever anything I can do— I've no idea what that might be—don't hesitate for a moment, or for any reason. It must be hell. I never know whether to talk about it or not, Harald; how you'd feel. Whatever kind of frame-up it is—it must be agonizing to deal with, knowing it just couldn't be, it's out of the question.—

Lindgard had washed his hands. He was pulling the roller towel fastidiously to serve himself with a dry length. Now he spoke in this tiled enclave devoted to humble body functions.

—It isn't out of the question.—

His colleague righted himself, stood in shock. It hadn't been said. There are some things it's not fair to have been told, the speaker will regret the telling the moment it has been done. He went quickly to the door and then turned and came back, put the flat of his hand on Lindgard's shoulder-blade exactly where the son had made his gesture of communication when he met his father and mother for the first time in the visitors' room.

Few of the doctor's patients connected her with one of the cases of violence they might have read about. There were so many; in a region of the country where the political ambition of a leader had led to killings that had become vendettas, fomented by him, a daily tally of deaths was routine as a weather report; elsewhere, taxi drivers shot one another in rivalry over who would choose to ride with them, quarrels in discotheques were settled by the final curse-word of guns. State violence under the old, past regime had habituated its victims to it. People had forgotten there was any other way.

She did not work within a group, colleagues who would have to form an attitude to what set her apart among them. There was only Queen, the pert beauty preoccupied with her own authority as sister-in-charge at the clinic, and in the private surgery, Mrs February—whose ancestors had been dubbed with the name of the month in which they had been bought in the slave market—sat at her receptionist's desk with the mournful eyes of a traditional dignified guise of trouble borne, in lieu of the doctor herself taking this on. It was a delicate expression of empathy that needed no passage of clumsy words. At the clinic and in her surgery hours, the doctor was within an unchanged enclosure of her life, a safe place; people who are surrounded by encroaching danger may be precariously protected for a time in areas declared as such by those outside threat, some agency of mercy. However she had difficulty in retaining the personal interest in patients' lives which she had always held as essential to the practice of healing. The first identification with another whose son is imprisoned soon disappears in the crowd of those who are in misfortune; once truly jostled, become one among them, there has to be a sense that if I had to listen to your trouble you would have to listen to mine.

She packed up with a food parcel the clothes Harald had brought home, re-folding them.

Why didn't you bring pyjamas?

Young men don't wear them, don't you remember? There weren't any. Don't you remember, from when he still lived at home?

How would I know what he slept in?

Didn't you see him walking around in shorts, underpants, in the summer often coming to breakfast like that?

Of course, and didn't she put away the clothes that came out of the wash, arrange their order in cupboards for the men in the family, the dutiful wife and mother expected, as well, of the doctor.

I didn't occupy my time entirely with underpants.

Seems to me there must be a lot of things. Much that we didn't remember. Don't remember.

I wish you'd say what you mean. It's difficult enough . . . to talk, to know what we're saying. I have the feeling you're in some way suspicious of me. You're trying to catch me out, get me to explain, because I'm his mother, I ought to know, I should know *why*.

And I'm his father! I ought to know!

They stayed up late as they could in order to shorten the intervening night before the visit to the prison. At random he put a cassette of a Woody Allen film into the video player. When the lugubrious face appeared, Claudia remarked that the cassette was Duncan's, lent to them and not returned. Perhaps it was an attempt, pathetic or ironic, to assert that she remembered something, a loose end, between them and their son. They heard each other laugh at parts of the film; and then it was over, the light on the screen drew in upon itself, vanished into the succubus of darkness. In bed, they lay in that darkness. Harald put his arm over her back, round her waist, but did not take her breast in his hand; it, too, lay there, open. Harald and Claudia had not made love since the night the messenger came. It was not possible for them. It might have been good, it might have helped—after all, they had been able to laugh—but there was witness, from a prison cell, closing her body, making him impotent.

He thought under cover of darkness he might tell her what he had read on the last page of the notebook. Under cover of darkness: the place to understand, for them to understand what Dostoevsky revealed of their son, and to their son, of himself. Claudia read medical journals, she probably had never read Dostoevsky, he did not reproach her for it, in his mind; she healed while he could ensure—'insure'—as a compensation for pain and disaster, only money; but how to expect her to be able to interpret a passage from the depths of a mind with whose workings she was totally unfamiliar.

In the darkness he could disguise the reference that was within him, as a mood of practicality, necessity; the sole action open to them was to find the next thing to do.

We've the right to expect her to come to us. We have to see the girl.

Harald kept the key Khulu had given him and returned to the cottage and took, in the silence of the deserted bedroom, the notebook. Read again the passage of text that his son had found—what?—so devastating, a judgment unable to escape; or was it such a confirmation of ego, of power, that he could make of it his text, flaunt it, live by it. Act on it.

Harald went again through the pages. There were a few lines he had missed the first time, among banal jottings; another quotation but nothing he could put a name to. It was scribbled in overlapping large script, the kind of result of something remembered and written by feel, in the dark, half-awake. 'I'm a candle flame that sways in currents of air you can't see. You need to be the one who steadies me to burn.' There was a dash, the initial 'N'. A piece of adolescent self-dramatization probably divided into the broken lines of blank verse in the original, and hardly in a class to be appreciated along with Dostoevsky. He took the notebook to his office and locked it in a drawer of his desk; it was confidential, between him and his son as the two lovers of literature in the family, in their knowledge that the terrible genius of literature can give licence. His son did not know of this confidentiality. He did not know that his father had sneaked into his adult privacy and stolen his cryptic quotes with the intention of deciphering him.

Hamilton Motsamai was already in contact with the girl—of course. He stretched behind his desk and turned a gleaming yawn into a smile, in tolerance of the ignorance of lay people of how lawyers have to think ahead of them. —We don't know this lady. You met her a few times? She has not put herself in a very good light, in view of her behaviour that night. There will be a certain reluctance I anticipate . . . ah-hêh . . . (he paddled the air with spread hands) to bring her little performance on the sofa out in court, that we're aware of. So I'm not disturbed at all that the Deputy Attorney General has put her on the list for prosecution witness. That means I can cross examine her. You follow?—I couldn't do that if I were to call her as a defence witness. But I've also made a request to the prosecutor which hasn't been refused. He's allowing me access—I can have her. Permission to bring her here to talk. Seems for the moment he's undecided whether he's going to use her or not, but I'm sure he will, in the end. He will. So he'll recall permission after I've seen her, but that's okay, that's fine. To cover her own hanky-panky she may try some damaging character allegations about Duncan that would be useful to the prosecution. But I expect to have all I'll need from her for when I get her on the witness stand. A lot depends on her attitude to your son. Is she still attached to him? Or is there some bad feeling, resentment towards him, so she'll try to make herself look blameless—never mind the sofa—in any provocation that led him to this act. What about *her* character. All we have is her name, Natalie James, she has worked at an institute for market research, she's been a hostess on a cruise ship to the Greek islands, she was at one time secretary to a university professor somewhere, and now she describes herself as 'free lance', I don't know in what. What field. She also writes poems. I have informed her you want to see her. She says she will only meet you here, with me. Not at your place.—

Claudia keeps herself turned away while Motsamai speaks, it's as if she would shut her eyes to concentrate best on what he is saying.

—Have you talked to Duncan about her?—

—He tells me they were lovers, but they 'lived their own lives'—these are his words.—

A day and time were set up to meet the girl at Senior Counsel's chambers. That morning Claudia telephoned Harald from her surgery to his office. A representative of the government Housing Commission was with him, they were discussing an agreement on terms of low-interest loans that would put up walls and a roof for thousands of poor people; there was a long negotiation about to come to a conclusion, or to risk being deferred yet again.

Harald, I'm not going. There's no need for us to meet her if the lawyer is handling her. I don't want to see her. We should leave it to him.

As if he had been shaken and dragged out of bed in the middle of a night; for a moment he did not recognize what he was being recalled to, his comprehension was torn in two. The man from the Commission picked up his papers in order to be seen to be not listening. Harald was possessed by wild irritation, with her, Claudia, her intrusion, her recall to *the* intrusion in their life that monstrously displaced everything else, his fifty years, eclipsed the sun and shut off the air of all he had learnt, the understandings he believed he had reached in knowledge of human beings and the mores he had tested, the satisfaction in work and the pleasures of accepted emotions, the love between man and woman, between parents and son, the ease of friendship; irritation that swelled and struck out—even at his son, Duncan, who had landed himself in prison. Yes! Clamouring forces were struggling to take over his innards, forces that if let loose outside were the kind that could be violent. He could not speak, not even pronounce oblique dismissive, soothing things to her that nevertheless would relate to a situation the other man in the room was completely remote, removed from, innocent of. He put down the receiver on her midsentence.

Natalie-Nastasya. Motsamai said she was already there, had gone to the ladies' room.

Received by a father's eyes as she came in she matched the young woman Duncan had brought to the townhouse once or twice. This was she, all right. She was closing the door with a hand curving gracefully behind her, Motsamai smiling acknowledgment of the consideration. So Motsamai, also, felt an attraction she apparently emanated for some—many—men.

The same sloping shoulders of a Modigliani model (and there was a print of a Modigliani nude, unremarked until it came to him now, in the bedroom he had plundered). He was not one to take much notice of women's clothes, only of the effect they produced, but it seemed she wore the same kind of garments she had worn, legs outlined in something like a dancer's tights and a loose shirt unbuttoned on a deep V of sun-stippled throat. The hair was somehow different—whatever colour it had been before it was now boot-polish black—but the eyes, the gaze on him, were unavoidably recognizable. Perhaps there was a place in memory, a cheap photo album of Duncan's girls that existed though never opened.

That was the impression of her: yellow-streaked dark eyes (colours of the Tiger's Eye paperweight on Motsamai's desk) secretive within extremely thick lashes on both upper and lower lids that tangled at the outer corners. And these outer corners of the eyes turned down slightly, whether by the nature of her facial muscles or by an expression she permanently arranged; the eyes were a statement to be read, depending on who was receiving it: lazily, vulnerably appealing, or calculating, in warning.

When Duncan brought girls—his women—to the townhouse it could not be thought of (really) as bringing them 'home', home was left behind where he grew up, was the house they had sold, abandoned as having become a burden no longer necessary. Dropping in for a meal accompanied by a girl did not mean that he was presenting her to his parents as someone to whom he had a serious commitment, but it also did not mean that she was a passing fancy; if those existed, they did not warrant the degree of intimacy implied by being admitted, however casually, to the area of his life he shared, committed to it by the past, with Harald and Claudia. He must have brought her at least because she was on a level of personality that interested him; come to think of it, that was how he, Harald, thought of the criterion on which a son introduced a lover to his parents. How Claudia thought of it—she had referred to the girl as 'that little bitch who shacked up with Duncan'. How could she have formed that impression in the few times Duncan had brought the girl to the townhouse—oh and the single occasion on which Duncan had bought theatre tickets and the four had seen a play together, an occasion when one listened and looked and didn't have much of an exchange. Women see things among themselves, about one another, that you have to belong to their sex to attribute, whether these attributions are just or not. Whatever this girl was, there was a judgment on her, by Claudia, as the cause of whatever terrible consequences Duncan's embroilment in her life had brought about. But how to believe, Claudia, at the same time, both that Duncan could not have performed that act, the final act of all human acts, the irreparable one, the irreversible one, and that this girl, little bitch, was important enough to him for her behaviour to cause him to be suspected of performing that act? The torturing preoccupation when such contemplation seized him was out of place here and now: he had lost attention to what was passing as the three of them, he, the girl, Motsamai, were sitting together in Senior Counsel's chambers. What had Motsamai just said? *Mr Lindgard and his wife are naturally concerned to have your version of what happened that Thursday night.*

Slender hands interlaced, fingers with up-turned tips, calmly on her thighs. —I've already told you. You can give them that information.—

She was responding to the lawyer but she was addressed to Duncan's father; under the wisps of fringe that moved on her brow those eyes gazed out steadily on him. If there were to be a malediction, it would come from her. He dismissed the context swiftly. —We are not interested in your behaviour that night. Only in your other observations. Duncan's state of mind. Leading up to that night, what has been his mood, lately, you were living with him—what kind of relationship was it?—

And his bared face before her gaze was saying, between them, what are you, what did you do to him?

—He was the one who asked that I move in with him. He was the one who decided.—

—That's not enough. Why did you move in?—

—I don't know. He seemed to be a solution. I'm sure you don't want to hear my life story.—

Although she, not the one in a cell, was the accused, here, she said this last charmingly, taking in with it the two men, her interrogators.

—Only insofar as it will help Mr Motsamai in Duncan's defence. Don't you know Duncan is in danger—we're talking here as if you're some stranger to him, but you were living with him, sleeping in the same bed, for God's sake! To be blunt, your life's your own, yes, but what you did that night couldn't have come out of the blue, what was in your relationship must have had something to do with it—what you did must have been a consequence of some sort? Were you quarrelling? Was it a crisis, or just another incident, that you'd both accepted, before? Don't you see this is important?—

She was listening attentively, meditatively, as to a voice indistinct on another wave-length.

—Duncan takes on other people. Forces. Can't leave them alone. He likes to manipulate, he can't help it. And he's pretty ugly when you resist, and you're resisting because what he's doing, what he's got to offer, isn't what you want. And the more he fails, the worse he gets. I think you don't know what he's like.— She gave a show of shuddering admiration.

—But you stayed. You stayed with him until you got into your car and drove off and left him alone that night and didn't come back.—

She was still looking him full in the face, her hands still calmly interlaced.

She closed her eyes a moment. The black lashes pressed on her cheeks.

—I was free.—

—So you were afraid of my son.—

—He was afraid of me.—

When she had gone Harald sat on in Motsamai's chambers, looking round the shelves of law books with their paper slips marking relevant pages that might decide—not justice—he was not able to think of justice as he used to—but a way out. The law as a paper-chase whose subsidiary clauses might lead through the forest. Motsamai called on his intercom for coffee, and then without explanation to his client countermanded the order. He came out from behind his desk and went to a brass-handled cupboard. In it were rows of files and an inner compartment where glasses hung by their stems from carved slots, as in an elegant bar. He lifted in either hand a bottle of whisky and one of brandy, questioning? Harald nodded at the brandy. Motsamai poured them each a good tot. It was a small gesture of kindly, silent tact that came unexpectedly from this man. Harald could say to him—So she believes Duncan killed the man he saw fucking her on the sofa.—

—She knows the sort of woman she is. That is for us to proceed on.—

Motsamai drew at his tongue to savour the after-taste of the brandy; here is a man who enjoys his mouth, has managed to retain the avidity with which the new-born attacks the first nourishment at the breast.

—Is it?—

—Man, she provoked him beyond endurance, drove him beyond reason, not only that night, with her exhibition, but for over a year or so preceding that night. Culminating in it.—

—That's not what she says. She says he was the one. He was the one to get, how did she put it, pretty ugly.—

—Ah, but you said it yourself—she stayed. And did you hear: he was afraid of me. That was her answer when you asked, after all her complaints, her allegations about him, if she was afraid of your son. She stayed, she stayed!—

Because he was more dreadful than the water, learned Senior Counsel. But that self-judgment of the accused was not for the ears of the lawyers; not yet, if ever. There is a winnowing process in preparing a case, to be learnt by a layman; Harald had some experience in picking up nuances in a very different context, the Board meetings he attended and sometimes chaired. Some facts would be useful to the lawyer, some would be detrimental to the argument he would present—how to proceed?

Motsamai slid between his majestic maroon-leather upholstered chair and his desk to seat himself again. What he had to say had to be said from there and not from the casual stance of sharing a drink. —Harald, it's not going to matter whether or not fingerprints can be discovered under the dirt on that gun. My client has instructed me.—

—Duncan has said so.—

—He has. Duncan has told me.—

—He's told you. And he's told you to tell us.—

—Yes. Ah-hêh.—

That drawn-out sounding from the breast can be, is everything, a recognition, a lament. When he heard the man call him by his first name, for the first time, he knew what was being expressed now in an articulation older and beyond words.

—So that's the end of it.—

—No, that's not the end of it at all. It's the beginning of our work.—

—You and his good friend, his attorney.—

The whole body tingling, the drug of an unknown emotion injected in this well-appointed chamber of announced damnation which now replaces the meaning of all other dwellings on this earth, in this life.

—Is a lawyer obliged to take a brief for someone who has said he is guilty? Already judged himself. What is there to defend.—

—Of course a lawyer must take such a brief! The individual has the right to be judged according to many factors in relation to his confessed act. *Circumstances* may affect vitally the weight of circumstantial evidence. The accused may judge himself, but he cannot sentence himself. Only the judge can do that. Only on the verdict of the court. In terms of the kind of sentence likely to be imposed, this is the beginning of the case, man! What we concentrate on is ensuring that the sentence is not going to be a day longer, not a degree more punitive than mitigating factors allow. He's opened up, Harald—your son's talking to me now—there're aspects of the affair to pursue for the defence, that defence still exists!—

The prison visit to a murderer.

When he came back from Senior Counsel's chambers and told her, her face broke out in scarlet patches as if in fierce allergy, it was shocking to look at. A raw indecency before him. He anguishedly wanted her to weep, so that he could hold her.

They went dully over what the lawyer had said about his brief, his task. The principle of law, innocent until proved guilty, which they held along with all those who are confident they will never transgress further than incur a traffic fine, was overturned. In its dust, bewilderment isolates; each spoke for the self rather than succeeded in reaching out to the other.

Any other woman surely would have wept, keened over her son, and he could have found some purpose, embracing her, joining her. He offered, of himself: We know less than before. Motsamai didn't ask him the only thing that matters. To me—us. It's not why—that's all Motsamai's concerned with, that's the defence. It's also how. How could he do it. Duncan could bring himself *to do it*, take a gun and kill. He's you and me, isn't he, and we can't know, can we. Not because he's not going to tell Motsamai or us or anyone; it's something that can't be 'told'. It has to be in you. In him.

Claudia went to the kitchen to find food because this must be about the time when they usually ate. He was not domesticated. He followed, out of some sort of courtesy which was all that was left for their situation. There was nothing further to say; he had perhaps said too much already. What Claudia had been thinking, framing in her mind in that burrowing silence of the kitchen, came next day when they were walking together down the path to the carport on their way to the prison. One of the stiff spatulate leaves of the Strelitzia caught at her hair and she dodged, breaking their inevitable progress, and he turned to see what was impeding her. A grin swiftly transformed her face and as swiftly shut away. You believed that night that he could do it. Didn't you? You'd decided. You didn't need to wait for any confession to a lawyer.

First there had been the persona of a prisoner on the other side of the table in the prison visiting room, this day there was the persona of a murderer, self-accused, self-defined as such. Duncan. Claudia, his mother, managed the half-hour within the format of her profession that she could summon, a surety no calamity could take from her; the confession of guilt a diagnosis. There was the

question of the lawyer yet again. Was the patient absolutely satisfied with the competence of the one in charge of his case, was
he sufficiently impressed with Motsamai, now that he had had talks
with him? Would he like to have another opinion called in, there
were many highly-experienced lawyers, wouldn't that be worth-
while? The nature of the diagnosis itself, what awesome malig-
nancy it has pronounced, is not under discussion. His father
confirms: —I've also had a chance to talk to Motsamai. I think
he's a clever man. And he knows you're going to need a clever
man. I think we should leave it to him, if he wants to bring in
someone else for consultation. If there's someone whose particular
experience in a certain kind of case he'd want to make use of.—

Their son—in his new persona, there he is, wearing one of the
shirts his father fetched from the cottage, their son who has killed
a man—he is not calmly observing them as he did during the
previous prison visits when they could represent to him the fantasy
their presence posited that he had not done what he did, someone
else would be found who had tossed the gun into a fern-bed. He
is distrait, restless of hands and eyes. She even asks if he has a
fever?—all she knows about, poor loving mother, poor thing.

What could she prescribe for this kind of fever.

—Motsamai's a bit of a pompous old bastard, but he's all right.
I get on with him. So you've been with him. You know what there
is to know.—

—No. We don't know what there is to know. Only your
decision. And that he accepts it. Can't offer an alternative.
Duncan.—

Abruptly Duncan puts out a hand, the hand of a drowning man
signalling from his own fathoms, and grasps his father's across the
table. His gaze falters between Harald and Claudia. —I would have
understood if you two hadn't come again, now.—

The nearest Duncan goes to admitting what he has done to them.

It is not only the man on the sofa who is his victim. Harald and Claudia have, each, within them, now, a malignant resentment against their son that would seem as impossible to exist in them as an ability to kill could exist in him. The resentment is shameful. What is shameful cannot be shared. What is shameful, separates. But the way to deal with the resentment will come, must come, individually to both. The resentment is shameful: because what is it that they did to him? Is that where the answer—Why? Why?—is to be found? Harald is prompted by the Jesuits, Claudia by Freud.

There is a need to re-conceive, re-gestate the son.

There was good sport at his making, that Harald knows. The transformation of self in the first sexual love is something hard to recall in its thrilling freshness—it's not only the hymen that's broken, the chrysalis where the wings of emotion and identification with all living creatures are folded, is split for release. Harald was Claudia's first lover when she was the youngest medical student in her class and he was in a state of indecision whether or not to leave the faculty of engineering for that of economics. Swaggering confidence of being in love gave him courage to disappoint his father and desert a tradition of engineers reaching back to the great-grandfather who emigrated from Norway.

Claudia's father was a cardiologist and her childhood games were playing doctor with an old stethoscope; she disappointed no-one, since her mother was a school teacher whose nascent feminism wanted a more ambitious career for her daughter.

Harald and his girl, Claudia and her boy (that was how their parents thought of them, in the Sixties) were lovers too young to marry but did so when she found herself pregnant. Sport at his making. What was so enthralling about the mating, what was the compulsive attraction of the partner is something that not only changes perspective from the view of what is revealed about one another as each becomes known over years, but also reveals something else, that was there at the time, to be seen, and wasn't. Claudia, so young, even then satisfied that healing the body fulfilled herself and all possible human obligations—a destiny, if you wanted to use outdated highfalutin terms. Harald, unable to commit himself to any such self-definition, choosing an occupation that interested him for its influence over his own existence, already picking away at meanings of life like layers of old paint. Neither was attracted to join the chanting flower-children of the era. Making love, making love was exclusive and serious—hopeless to understand now what it meant to them then—how could they have at the same time kept aware of the oddness that mismatched them even while their bodies matched in joyous revelation. And they had overcome, too—no, managed—these incompatibilities through the different stages, in marriage, of loving one another as distinct from being in love—incompatibilities which were ignored at the moment of conception: but present. The son was born of them.

The wriggle of a sperm and its reception by the ovum—what comes together in conception is what parents are, and their two streams of ancestry. But you could go back to Adam and Eve for clues in pursuit of that. Hamilton Motsamai, to whom their son's life is entrusted—and theirs—can no doubt trace his through a language spoken, through oral legend, song and ceremony lived on the same natal earth. For those whose ancestors went out from their own to conquer, or quit their own because of persecution and poverty, ancestry begins with grandfathers who emigrated. There is an Old Country and a New Country; the heredity of the one who is conceived there begins with the New Country, the mongrel cross-patterns that have come about. The Norwegian grandfather was a Protestant but Harald's father, Peter, mated with a Catholic whose antecedents were Irish, which is how Harald comes to have a Scandinavian first name but was brought up—his mother's duty to do so, according to her faith—as a Catholic. Claudia's parents had been to Scotland only once, on a European holiday, but her father, the doctor whose disciple she was, was named for a Scottish grandfather who emigrated on a forgotten date, and so Claudia's son has received the genetically coded name Duncan Peter Lindgard.

A fish-hook in his finger.

When did certain things enter, work their way in to join the inherited, couldn't be removed?

He did more with his father, shared more activities. She supposes that is natural, when the child is male. So there is a particular responsibility on the father. His father had him with him, fishing, and the fish-hook was embedded in the soft pad of his third finger, he was perhaps six years old. Or less. He was brought home to his mother the doctor so that she could gently remove the hook as she had the skill to do, hurting him as little as possible, an early example to him. The human body must not be wilfully damaged.

As a child he had the perfect balance of a bird on the topmost frond of a tree.

The image came to Harald from the times he took him bird-watching. She would make excuses not to come, too slow for her, the extended waiting for something to alight, sweeping the empty sky for a cut-out shape to pass across binoculars—the boy importantly looking up the appropriate illustration in the bird manual even when he was still too young to read the text. An image drew close, from time, as the lenses of binoculars do from distance: sunlight fingering the spindly forest (where, what year) and his figure striped with it, like a small animal himself as he moved carefully, not to be a disturbance to any creature in nature; such a respect for life.

When a dog had to be put down—alone, how could she not re-examine this, she was the one who had to do it because he begged her not to let the task be left to the vet. He was ten or eleven, he wanted his doctor mother to do it because he trusted her not to inflict pain, to 'put to sleep' (he was protected from killing by the euphemistic phrase) the pet who, while he was growing taller and stronger, had grown too old to walk. She did it without delay because of his painful, almost adult indecision about taking the old animal's life; and after, in his subdued face, there was his conscience over their having done so, reproachful of her for having been his accomplice; adults should know how to make creatures live forever, abolish death.

This sentimental searching back to what he was is something each, Harald and Claudia, is alert to in the other, not because each seeks the weakness of comfort from the other, but because something vulnerable, incriminating to either, might be revealed. Someone must be to blame. If Duncan says he's guilty. Sometimes, the hint of a search slips out: while they are taking the dog for a walk (they decided to defy the ruling against animals in the townhouse complex, least they could do, for their son) she remarks suddenly on the way the child would express himself, particularly when he was intrigued by what he had just learnt. *Paper is trees, rain is the water that comes up from the earth when the sun heats it. So everything is something else. And tears? When I cry?*

I don't remember he ever had much reason to cry. A happy kid. Never what you'd call punished.

She saw him when his face went into the scarlet paroxysm, white round the mouth, of childhood.

Because that was always left to me.

So you caused the tears.

To answer back was to engage. She let the dog on his leash tug her forward. Both parents were concerned with the preservation of life. Even he, in a manner, assuring that people (at a profit, yes; but she also was paid for most of her services, wasn't she) would be compensated for misfortunes that befell them, and, lately, providing money for the homeless to house themselves. The army—the army. *That* was where the life-ethic the son had absorbed from his parents was reversed. When he did his army service he was taught to kill; whether disguised as parade ground drill, field manoeuvres, ballistics courses (the calibre of the gun found in the bed of fern has been established), what was being given was licence to cause death. That there are circumstances in which this is justified by the law of both man and God—though God's supposed sanction might not have worked its way in, for Duncan, because although Harald had made him a reader, had he succeeded in making him a believer?

War, the right to take life: a truism.

If Harald brings it up, he also tramps it out of relevance under their feet.

Did he really see action? We know he didn't, we thanked God he didn't.

You said to him the army was going to be a brutalizing experience.

All right. The alternative we could have taken? You didn't want us to send him away, did you? Out of the country. A brutalizing experience, a moral mess: but millions have resolved it. He only fired at targets.

He told us they were in the shape of human beings.

Something terrible happened.

Dear Mum and Dad,

  A terrible thing happened. It was on Saturday, we were playing football, 2nd team, the one I'm in. A kid from junior school went into the gym to fetch something and suddenly there was screaming, we even heard it on the field. He saw someone hanging from the beam where the punch bag is. It was Robertse in Form 5. He was hanging by the neck. Old McLeod and the other masters went in but we were kept away. But we saw them bring out something carried in a blanket. There was an ambulance and the police. But we were told we must stay in our cubicles or the common room.

  The second page of the letter is lost, although she must have kept the letter as something whose validity was meant to outlast schooldays, boyhood. It was among documentation of the protection parents provide for a child, the commitments they assume, for him. Boosters for polio inoculation, record of orthodontic treatment, anti-tetanus and hepatitis inoculations as precautions taken when he went on some school camping trip in Zimbabwe. This letter came back to her, now, she went to look for it among these other bits of paper which, perhaps, there was really no reason to keep.

When Claudia and Harald received that letter they had been strangely disturbed; she saw, now, that this was the forgotten *other time*, first time, they were invaded by a happening that had no place in their kind of life, the kind of life they believed they had ensured for their son. (A liberal education—whose liberalism did not extend to admitting blacks, like Motsamai, they realized now.) What could it be that led a schoolboy, a companion of their own son, protected in the same environment, the same carefully limited experience, the same selective civilized mores—they would not have confided Duncan to any school that practised corporal punishment—what could it be that brought a boy to put a rope round his neck? The contemplation was horror—once removed, that's all. The unease they felt came from revealed knowledge that there are dangers, inherent, there in the young; dangers within existence itself. There is no segregation from them. And no-one can know, for another, even your own child, what these destructives, these primal despairs and drives are. Harald and Claudia—they could have been the boy's parents, they were their clones, paying the same school fees, approving the enlightened educational philosophy of the worldly teaching staff, choosing a co-educational school so that a male child without sisters should mingle naturally with the other sex. What came to them was fear—fear that there could be threats to their son about which they could not know, could do nothing. They wrote to him—she wrote?—or they went to see him. She heard herself saying to Harald, I want you to tell Duncan, whatever happens to him, whatever he has done, no matter what, he can come to us. *There's nothing you cannot tell us. Nothing. We're always there for you. Always.* And so they could feel Duncan was safe. They had made him so.

D'you remember that time with the Robertse boy, what you told Duncan.

I remember *you* telling him, we got permission to take him out to lunch. We were in a garden restaurant somewhere—there was nowhere else to go. Didn't seem the right place. Anyway.

No, no, we'd gone over the whole thing, decided we must say something to him he wouldn't forget, and you were the one.

Why should it have been me? It came from his mother, that would be the obvious way.

Because you're the man and he was the boy. Perhaps the idea that you would have—I don't know—some kind of shared male experience, something likely to happen, I wouldn't have.

What did it matter who uttered the pledge to the boy; it was made by both. It was the document produced when he said in the prison visiting room, I would have understood if you two hadn't come back again.

When you have been given a disaster which seems to exceed all measure, must it not be recited, spoken?

Harald's dependence on books became exactly that, in the pathological sense: the substance of writers' imaginative explanations of human mystery made it possible for him, reading late into the night, to get up in the morning and present himself to the Board Room. He turned to old books, re-read them; the *mise en scène* of their time would remove him from the present in which his son was awaiting trial for murder. But like his son, he came upon his own passages, to be omnipresent in him if not to be copied out alongside the others in the notebook locked up in his office. " '. . . the man is as he has wished to be, and as, until his last breath, he has never ceased to wish to be. He has revelled in slaying, and does not pay too dear in being slain. Let him die, then, for he has gratified his heart's deepest desire.'

'Deepest desire?'

'Deepest desire.'

'It is absurd for the murderer to outlive the murdered. They two, alone together—as two beings are together in only one other human relationship, the one acting, the other suffering him—share a secret that binds them forever together. They belong to each other.' "

Thomas Mann's Naphta spoke to Harald in the silences that accompanied him everywhere: the accusatory silences, protectively hostile, between him and his wife; the silences he occupied even while he drew attention to anomalies in decisions being considered at business meetings or discussed the effect of new fiscal policies on the financing of mortgage bonds; susurration in the mind like a singing in the ears. The off-hand manner of the girl, at the lawyer's chambers, when Motsamai said, You were afraid of him; and then—almost a boast—He was afraid of me. Afraid of each other?—in what is fearful, surely there is always one who menaces and one who fears. How can menace be equalled? In deadlock; and that is exactly what it will be, deadly; so if it had been Natalie/Nastasya his son had killed there would have been an answer: they belong to each other. The reverse side of the conception of sexual love that romantically defines it as the blissful state of union, to which that good old-style marriage ceremony gives God's blessing as one flesh. But he didn't harm her; it was the man who lay, shot in the head, on the sofa, and it was known to the friends, to the lawyer, apparently to everyone, that he was not the first or the only other man she'd lain back on a sofa for, any one of them could have served as victim of the lover with whom she belonged in the intimacy of menace. There were times when Harald had the impulse to seek out the girl again, but Motsamai, who knew where to find her, discouraged this.

—I can't afford to get her back up in any way, y'know what I mean, Harald, she feels that you and your wife blame her—

—How could we blame her. He did what he did.—

—Because you must blame someone. Your son in trouble. It's human nature, nê? Because I must blame someone! His Counsel must prove circumstances that are causal, that will spread the guilt so that the burden of it rests on others who will never be arraigned.—

In the surf of silence that is with him, here in the familiar room where innocence and guilt are annotated by paper slips in tomes —this chamber and the prison visitors' room are extensions of his townhouse now—Harald knows: us. On us. Harald and Claudia, who made him: the birds and the bees, don't steal another's toy, never read other people's letters, thou shalt not kill.

—I have a very special kind of approach to her. Oh yes. Ah-hêh.— Motsamai's lips struggle with something like amusement and self-approbation. —With women, you know; they're very shrewd. And she, she turns on the charm—like a tap!—when she feels she's being cornered. I have to coax her, without her realizing it, to condemn herself while she thinks she's telling me about him. You have to know how to deal with such women. One moment they're poor little victims, the next they're showing off how they can dominate anyone and any situation. The weaker sex, they give us lawyers a lot of trouble. I can tell you.—

Harald's distaste for the assumption that he will share, as an aside casually confidential among males, a patronizing generalization about women, is something he has to dismiss. It doesn't matter, now, what this man thinks about anything except the case he says he is defending. Prejudices seem unimportant. Duncan was taught not to be prejudiced against blacks, Jews, Indians, Afrikaners, believers, non-believers, all the easy sins that presented themselves in the country of his birth.

—What did she tell you.—

—Don't take this too seriously—from her. She says he is a spoilt brat. Her words. A spoilt brat. She also uses big words, nê: 'over-protected', so that he's not used to any opposition, anything that threatens his will, the way he thinks things ought to go. The rules are his rules—I questioned this, I suggested that the kind of set-up these young people have has no rules except perhaps the most basic ones, you know, who has the right to take the beer out of the fridge—and of course they had the black man Petrus Ntuli to do the dirty work for them. No, she says, his rules were made for himself, it didn't mean they were the kind of conventional rules someone like me, a lawyer, would think of. Then what were they? Well, they were about who went with whom, and so on. Sex, I gather; but also friendship, she insisted, the set living on that property seem to have complicated friendships, what you'd call loyalties. He 'went along' with the way everyone lived on the property, he thought this coincided with his ideas, his rules, if you prefer, but at the same time he was the 'spoilt brat' who couldn't tolerate it when this style—which he'd taken on for his own, mind you—came into conflict with the other rules he'd freed himself from. From the older generation. Yours. She says these were still there in him although he believed they were not. She said something: he's in prison now, but he was never free. And of course she means *she's* free.—

—That doesn't say much of what happened between them. From what you tell me, you'd think she had nothing to do with the couple there on the sofa.—

—You're right. You're right! She somehow distances herself, that is so. Ah-hêh. And she seems to have, well, no feeling for the man who died as a consequence of her act with him that night. She doesn't show any particular signs of sorrow . . . for this terrible thing. Which of course is very good, excellent for my case. When I cross examine her. *She* could have been the one to die. Why not? She doesn't even consider it. Why not? It takes two, nê? To get going . . . Yet she shows no remorse that she was at least half the cause of the man's death, if we grant that he was well aware that he was busy with his friend's girl. It's difficult to understand her detachment. As if she's sure it wouldn't have been her. I'm aware there are things I won't get out of her, perhaps—not even with my means.—

And he has a flashed laugh in appreciation of that skill, at once returning to the seriousness the face of the father, fixed on him, may trust.

To recount what passed at a meeting like this with the lawyer means that Harald, who is informing her, and Claudia, who is the listener, both must first tell themselves again, as they must many times, every day, that Duncan has killed someone. Accept that. The man lay in the mortuary, there was a post-mortem which confirmed death by a bullet in the head, and he has now been buried at a funeral arranged by the friends with whom he shared the house; his body was not flown back to Norway, the man Duncan killed is still here, under Duncan's home ground.

Harald found Claudia talking on the telephone, making contrivedly interested enquiries and comments about someone else's life; one of the kind friends who make a point of calling regularly to show that the Lindgards are still within society although something terrible has happened to place them out of bounds. She stares at him while she continues to talk and smile as if the friend could see her, not aware of what she is saying; she wants something he does not have, to give. The incongruity between the smile and the stare is anguish he has to harden himself to observe. He goes to the kitchen and watches the water overflowing the glass in his hand as a measure of time. When he comes back she is on the small terrace, waiting for him.

How far has he got?

What is the point of her aggression; as if he, along with the lawyer, were responsible for the lawyer's request for postponement of the trial so that evidence may be prepared.

We talked mostly about the girl. He finds her a complex character. She hasn't a good word to say for Duncan—he's a 'spoilt brat'—but Motsamai seems to think there's an advantage in that. It's difficult for us to follow this kind of legalistic reasoning. He thinks he's getting her to condemn herself out of her own mouth —something like that.

Condemn herself—she's not on trial! He wants to show you how clever he is. And were you satisfied that's all? All he's doing!

It's just that he sees her as a key prosecution witness. We have to trust his judgment, he quoted a stack of precedents for the kind of case he's preparing. You and I know nothing about such things.

We haven't exactly had experience, have we, we could read about them in the newspapers or ignore they ever happened . . . He agrees with you, anyway, if not in so many words. She's a bitch. The more he inveigles her to reveal herself the better his 'extenuating circumstances' can be cited. He says she's entirely cold about the man who died, no conscience, not even the sense that she might have been the one in his place. So sure of herself, she wouldn't be harmed whatever she did. God knows why.

Because Duncan was in love with her.

At what she has just said Harald feels a rising disgust, distress that he cannot suppress.

So you believe in that kind of love, she fucks with another man, so her lover kills him! Proof of love. I thought you had a better opinion of your own sex, you're responsible for your actions, as we men are. You call that love. Where did he get that love from!

I'm trying to understand, Harald. Haven't you been in love.

What a bloody stupid question. You ask that. I was in love with you. I thought I would have died for you, though I suppose that was a safe illusion of youth, knowing I was unlikely to need to. But to imagine I would have killed anyone. Even myself. No. Love is life, it's the procreative, can't kill. If it does, it's not love. It's beyond me, beyond me to imagine what he felt for that woman.

Then maybe he hates her. Punished her by doing away with the man she wanted. If you kill her you spare her suffering.

We're not talking about some euthanasia debate among doctors. As if he doesn't know that if she loses one man she'll find another.

We were in love, you were in love with me, rather crazily, you say—what if you'd ever found me the way he found her?

Claudia. How do I know. I can't feel again as I would have felt, then. I would have walked away from you, we wouldn't have been here, there would have been no Duncan—that's what I say now. Oh but maybe I'd have claimed you back and fucked you myself, how do I know what I would have done, in love. Spoilt brat or not, that kind of love doesn't come from me. I wouldn't have taken anybody's life.

You can say that because we know now that you have to live on through any disaster.

Could you have done it? There are women who say they've killed 'for love'—what a question to you, who spend your life keeping people alive. What an insult, to ask.

But it was more like a jeer.

There are also women who when they have something to say that never should be said, raise their voices, fling out the words, and there are other women who are drop-voiced as if communicating with themselves and are overheard on such occasions. Claudia's one of them.

I understand now I've never been in love like that—crazily, as you say. Never.

Stop the clocks, lock the doors, but every summer night there is repeated the afterglow they used to come out to enjoy as it raised the sky with light from the bonfire of the day. Another day; awaiting. They still come out. Awaiting trial. They pass the newspaper between them as people do who are not on speaking terms but recognize one another's presence. They are here, there is no remedy. When there were the usual disappointments and setbacks in their lives—small, small, dwindled to the trivial—they would come home and burrow into each other in bed. He drinks his nightly alcohol ration while the birds (Black-faced Weavers, common to the region) make conversation like foreigners in a bar.

Spoilt brat.

She looked up, at the quotation.

Oh that's passing the buck from adult responsibility for what you do. The toilet-training syndrome. I would never have tolerated a child of mine as spoiled.

'Spoilt'. Over-indulged. Chocolate and toys. But there's another meaning to the word; to spoil something is to damage it for good. Like that burn in your carpet.

You know everything—you've read everything, do people

commit crimes out of self-hatred? Is it true? Isn't that another explanation people give? Why should he hate himself? What had he done to make him able to do what he did.

He passed her another section of the paper and returned to the pages he had. To think—thinking—of things to which were given only a moment's skimming attention, before: an intelligent person reads selectively, no real interest in following the sex adventures of pop stars or the lurid crimes that must have been performed by the deranged. But now—here was that woman who strapped her two small children into their safety seats in her car and got out and let it run off a wharf into the water, drowning them.

Other people! Other people! These awful things happen to other people.

It doesn't matter whose thoughts these were, Harald's or Claudia's; they were in the evening air on the terrace, they were in the rooms of the townhouse like the clinging odour of cigarette smoke in curtains and upholstery.

He was aware that he and she were thinking of these things in terms of happening *to* the perpetrator, not the victim: as if the motive, the will, came from without. But it came from within. 'The man is what he wished to be, he has gratified his heart's deepest desire.'

Claudia went alone to the prison. Harald was a delegate to a conference of bankers and insurance brokers called by the Minister of Economic Development; he could not continue to subordinate everything in his engagement book to the susurration in his mind: without the outward performance of normal occupations life could not be even materially sustained. Senior Counsel Hamilton Motsamai, the stranger to whom he was coupled in the processes of the law, would cost six thousand rands a day for appearance in court, and half as much for time spent working on the case in his chambers.

Claudia found herself considering what she should wear; as if, without Harald, there would be a concentration on her presence in which her clothes would reveal an attitude—to her son—her attitude. In winter she wore trousers, shirt and pullover under the white coat of her working day, in summer a cotton skirt and whatever went with it was in the shops each year, she liked to be in contemporary fashion while her profession was old as human history. The healer does not have to be dowdy; the ancients, like sangomas and shamans of the present, wore beads and feathers. If she went to the prison in her work clothes this would, in a sense, be fancy dress; she would not be consulting at her rooms that morning. If she put on the kind of outfit she wore when she attended some medical conference (as Harald wore a dark suit for his) or went to a restaurant with Harald at the invitation of one of his colleagues, it would seem undue respect granted to the authority of the grim place that held her son. If she wore the jeans of her weekend leisure (a euphemism, a doctor's beeper could recall her to her patients at any time of day or night) this might look like a thoughtless reminder that out there, outside the walls and lookouts with armed guards, people were walking on grass under trees, the Strelitzias were perched in bloom over the townhouse terrace where his parents sat in summer, the man Petrus Ntuli was watering the bed of fern. She dressed, finally without awareness of it, to please him. To be the kind of mother he would want; neither expressive of the judgmental conventions of a parental generation nor attempting to project into his own, to reach him by trying to look young—she knew that she sometimes took unwise advantage of the fact that she did look younger than forty-seven to choose clothes that were meant for younger women. What she wore should confirm: whatever happens, whatever you do, you can always come to me.

Duncan did not remark on Harald's absence; it was as if he expected her. She was the one to bring up the circumstance of his father's obligation to respond to an invitation from a government ministry. He sends his love. It was the line scribbled as an afterthought at the end of a letter, even if the supposed message had never been requested to be conveyed.

He said he'd heard something about the conference, on the radio. This tenuous connection somehow bewildered her, as if what he was claiming was a faint voice from the earth being received by someone strapped in a space craft. She could not picture how someone would sit—no there would be no chair in a cell—lie on a mattress on the floor and listen to the *living* going on. Outside.

She had not noticed, on previous prison visits, that Duncan

raised and lowered his eyelids, slowly, while others—she and Harald—spoke to him. It was not blinking, exactly. It was a patient, distant, stoically fanning movement. He hears us out. She was observing him much more intently and clearly this time than she had done before. When Harald was there, she and Harald had between them sensors invisibly extended, like the raised hairs on certain creatures that pick up the impulses of others towards them, which distracted from perception of their son. Each was tense to what the other's reactions to him were; there was static interference with the reception coming from the son.

Harald was not there; after a number of visits, it was as Motsamai had said, the warder was no more than the presence of the scarred and scored wood of the table. On it, she was suddenly able to take both Duncan's hands in hers. She had always admired his hands, so unlike her own with their prominent knuckles and leached skin of doctors and washerwomen; when he was a small child she would spread his fingers and his long thumbs and display them to Harald, look he's got your hands (and laugh cockily) I made sure he didn't get my own, didn't I. She turned them palm-up, now, in that gesture, but he pulled them away and made fists on the table, throwing his head back.

Claudia was appalled. That he should have thought the gesture was a reminder of what he had done with those hands. Here, to him, in this place, you could not explain to him, this was one of those female reminiscences, sentimental, indulgent, that adult progeny rightly find an unwelcome fetter and a bore. It was a moment to get up and run from a room. But this wasn't that kind of room. Walk out, you can't walk in again. Can't come back until the next appointed visiting day. This is not home, where misunderstandings used to be explained away.

The irreparable made her reckless.

—You've told him you're guilty. The lawyer. I can't believe you.—

—I know you can't.— He moves his head from side to side, side to side, it's measuring the four walls, he's enclosing himself in the walls of the prisoners' visiting room. She has never seen the cell where he is kept but he has its dimensions about him.

—Do you want me to believe you.—

—Sometimes I do. But I know it's impossible. Other times I don't think about it, because whether you'll accept it or not—

Something terrible happened. She cannot remind him of the letter he wrote so long ago, and the pledge she—his father?—they made.

—Wouldn't it be better if you tried to tell me something now instead of Harald and me hearing—things—when you have to answer in court—

He continues to move his head like that, it's unbearable to her.

—so I could tell you now, I'm telling you now that it doesn't matter what it was that happened, whatever you might have done, you can come to us.—

He gazed at her with deep sorrow changing his face before her, the nose pinched by the grooves that cut into the cheeks on either side, down to the mouth. Better not claim me, my mother.

He did not need to say it.

Slowly, cautiously, she took one of his hands again. —Remember, while you're shut up here. All the time.—

He did not withdraw the hand.

—You can imagine all the things we want to ask. Harald and I.— She avoided referring to 'your father'; any reminder of that identity with its authoritarian, judgmental connotations—Harald with his Our Father who art in heaven—could destroy the fragile contact. —Could I say something about the girl?—

—Natalie.— He pronounced the name rather than prompted. As if to say, that's what stands for her; what has it to do with what she is.

—I didn't have the impression your affair with her was particularly serious, I mean the few times I saw her with you. And I can tell you I didn't take to her much. But you probably saw that. Mama being carefully nice when she was really disapproving. Of course.— The slackening of a slight smile, between them. —I thought the other one, the one before, was more your likely choice to live with. This one. I'd look at her when she wasn't aware of it and I'd see she had the childlike manner of many promiscuous women. They're the hunters—what would you call it, the predators who look like the hunted. I see a lot of them in my practice, black and white, they have that same manner. I'm not disapproving of her because of promiscuity, you know. My only objection would be on grounds of what it can do to the bodies I have to deal with. I've always supposed you've had plenty of experiences of your own. When Harald and I were young there were only diseases you could cure with a few injections. Now there's the one I can't cure with anything. At the clinic they bring me babies who've begun to die of it from the moment they're born. But I thought—oh I suppose all middle-class people like Harald and me have that snobby notion—you'd mix with the kind of women who'd be as, well, fastidious as you. Fussy about partners. It wasn't the promiscuity that put me off, it was the manner, the disguise, the childlike manner. My experience is that there's something quite different underneath. And I must tell you something else. Harald met her at Motsamai's chambers, and it showed. It certainly wasn't childlike.—

—What is it about her you want to know.—

—Whatever you'll tell me.—

—Natalie had a child—not from me—given at once for adoption and then she tried unsuccessfully to get it back and she had a nervous breakdown. That's when I met her. She recovered, she was full of—you know—the joys of life, return to life. She moved into the cottage with me. She has energy she can't contain, she wouldn't ever try to.—

—You knew that?—

—I suppose so. Knew it and didn't know it. But if you ask about her you have to ask about me as well.—

The warder stirred like a sleeping watchdog. Agitated, she lifted her hand away to look at her watch. Was there time, was there ever time, for this; years had gone by separating the two beings they were, blood counts for nothing.

—You told him you're guilty.—

—Could you bring me more books. Ask Harald. You don't have to wait for next week, you can deliver them to the Commissioner's office.—

But he embraced her, across the table, she took with her on her cheek the graze of what must have been several days' beard; shut away there he was doing what she knew men did to change their picture of themselves, growing the hair on their faces. There would be no mirror in a prison, shards of glass are a weapon, but he could put up his hand and feel the image.

Driving herself back to the townhouse she was tormented by what she had failed to ask him. The loss of an opportunity alone with him that might not come again; a connection that broke, but that had come briefly, irresistibly into being, no doubt about it. Did he—did he *not*—think of consequences? How could he not know he would be where he was?

Perhaps he meant to kill himself, after what he had done. No-one had thought of that. He lay on his bed in the cottage and waited for them to come for him. Only resistance was to sleep, or appear to be asleep and not hear them when they hammered on the door. Didn't he think about what would happen to *him*? To her. To Harald.

Awaiting trial. Now there's been a postponement.

When Harald tells his secretary he will not be in that afternoon everyone in the company knows this must be the day of visiting hours at the prison. If his absence has to be remarked among his peers—apologies from absentees are read out in the routine formalities of a board meeting—there are solemn faces as if a moment's silence is being respectfully observed; secretaries at their computers and clerks at their files exchange among themselves the country's lingua franca of sympathy: Shame. The utterance has exactly the opposite of its dictionary meaning, nobody knows how this came about. And in this particular circumstance the reversal is curiously marked: no-one is casting opprobrium at Mr Lindgard for his son's criminal act; what they are expressing is a mixture of pity and a whine against the injustice that such things should be allowed to happen to a nice high-up gentleman like him.

Harald and Claudia had close friends, before. Although these are eager to be of use, of support, they cannot be. Harald and Claudia know they have little in common with them now. There is her patient endurance of the telephone calls; without discussion,

both avoid invitations, which are more than kindly meant: these
few close friends, shocked and genuinely concerned by what has
happened, feel left out of the responsibility of human vulnerability,
the instinct to gather against it huddling together in some sort of
mutually constructed shelter, the cellar of the other kind of war,
from the bombshells of existence.

The only person with whom they have something in common
is Senior Counsel Motsamai; Hamilton. Without bothering to ask
permission from them, he had established first-name terms. The
fact that he himself was prepared to address Harald by first name
was licence granted. He has the authority. Present within it, he
has complete authority over everything in the enclosure of their
situation. Motsamai, the stranger from the Other Side of the divided past. They are in his pink-palmed black hands.

The Lindgards were not racist, if racist means having revulsion
against skin of a different colour, believing or wanting to believe
that anyone who is not your own colour or religion or nationality
is intellectually and morally inferior. Claudia surely had her proof
that flesh, blood and suffering are the same, under any skin. Harald
surely had his proof in his faith that all humans are God's creatures,
in Christ's image, none above the other. Yet neither had joined
movements, protested, marched in open display, spoken out in
defence of these convictions. They thought of themselves as simply
not that kind of person; as if it were a matter of immutable determination, such as one's blood group, and not failed courage. He
did not risk his position in the corporate establishment. Claudia
worked at clinics to staunch the wounds racism gashed; she did
not risk her own skin by contact, outside the intimate professional
one, with the black men and women she treated, neither by offering asylum when she had deduced they were activists on the
run from the police, nor by acting as the kind of conduit between
revolutionaries her to-and-fro in communities would have made
possible. What these people called the struggle—she recognized its
necessity, their courage, when she read reports of their actions, in
the newspapers; kept away from them outside clinic and surgery

hours. Stuck to her own struggle, with disease, and the damage other people caused: *yet other people*, who tear-gassed and set dogs upon blacks, evicted them from their homes to live in shacks from which old men and women were brought to her dying of pneumonia and children were brought to her dwarfed by malnutrition. She had kept clear of those others, too.

Harald left her asleep on Sunday mornings and went to the cathedral to take Communion. It was down at the east end of the city where the business district ravelled out into blind-front clubs where drugs were peddled, and stale-smelling hotels rented rooms by the hour. In the congregation there was no-one who would recognize him with sympathetic smiles of greeting he would have to meet at the suburban church in the parish of the townhouse. He was alone with his God. It was none of Claudia's business. It was nobody's fault but his own that he had not seen, when they married, that she could never change, was ignorant, a congenital illiterate in this dimension of life where they might have been together now in unforeseen catastrophe. The nameless congregation was of all gradations of colour and feature. Paper-white old ladies from pensioners' rooms and adolescent girls with mussel-shell eyes and cheeks smoothly brown as acorns, thin black men lost in charity hand-me-downs, women in heavy-breasted church black, young men of the streets with Afro-heads like medieval representations of the sun. Phoebus framed in tangled aureoles of hair and beard. He took his turn behind a man the age of his son who breathed the odour of last night's drinking and scratched at a felted scalp. He took the wine-moistened Host as did this man blessed in Creation with what not long ago had been an affliction, under the law's malediction of a mixture of both skins, the suffering of black, and the apostasy of white.

Harald's religion surely protected him from the sin of discrimination. True, he had never done anything to challenge it in others; not until the law had changed society to make this safe and legal for him. All the years he was, as the convenient phrase goes in praise of private enterprise, 'climbing the corporate ladder', he had accepted without questioning that black people could not be granted housing bonds; they could not afford to meet payments. A bad risk. That was the fact. The government of the time should house them: so he voted against that government, who did not do their duty. That was the extent of his responsibility. Now the new laws were addressing many of the factors that had made poverty black people's condition as the colour of their skin had been their condition. He was one of those who did not initiate but could respond; he was prominent among members of the insurance and bond industry working with banks who were under a similar obligation to take the risk of putting a roof over the heads of people whose only collateral was need. It gave him some satisfaction to think that he was able to be constructive in improving the lives of his fellow men, even if he had failed to follow Christ's teaching in destruction of the temples of their suffering. He served on a commission comprised of representatives of the new government and of the finance industry. The members were blacks and whites, of course; the bad risk was shared now. At least, if nothing else brought them together, they were on comfortable terms in business philosophy.

It is very different with Motsamai. Hamilton. Servants used to be known to their employers only by first names, everyone knows now it was intrinsically derogatory. *This* use of a black man's first name is a sign not of equality, that's not enough—it's a sign of his acceptance of you, white man, of his allowing you unintimidated access to his power. In this relationship the comfortable terms, quite accustomed now, of taken-for-granted equality once the appropriate vocabulary and the same references are understood, draws back from an apparition that must have been waiting in the past. In those hands, now. Hamilton. All that exists, in the silences between Harald and Claudia, is the fact of the life of their son. Every other circumstance of existence is mechanical (except for Harald's prayers; the sceptic resentment Claudia feels when she senses he's praying). Because of the old conditioning, phantom coming up from somewhere again, there is awareness that the position that was entrenched from the earliest days of their being is reversed: one of those kept-apart strangers from the Other Side has come across and they are dependent on him. The black man will act, speak for them. *They* have become those who cannot speak, act, for themselves.

The relationship between the lawyer and his clients is not a business relationship of any kind Harald has known although the best available Senior Counsel is highly paid for his services. Claudia should understand it better; it must be more like that of patient and doctor when disablement threatens. But she was dismayed by the lawyer's suggestion that she and Harald come to his house— for a quiet talk, Harald told her he had said.

What Hamilton had said to him was confidential. —I don't think Dr Lindgard—Claudia—and I have really hit it off together, yet. I don't feel she has confidence—you know—in what we lawyers are doing. Ah-hêh. Yes. I want her to get to know me not here, this room reminds her of what is happening to Duncan, this place with the nasty smell of a court about it—isn't that so? Nê? I want to talk to her in a relaxed way, get her to tell me the kind of thing women know about their kids that we don't, my friend . . . I see it with my own youngsters. They'll run to their mother. We men bring our work home with us in our heads even if we don't bring it in our briefcases, we don't seem so sympathetic, you follow. Any childhood traumas are useful to me in this kind of defence where there isn't the object of proving innocence of a crime—no option for that—but of proving why the defendant was pushed beyond endurance. Yes. To an act contrary to his nature. Ah-hêh. Anything. Anything the mother remembers that would support, say, a deeply affectionate, loyal nature in the defendant. Anything that will show the *extent of the damage* done to him by the woman Natalie. How she betrayed these attributes he has and wilfully destroyed the natural controls of his behaviour—think of that scene on the sofa! Not even to go into a bedroom, man! She knew anyone could walk in and see what she was up to there, she knew—I believe it—he might come back to look for her, and what he'd find!—

A brief preview offered of what eloquence Motsamai was going to produce for his clients, in court.

Harald had to grant it as such with a gesture.

—Claudia spent as much or as little time with him as I did. A doctor also brings preoccupations home and doesn't even have regular hours. And he was in boarding school . . . if you think of it, how much time did we have of him. I don't think she knows anything about Duncan I don't.—

—I think I know better. Sorry! I'm working on Natalie, I'm satisfied with that, and what I am looking for from Duncan's mother is the other side of the story, what the young man was before that particular young woman got hold of him.—

Harald has learnt that when Motsamai has something to tell that is likely to rouse emotion and dismay he uses the tactic of sudden rapid development of the subject so that there is no warning pause in which apprehension speculates on what might be to come. He does this now without a change of tone or voice level. —I've made an application for Duncan to go for psychiatric observation. To tell you the truth, that's why I didn't quibble over postponement. Among other reasons . . . I need time, I need a full psychological report for my submissions. Absolutely essential. I need to know everything there is to know about Duncan. As I've told you—from you, from Claudia. And I need to know what neither of you knows and what I'll never get from him myself. There'll be a State psychiatrist and one we'll appoint privately, ourselves. I've engaged a first-class chap, your wife will have heard of him. Duncan will go to Sterkfontein—that's a state mental institution, yes. Ah-hêh. Don't be alarmed. I know you won't like the idea. He'll be there a few weeks—well, four weeks. And it's better if you don't visit. Don't be upset. It's a routine procedure in a case like this. Your son's not mad, man! That is certainly not my submission, no! Something different—what propelled the accused to act as he did.—

Duncan Duncan. Again the branding iron descends. —He's guilty. In his right mind.—

—No no Harald, the plea is 'not guilty'. That's the form. While we admit *material facts* which prove guilt, we submit our argument of momentary loss of capacity to distinguish between right and wrong.—

Your son is not mad.

—Only a few weeks there. And it so happens—it's advantageous, point of view of timing. The trial. Yes . . . Ah-hêh. I have my sources.—

The glassy whites of his eyes signal a quick nudging smile, for himself, not directed to the man in trouble. —It's good to find out what judges will be on the bench during what period. There's an old precept we lawyers have—well, call it a saying—you must meet the judge in the moral climate he occupies. I want the judge whose moral climate is one I can count on meeting in this exceptional case.—

Your son's not mad, he said. She, Claudia, understands better. I expected it, she says.

What kind of place is it.

Pretty unpleasant, she says.

That's all, from her.

At the remove of the telephone, Harald told the Senior Counsel that Claudia was stressed and wanted to rest over the weekend. Motsamai sounded as if he took no offence, but asked Harald to come to his chambers whenever convenient that afternoon.

For Harald's part, it still was necessary to show no offence was intended—after all, the man had offered his hospitality, if with professional motive.

—Claudia's become unapproachable.—

But Motsamai understood Harald did not know what he was saying, did not know his was an angry plea for help, not a warning to the lawyer that he would have no success with the wife. Motsamai is accustomed to the erratic attitudes of clients—people in trouble—alternating between confidence and distrust, dependency and resentment.

—The very one who's in the same boat with you isn't always the one you can talk to. I don't know why. But there it is, I see it often. Don't worry that she won't get through to you. Don't be disturbed, Harald.—

Ah-hêh. In the silence there is the resonance of his soothing half-sigh; sometimes it is like a human purr, sometimes a groan you cannot express for yourself.—

And Harald at once felt a new anger; at himself, for having revealed himself. Too late to recall the image that should have remained private between him and his wife, to rebuff the recognition expressed (urbanity speaking clumsily for once) by this third party for whom nothing must be private because it might be useful. There is no privacy for anyone, in what has happened, is happening. Soon the prisoner's utter privacy of isolation will be broken into by doctors. Night-notes at the bedside are discovered by prying eyes.

—I'll have a good chat with her anyway. I'll make a date when you and I are sure you'll be busy somewhere. Maybe I should drop in at her surgery, end of her day.—

—I wish you luck.—

He did not know it was the day the Senior Counsel had arranged to visit her. There was no regular hour for her return in the evenings, emergency calls on the beeper could delay her any time; she came in now lugging a supermarket bag from whose top the spiky headdress of a pineapple stood up. He half-rose to unburden her but she was already passing into the kitchen.

He poured her a gin-and-tonic, relic of those evenings when they used to enjoy sitting on their terrace, watching the colours of mixed vapour and pollution wash out in the sky and listening to the raucous plaint of shot-silk plumaged ibises perched tottering on the treetops of the landscaped enclave.

D'you want it in there?

She came back into the room with the pineapple in her hand and signalled with a tilt of her head for him to put down the glass on a table. She was preoccupied rather than ignoring him; hesitated, placed the pineapple in space pushed aside for it in a bowl of apples, then took it out again and went slowly back to the kitchen.

One of the displaced apples fell and rolled to the floor; it stopped at his feet.

What was Claudia going to do with the bloody pineapple? Decide they mustn't eat it? Everything they ate, drank, everything they did, the air they breathed, *he* was deprived of, they took while he did without, they took from him because they indulged themselves with these things while he, their son, Duncan, was about to be shut up among schizophrenics and paranoids. She'll get Motsamai to deliver it to that other kind of prison, maybe they'll allow him to have it. Maybe they'll examine it to see if there's a knife suitable for suicide or a file suitable for escape buried in its flesh; these cheap detective yarn tricks of tension are a fact, for us. If it isn't a pineapple it's a salad to be wrapped in plastic, a bunch of grapes, a goat cheese—does she know how irritating these futile attempts to take our kind of life into his are?

May God grant patience with her. Tonight while she lies beside him in her ignorance.

Did you ask Motsamai to come and see me?

Claudia has come back and picked up her drink. She rattles the ice in the glass and her gaze wanders the room.

Why should I? No.

About Duncan.

It was his idea, he wanted it. I couldn't say no on your behalf, could I? It was for you to say whether you'd see him or not. I simply told him you didn't feel like coming to his house at the weekend, I said something polite and plausible.

Why me? What's the difference between that, and talking to us together?

But he's talked to me alone, too, hasn't he? Times when you didn't turn up. And you didn't mention you'd agreed to have him come to the surgery today—I don't know why you didn't, some reason of your own.

She is gazing at Harald with great concentration as if waiting for some move in him to be detected.

I don't understand you, Claudia.

He wants to know everything, Duncan's childhood, his adolescence, everything—from me. As if I produced him by parthenogenesis. Only me.

That's nonsense. That's not so. You know the reason he has to question us both, everything we remember, everything we know —our own son, who else could know it! So that he can show what awful pressures ended up in him doing what he did. Against his nature, his background. What our son says he did. But Motsamai does have some sort of patronizing attitude towards women, so you . . .

I didn't find him patronizing.

Then what is it?

As a little boy, was he happy at school, at home, was he ever aggressive, did he confide in me. Of course he was happy! What else could he be, loved as he was. The question could only be asked by someone whose kids get beaten.

She is searching among her own words. He tries to find the right ones for her.

He has the idea that women, somewhere in the background, are more accessible than men, children turn to the mother—it obviously comes from the way things are in his own house. I'll bet he's an authority to be reckoned with, there. It's their style.

She has come upon something.

Did the child have a religious upbringing. Did he go to church.

Harald smiled. So what did you say.

That you were Catholic and took him with you but so far as I know he stopped when he was old enough to decide for himself. I didn't try to influence him one way or the other.

Well, that's something we won't go into now.

And does he believe in good and evil. Does he believe in God. Does he?

You know that kind of question wouldn't come up between Duncan and me.

Harald raises his hands stiffly and places the tent of palms from nostrils down lips to chin; his regular breath is warm on the tips of his fingers.

Neither knows whether the man, Duncan, believes in a supreme being by whom he will be judged, finally, above the judgment of the court.

The barrier of hands is discarded.

Perhaps Motsamai's playing us off one against the other. Has to. So what the one (Harald swiftly censored himself from saying 'who doesn't want to remember')—what the one doesn't remember he may get from the other. That's all.

The townhouse is a court, a place where there are only accusers and accused. She leans back in her chair, arms spread-eagled on the rests, preparing, baring herself.

What have I done to Duncan that you didn't do?

Of course what the lawyer's getting at—what he wants is to be able to convince the judge that the self-confessed murderer is one to whom, because of a devout Catholic background, his own crime is abhorrent. The confession itself is certainly a strong point; he confesses his sin, through the highest secular law of the land, to the law of God. He throws himself on God's mercy. Jesus Christ died for all others, to kill another is to act in aberration against the Christian ethic in which the boy was brought up, and which is within him still.

And perhaps if she—seated across the room, outside walking the dog, hanging up her clothes before bed, lying beside him with her beeper handy (to hell with them)—if she could have gone beyond the intelligence of the microscope and the pathologist's finding to intelligence (in its real sense, of true knowledge) that there is much that exists but cannot be known, proved in a test-tube or by comparison with placebo results—if she had not been stunted in this dimension of being, the boy might have been the man who at twenty-seven could not possibly bring himself to kill, to have become someone more terrible than the water. 'Didn't try to influence him one way or the other.' But wasn't that statement her very position? Its power. Mother managed perfectly well to be a loving mother, to do good and care for others by healing the sick. She could look after herself. She quite evidently needed no-one to be accountable to for control of any of the temptations every child and adolescent knows about, to lie, to cheat, to use aggression to get what you want. 'They turn to the mother.' Then what he found there was a self-sufficiency of the material kind—and that includes the doctoring, expert preoccupation with the flesh—which if it was enough for her wasn't enough for him. If that's what he did settle for when he stopped coming to church.

Stopped; oh but that doesn't necessarily mean he stopped believing, lost God. That's something this father does not know any more than does his mother. Even though, while he himself finds communion not only with God but with the unknown people around him in the cathedral in the wrong end of the city, a communion with life which guards him against the possibility of harming anyone, any one of them, no matter what they may be, he knows that there are men and women who remain close to God without partaking of the ritual before a priest. Her son may still believe, in spite of her; my son.

And then again that other special intelligence: of the lawyer, the best Senior Counsel you can get. *He* knows what he wants, what will serve. It could be that he'll want to present *two* moral influences; religious faith from the father, secular humanism from the mother. The two sets of moral precepts the whole world relies on—what else is there—to keep at bay our instinct to violence, to plant bombs, to set ablaze, to force the will of one against the other in all the kinds of rape, not only of the vagina and the anus, but of the mind and emotions, to take up a gun and shoot a friend, the housemate, in the head. What a strong argument for the Defence a dramaturge like Motsamai could make of that: the force of perversion and evil the woman Natalie must have been to bring this accused to fling aside into a clump of fern the sound principles with which he was imbued: one, the sacred injunction, Thou Shalt

Not Kill, two, the secular code, human life is the highest value to be respected.

A visit before he goes from one destination to another he's made for himself; prison to madhouse.

The meek trudge along the corridors where some black prisoner is always on his knees polishing, polishing, the place where all the dirt and corruption of life is quarantined must be kept obsessively clean. If only there were to be disinfectants to wash away the pain, of victims and their criminals, held here. What is Claudia thinking: that he couldn't have done it? Does she still hang on to that. Much use. Much good it will do any of us.

In a house, in an executive director's office, in a surgery, each day nothing is ever the same as at the last entry. A flower in a vase has dropped petals. The waste baskets have been emptied of yesterday, an ashtray displaced. A delivery of pathologists' reports has been made.

The visiting room and the table and two chairs and the watching walls are always exactly the same. Two warders, one on either side of the accused, now, are the same nobodies; only Duncan is the element out of place, doesn't belong here. Duncan is Duncan, his face, the timbre of his voice, the very angle of his ears—the visitors' attention sets about him a nimbus, the existence of his presence elsewhere, as it surely must be if there is any continuity in being alive, in the places in the city that know him, in the townhouse, come for Sunday lunch; in that cottage. They bring with them *himself*; having never experienced prison before, they do not know that this is what a prisoner receives from visitors.

He is all right, yes; they are all right, yes. His mother lightly strokes her hand down the side of her cheek to convey appreciation of his beard, which has grown out wiry ginger-bright rather like the filaments of light-bulbs. The preamble is over.

No mention is made of the place to which he has been committed by Motsamai to be observed and assessed for his capacity to know what he learned from them, to distinguish right from wrong. They talk obliquely round it.

—The lawyer's been to see me at the surgery. Quite an interrogation. Asking me all about what you were like, as a child and growing up.—

—Yes.—

Harald made as if to speak. The distraction was ignored by mother and son.

—Duncan, do you think I've had any particular influence on you? Anything I did?—

—My mother; of course. But you both had an influence on my life, how could it be otherwise. It's not a question. Everything you've done for me. And why you did it. What do you want me to say? You've loved me. You know all that. I know all that.—

This kind of statement would never be made anywhere else but in this dislocated anteroom of their lives.

He looks at them both waiting, each for accusation or judgment from him.

—The letter.—

That's all he has said. But it is as if with the sureness of his architectural draughtsmanship he has drawn lines confining the three of them in a triangle.

—So you do still remember when your father and I came to see you at the school after what happened that time.—

—But you'd first written a letter. I might even still have it somewhere.—

—D'you remember who signed it?—

—Dad . . . it's so long ago.—

—But you remembered about it.—

He was suddenly gentle with his mother. —You repeated what was there—you've forgotten—when you came the other day.—

—The lawyer—he asked whether you believe in God.— Claudia brings it out.

But he smiles (it is always disturbingly extraordinary when he smiles in this place, an indiscretion before the two lay figures of warders), and so she can smile with him.

—Yes. Nothing's irrelevant to Motsamai. He's a very thorough man.—

—I had the feeling he was fishing for something. Expected to find, with me. Well, you've been an adult a long time.—

It was to his father he said as usual, his form of farewell this time as any other, that he was running out of books. —I'll need them, in that place.—

—Apparently we're asked not to visit you although as a doctor they can't really prevent me. Remember that. If anything—anything at all—something goes wrong, insist on your right to call us.—

—Have you ever read Thomas Mann? I'll bring you 'The Magic Mountain'.—

In the car, Harald speaks.

He didn't answer you.

About what?

But he knows she knows.

Faith. God.

It was pretty clear, wasn't it. If 'nothing is irrelevant' to Motsamai, this—question, whatever—is something irrelevant to Duncan, doesn't exist in his life.

That's how you want to understand his dodging what you suddenly sprang on him out of the blue. The most intimate question. You put him in your dock.

But Harald, also, has not answered what she put to him, elsewhere. That must mean he does believe she is more responsible than he for what has happened to Duncan, what Duncan has become. She follows the thought aloud: What Duncan has become —whatever that is, neither of us wants to admit what it might be. I mean, how could anyone, how can we be expected—

He, great reader, corrects her imprecision with his superior vocabulary.

Too naïve in our security.

Claudia resists the impulse to say thank you very much; self-disparagement is damaging to health, let him indulge in it on his own.

All their lives they must have believed—defined—morality as the master of passions. The controller. Whether this unconscious acceptance came from the teachings of God's word or from a principle of self-imposed restraint in rationalists. And it can continue unquestioned in any way until something happens at the extreme of transgression, rebellion: the catastrophe that lies at the crashed limit of all morality, the unspeakable passion that takes life. The tests of morality they've known—each has known of the other—are ludicrous: whether Harald should allow his accountant to attribute so-called entertainment expenses to income tax relief, whether the doctor should supply a letter certifying absence from work due to illness when the patient had succumbed only to a filched holiday. But what is trivial at one, harmless, end of the scale—where does it stop. No need to think about that, all their lives, either of them, because the mastery has never needed to be tested any further. My God (his God) no! Where do the taboos really begin? Where did their son follow on from their limits beyond anything they could ever have envisaged him—their own—following. Oh they feel they own him now, as if he were again the small child they were forming by precept and example: by what they themselves were. Parents. Since they were once in this adult conspiracy together, neither can get away with absolving him- or herself of their son's extension of their limits, any more than they can grant absolution from the self-accusations that preoccupy each. Separately, they have lost all interest in and concentration on their activities and are shackled together, each solitary, in the inescapable proximity that chafes them. Incongruous invasions dart each in the midst of conversations with other people which concern, naturally, the normal world they move about in without right. Targeted, they carry these strikes home to the townhouse, and out of the silence, against the touch of cutlery on plates or the voice of the newscaster mouthing from the TV screen, statements without context burst forth.

You've got a good holding in tobacco shares, haven't you? You know people who've died of lung cancer. You have No Smoking signs all over your offices. But the dividends are fine.

There is a context; they're in it. He would never have believed she could be a spiteful woman. He prepares himself, although he is not sure of the exact issue, it must belong somewhere to the only subject they have.

He laughs. Dull-weary. We're eating chicken and you bought it. I suppose it's one raised in cruel conditions. Caged.

The last word hits home. What concern is there for chickens while you talk to your son within the walls of a prison.

I'm asking you, it happens to interest me, is to kill the only sin we recognize.

It's the ultimate, isn't it. Is that what you mean.

No I don't.

Lies, theft, false witness, betrayal—

Go on. Adultery, blasphemy, you believe in sin. I don't think I do. I just believe in damage; don't damage. That's what he was taught, that's what he knows—knew. So now—is to take life the only sin recognized by people like me? Unbelievers. Not like you.

Of course it's not. I've said: it's the ultimate. Nothing more terrible.

Before God. She pushes him to it.

Before God and man.

I thought for believers there is the way out by confession, repentance, forgiveness from Up There.

Not for me.

Oh why? She won't let him off.

Because there is no recompense for the one whose life is taken.

Nothing can come to him. It's only the one who killed that receives grace.

In this world. What about the next. Harald, you don't accept your faith.

Not on this issue, no.

So you sin with doubt. Is that only now? Her gaze is explicit.

No, always. You don't know because it's never been possible to talk to you about such things.

Sorry about that, all I could do was respect your need for that kind of belief. I couldn't take up something I'm convinced doesn't exist. Anyway—you've allowed yourself the same latitude I have between what does and what doesn't count. Even with your God behind you.

Oh leave me alone. I'm a killer because you see people die of lung cancer.

At what point does what's let pass become serious. Harald? If God allows you to condone so much in yourself how do you decide someone won't take the example that you don't have to follow the rules because the people who've taught you to don't do so themselves. Of course they know when to stop. Because nothing in their lives goes any further. They're safe. Making money out of cigarettes, that's not much of a sin for a good Christian.

Claudia is not looking at him as she speaks. Her head is turned away. If it were to control tears it would break the tension which is both hostile and exciting, his heart gushes like a geyser at his breast, against her. She does not offer tears; she asserts the severance of not seeing him. What has happened has brought into the order of the townhouse what it wasn't built to contain; she's right, there—their life together was not equipped to sustain itself so far, to this edge. People have ambition that their sons should go further; theirs has made of this a horror.

She said once, What did I do to him that you didn't do? He wanted to say now in his controlled voice that he could use with the force of a shout, And what is it I *didn't* do for him that *you* didn't do? Why me? *Because I'm the man*. That sudden resort to the female tactic. Putting on the sheep's clothing of weakness when it suits you. I'm the man and so I'm responsible, I buy shares whose profits you spend, money that kills, I made him a murderer, a dead chicken and a man with a bullet through the head, it's all on the road to hell.

Hostility had sucked all communication into its vacuum. If he'd opened his mouth, God knows what would have come out.

So Harald is able to believe his son did it and that he must be punished. No confession (already made), repentance in exchange for forgiveness possible. So much for the compassion of Harald's God and of his Only Son who was conceived not of penetration and sperm (because that's human and dirty) but who took on himself all human sin to cleanse all others who sin. So much for the religious faith that the father had lived by in moral superiority, going off to pray and confess (what?) every week, and every Sunday taking the small boy with him to give him the guidance for his life, the brotherly love and compassion decreed from on high while the mother turned over in bed and went back to sleep. She carried about within her the wretched apostasy of the father as she had carried the foetus he had implanted when she was nineteen.

The great eye of the sun bleared under a cataract of cloud: the diffused glare confused the planes of the face so that for a few moments Harald and Claudia were not sure which black face this was. They were in the parking ground among police vans, he locked the car with the touch on the electronic device, out of habit, they were turned to the fortress. There was recognition acknowledging them, in the face; they and the man approached each other across the space between arrival and the entrance doors that always seemed so long to cover. Khulu. What was it again: Dladla. From the property where the cottage was. From the house, the sofa. He was leaving after a visit to Duncan. Duncan was back in a cell from the madhouse. They were going to Duncan. A strange suffusion of warmth accompanied their coincidence. Harald had not seen the man since waiting in the house stared at by that other eye, the computer, Claudia probably had not seen him at all since some invitation to the house given by their son in a time before what happened. She found no purpose, nothing to be learnt in going to be confronted by the place, it could only be like being forced to look at a grave where after a post-mortem duly performed a man had been stowed out of mind. The victim disappears, the perpetrator remains. It could only rouse revulsion at what the room had witnessed, and she couldn't risk this revulsion against the one who said he had performed the act.

Nkululeko 'Khulu' Dladla. He, too, brought to the prison what was missing, Duncan *himself*, somewhere existing outside. Any grim redolence of the house he had about him was evaporated in the glare on prison gravel; they felt some sort of gratitude. They had no-one else; only Hamilton.

A curved tooth of some captured feline set in gold tangled with an ornate Ethiopian cross on the broad breast in the opening of a shirt left unbuttoned. A gleam of cuff-links and a red-stone ring —these elaborations along with the other, anti-materialist convention of frayed jeans and sneakers—he was normality, a variety of contemporary ordinariness made surprising, simple freedom appearing in the sterility of this space before blind walls, like a daisy pushing up through stones.

—No, man, he's okay. I think so. I really do. I would have come before but, like, I didn't know how he'd feel. To see me, and so on. He's all right.—

This was one of the two friends who had found their friend with his sandal hanging from the thong on his foot, killed by a bullet from a gun that belonged casually to all who used the house, shared brotherly as the cigarette packs lying about and the drinks in the kitchen. He was one of two friends who ran to the cottage to tell their other friend something terrible had happened.

And suddenly, as they stood so close together in shelter before the prison he'd left and they were about to enter, his face very near them struggled with a changing tension of muscles and his eyes, appalled by what was overcoming him, grew large, brimming. He drew tears through his nose with the unashamed snort of a child.

Claudia put a hand on his arm.

But a man must not be patronized or humiliated by the hiatus of another man's silence: Harald himself had been blinded in this way, once, driving back from the prison at the beginning of await-ing trial. —I'm sure he was glad to see you. It was good of you to come. Thank you.—

Duncan's manner stopped their mouths against any concern about how the ordeal under scrutiny among the schizophrenics and demented had passed. And he did not acknowledge to them that there had been a visitor before them. He had ready a list of things he wanted attended to and time was on his heels, they must know as well as he did, by now, how soon the warders would shift from one heavy foot to another: back to the cell. There was a distanced practicality in his delivery. As if the probing of doctors had shaken him out of some stunned condition, in there, that place where the human mind in all the frightening distortions of its complexity is exposed. They were to get in touch with Julian Verster (they would know how to do that? If not at home, then at the firm, the ar-chitects' office) and get him to remove what was still on his, Dun-can's, drawing board. Plans. The work he was in the middle of. —I can do it here. They can't stop me. Motsamai's arranged it. And tell Julian to bring everything I need, everything, down to the last pen. Motsamai's arranged for a table.—

Harald noted dictated payments that had to be made: overdue. Time must have been destroyed with everything else in Duncan's life, and now the sense of what had passed, stopped dead at the moment of the act, had to be reckoned with. Insurance for the car. And it ought to be put up on blocks. To protect the tyres. The battery disconnected. Unless she would like to use it—for a moment the son was aware of her, remembered as if it were to be taken seriously his mother's jaunty enjoyment when she once tried out driving the second-hand Italian sports car; a vehicle for the transport of a young man's past life.

—The policy should be in a drawer. The bedroom. A file with other things.—

Harald has no need to make a note of this, he has been there before, looking into what was not for his eyes.

There were letters for posting. These were allowed by the prison authorities to be handed over, awaiting trial there are still some personal rights left, and Harald put the envelopes under the flap of his jacket pocket without looking at them. His son watched the letters stowed, as if a ship were disappearing over his horizon; no horizon within prison walls. And he knows these two will look to see to whom he's writing letters, once they're away from this place. And they'll want to know, desperately want to know what's inside, what someone like him has to say to these names they recognize or don't recognize. (Everyone wants to know what's inside him, everyone.) They'll want to know because what he's thinking is what he'll write and what he's thinking in the cell is what he is, the mystery he is for them, my poor mother and father.

They promised a twelve-year-old boy that whatever he did, anything, whatever he was, anything, they would always be there for him. And here they are, sitting facing him in the prison visitors' room.

Plan.

The plan their son is going ahead to draw in a prison cell— office block, hotel, hospital—what is it—predicates something that will come about. Ahead. Belief. Steel and cement and glass, in this form; yet an assumption of a future.

Messengers.

The Senior Counsel's secretary faxed the message and Harald Lindgard's secretary brought the missive to his desk. She entered softly in consideration and laid it before him just as she would a letter for signature but of course she knew what such messages concerned. Mr Motsamai had set aside 'the afternoon hours' for them, three-thirty onwards. As usual, the attendant at chambers' underground garage would reserve space for their car if Mr Lindgard's secretary called to give the registration number. Whatever portent messengers bear they have no responsibility, cannot help; all she could do was call the attendant with the necessary information which, of course, she memorized as part of her job.

Harald picked up Claudia at the surgery. Although the message had come at short notice—he heard her receptionist, Mrs February's question, what should she do about patients' appointments, when would the doctor expect to be back, answered with a gesture of dismissal. From Claudia, this time: to hell with them. But he saw it detachedly as the deterioration of her personality, since without the ethics of her doctoring she had no support.

What did they talk about in the car? Neither would remember. Maybe they hadn't spoken at all, each preferring it that way. They were already seated in the room when Motsamai—Hamilton— came in with the animation of a long lunch, like an actor backstage after leaving an appreciative audience.

—Got caught up!—

Dumped a raincoat, flung hands apart, a smile that seemed to belong with the last pleasantries and witticisms exchanged at a restaurant door. Wine in him maybe.

It was as if he had forgotten whatever it was he had called them together for. He calmed while ignoring them, flitting through papers that had arrived on his desk in his absence. And then became really aware of their presence; turned from where he stood and shook Harald's hand, clasped it doubly, covering the fist, and presented himself before Claudia. —Tea. You'll have some tea. Or you'd like a fruit juice?—

The tray had been brought and the obligatory ritual was followed in preparation for—what? 'The afternoon hours'. A considerable weight of his time to be given to whatever it must be he had to say to them.

—You've seen your son this week, yes? I have the impression he's standing up well.—

—Whatever that means.—

She may not know, but he, Harald, impatient, does: why pretend! —He's determined to finish the plan he was working on, you've arranged that, I gather. I don't know what the firm will feel about it.—

—Oh he's still on the payroll. Man! I should damn well hope so! They'd look fine if they struck him off before he faces a charge that hasn't been heard. I would not be prepared to let that pass, you can be sure.—

—If the man himself does not wait to be judged guilty.—

—Oh come now, Harald, I've told you again and again. That's not the principle. The facts still must be examined by the court, verified. You must bear in mind there are cases where an accused may be taking the rap for someone else—a matter of big money, or even, certainly where a capital offence may be involved, a matter of love, something where one party will do anything to protect the other.—

—You don't think there's any possibility here, do you.—

Claudia is not asking, she is drily pre-empting any baseless encouragement in herself.

—I do not. No. I'm reiterating from another aspect what we know our case rests on—circumstances. Circumstances that will be revealed in court. As I've already discussed with you. As I've been studying in the psychiatrist's report. As I've been following up in the talks I've had with people I've called in this past week. Verster. David Baker and so on. People from the house and those who frequented the house. What must and what should not be expected from cross examination. If I think it necessary to call this one or that as witnesses.—

—There is only the man, the gardener. If you can say witness is what he says he saw and didn't find.—

Harald contracted his calves against his chair to control irritation with Claudia. The lawyer was working up to whatever it was he was going to tell them, it was signalled in the way he leant back and then brought his body forward over the expanse of desk that held him at professional remove from them, his people in trouble; an intimacy with which, while inspiring their confidence must always leave him with a clear head above theirs. He could have summed it up for them: the definition of a best available Senior Counsel is one who thinks for those who do not know what to think.

—I've had them all in this room, one by one. With the exception of Baker, Jespersen's lover, they don't seem to feel anything particularly violent against Duncan, which surprised me, I must admit. Even if they thought they were concealing from me —I have my ways of seeing through the faces people put up. After all, one of them is dead, you could expect them to reject absolutely—never want to look at Duncan again. Ah-hêh . . .—

—One of them's been to visit Duncan. We bumped into him outside.—

Motsamai tilted his head at Claudia in confirmation; must have sent him there.

—Ah-hêh. It was necessary for someone to go to him. From the house, the two men who are left of the little set that lived on the property. Kind of family. Whatever in the house might have happened.—

—He never mentioned Dladla who'd just been with him.—

—I suppose it was a bit of a shock. But also something to give him courage, you know what I mean. Later. When he could bring himself to think about it, in there. There's so much time, so many hours when you're inside . . . Well. Dladla was with me last week and again yesterday. We've talked. Long talks. He's told me what Duncan hasn't, and what I didn't get out of the girl. Miss Natalie James didn't tell me the particulars of her relationship with Duncan. Dladla says she tried to kill herself after the affair of the birth. I don't know exactly what she did, pills, walked out into the sea, it was in Durban, he says, but Duncan found her and took her to hospital. He brought her back to life. Literally. She owes her life to Duncan; or she blames him. Depends which way it was, for her. Given my impressions of her, she could punish him for it. That could have been what the display of intercourse on the sofa was about. Oh yes. With a woman like her. A proven unstable character. I've said before—I suspect she wanted him to discover her. And now it turns out there's another reason why she would choose this particular way to get at him.—

The discourse is slowing down. All three were on some reckless vehicle together and it was braking as it approached a dangerous blind rise over which there would have to be a new surge.

—Well. Dladla, yesterday. Yes. We were talking. In English and also, yesterday, in our language, when there are difficult things to say it's better to use the words that are closest.—

Motsamai struck the flat of his palm at his chest.

—He told me many things. I thought I had it all straight from my sessions with Duncan—but this man told me. He told me something else. I don't think you know. You would have said, you'd know I'd need to know, that's so.—

He is looking at the two of them with the patronizing compassion of an adult who suspects a child of maybe not being entirely open to him. His head is lowered but the gloss of his eyes under fold-raised forehead glistens at them.

They knew nothing. Nothing. That was it, that was so! It was an accusation, not from the lawyer, but from each to the other, Harald, Claudia, another killing, a common life speared through, flung down: you, a father who knew nothing about your son, let him share a gun like a six-pack of beers; you, a mother who knew nothing about your son, let him fire it.

But Hamilton, their Hamilton Motsamai, had no part in this fierce flash of animus between them, although, diagnostician-priest-confessor that he was, he might have sensed it, brought from the Other Side his particular kind of mother-tongue prescience.

—Khulu knows something else.— He is racing the three of them down the steep descent now, can't stop. Don't speak. —Natalie was not the only lover on the sofa. Khulu says Duncan and Carl Jespersen were lovers at one time. Jespersen broke up the affair, not Duncan. Khulu says Duncan took it badly. He didn't move away, out of the cottage, although the other one—Jespersen had stayed there with him—went back to live in the house. But he was hurt, Khulu says he saw it. Depressed. Even if he wanted to show he wasn't any less free than the others—'for us, people can change partners, no big deal, still friends' that's how the fellow puts it—Duncan somehow underneath didn't have the same facility, the same attitude. And then it so happened that he went to the coast and found the girl to save. Saved himself. Khulu suggests. He doesn't know if Duncan had met her before, he thinks he might have, somewhere, when she was still with the other man, the father of the child she had. So he came back in love with a woman and brought her into the set-up. Nobody minded, no prejudices, he was free to do as he liked, and everything's fine, Miss

Natalie James fits in very well. There is the heterosexual couple in the garden cottage and the gay trio in the house. David Baker and Carl Jespersen are lovers, Jespersen's fling with Duncan is a thing of the past, for Duncan just as these episodes are for the others. And then, and then . . . Jespersen is the one who makes love to the woman. Duncan's woman. A wife, I call it, living there like any ordinary couple in that cottage. Oh we're told there were other little adventures she had. But this is Carl Jespersen. First he rejects the man and then he makes love to the man's own woman. He's there to be found on top of her—I'm sorry Claudia—right there on the sofa in the room where they're all such good friends!—

Motsamai is hearing applause, excitement moves his shoulders under the padding of his jacket which keeps them so elegantly squared. In an earlier generation, on what the law decreed as his Side, he would have had no recourse for this spirit but the pulpit. He had commanded them completely so that they could not have interrupted him; now he expects something outspoken from them. But all there is in this chamber, a familiar of the many emotions of people in trouble, is his rhetoric; and his clients' estrangement, neither wishing to admit any reaction to the other.

At last, it was Harald who spoke. Words are stones dropped one by one.

—Does it make any difference whose lover he shot.—

In their absolute attention that magnified every detail of his demeanour, both saw Motsamai's muscles relax beneath the jacket and the encirclement of his shirt collar and tie-knot.

—Ah, I'm glad you take it like that. Harald, Claudia. (He summoned and commanded each, formally.) That's how it should be. I'm impressed. That's what we need if I am to proceed in my client's interest, effectively, no nonsense. I have difficult decisions ahead. Because it does make a difference! It could make a crucial difference! This factor. The prosecutor—he'll have no purpose in calling any of the friends: as witness to what? The State's case rests on the confession. That's sufficient. It's the Defence's decision whether or not to put Dladla on the witness stand. Dladla's not going to be questioned about this aspect unless the Defence decides to bring it up. What matters is my and my colleagues' decision. That's the way to look at what you've just heard. That's all that matters. You are wise; believe me. Oh you are wise.—

Harald stood up as if someone had beckoned, so that Claudia turned towards the door. *Which way, which way.* She rose. Motsamai—Hamilton—came gently over to guide them.

—Don't discuss this with anyone.—

Claudia lifted a strand of hair off her forehead and looped it behind her ear, looking at him. —If you call Dladla to the witness box what is the effect on the judge going to be. How are you to know his attitude to this sort of complication.—

—Oh just like you two and myself, anyone is aware of the kind of set-up there apparently was in that house. Men with men. Nothing special about that, nothing to be ashamed of, condemned, these days—the new Constitution recognizes their right of preference. That is so. That's the law.—

Sinking.

Sinking down in the lift they were alone. Enclosed together. What a mess.

In contemplation, as if it had been come upon by chance in somebody else's life.

Did you mean what you said, what does it matter whose lover it was that was killed?

The cloth of her sleeve and his were touching.

I mean it. Why did he take on a kind of life, a range of emotions he just isn't equal to. Who did he think he was.

Harald is able to speak it out, to her.

Claudia hugged her shoulders against her neck; about to shame herself with an ugly giggle. Hamilton has the idea we'd be more concerned about the homosexuality than what happened.

Buggery may be criminal to him.

The mirrored box that caught their private images from all angles, a camera identifying them, halted with a shudder and Harald stepped back in an exaggerated gesture of convention for her to precede him.

In the car he released the locking device which secured it against thieves; they buckled their safety belts. That's what I asked about the judge. I was thinking of the old guard, the good Christians of the Dutch Reformed Church, some of them are surely still on the bench. But a black judge might be much the same, anyway, when it comes to that.

A mess is something before which you don't know where to begin: what to turn over, pick up first, only to put the fragment down again, perhaps in a place it never belonged. This 'discovery' of Hamilton's could not stun where already the blow of that Friday had made its iron impact; punch-drunk, after that has been survived, everything else is its fall-out. As the sight of Duncan coming between two policemen into the court was, as the first visit to the visitors' room was. What more could happen after something terrible has happened; what could measure against that fact. At night they talked in soft voices although there was no-one to hear them in the townhouse; expensively built, the walls sound-proof against the curiosity of neighbours. They lay in the dark, no longer in isolation. Sorting together through the mess. You cannot do this on your own.

That's what Motsamai was fishing for when he came to see me at the surgery.

I don't think so. He didn't know, then. It was before he'd seen Dladla.

But he may have got some idea, from all the times he's been probing Duncan. He has his ways of getting out of people what they don't know they're revealing. He says. It's a boast but there's some truth in it, it's like the gift for diagnosis some doctors have and some haven't.

They could take up where they left off; the weekend; any night. In the living-room Harald wandered, might be going to set the burglar alarm before bed, stood before a picture, found himself at the cupboard where liquor was kept and began to displace the bottles, jostled against each other. He came upon one that had been pushed to the back, only a thumb's-high level of some spirit was settled at the bottom of it. He poured the colourless stuff into a glass the size of a medicine measure and sniffed at it. The rest —the bottle turned upside down to empty it of the last drop— went into another glass; held up to her, but she shook her head.

He could have experimented at school. In boys' schools it's difficult to resist. But I would have thought—certainly we thought!—at a school like his, first sex would be with girls? There were enough girls available . . . Sex education. Girls would have been on the pill already, then, wouldn't they?

He came over to her with the glass, and she took it. They drank and grimaced at the potency of a distillation from the frozen North of his ancestry. The only link with it now was the identity of the one who was shot dead on the sofa.

You think it was an experiment. That's what it was?

Well, he was always attracted to females, wasn't he? If we can judge by the crushes we saw he had when he was only fifteen or sixteen, the hours on the phone, the necking with little blondes I'd come upon if I walked into his room at the wrong moment.

Claudia felt for the glass of water on the table beside her and washed down the spirit in gulps. 'Necking' belonged to the vocabulary of their youth, hers and Harald's; perhaps it was originally derived from the intertwining foreplay of birds—those mating dances Harald had the patience to teach his son to admire through binoculars.

That's what we saw. What we were meant to see, but there could have been something else. Perhaps he wanted to have some secret. When you grow up—I remember—part of it is having some area of your life no-one can look into, even to say—to take it over—that's fine-as-long-as-you're-happy-my-darling.

But he was madly in love with a woman. This woman. There's no argument about that. Verster told us enough. A serious commitment. Putting up with her capers on the side, no-one knows what else. He seems to have been besotted with her. Sexually there must have been something very strong between them . . . even devastating, the way I suppose it can be if . . . That business with a man, before her. Wasn't it a matter of being fascinated by the set in that house? Fashion that's been around for his generation, the idea that homosexuality is the real liberation, to suggest this as superiority beyond the ordinary humdrum. Why did he choose to live with those men? It turns out he didn't take the cottage because of the girl. Moved in with them on the property because their freedom claims to go beyond all the old trappings between men and women, marriages and divorces and crying babies.

He didn't suffer any example of divorces and crying babies with us.

Wanted to be one of the boys. Those boys. Emancipated. Superior. Free.

Or he wanted to try everything. Who knows. I have patients like that, drawn to drugs for example. Not really addictive by nature, some physiological or genetic disposition, just daring themselves for experience' sake. And what a mess, afterwards.

A lassitude, itself some benign drug, held them in their bed and in their movements about the townhouse, a kind of hiatus. They saw themselves, Harald, Claudia, Duncan, listlessly, from afar. She went to her clinic, he went to his Board Room. Duncan was in his prison. Discovery is not an end. Only a new mystery.

When they sat in the visitors' room they did not have the anguish that he told them nothing, although there was the covenant, he could always have come to them . . . short of killing; what does what he did with his sex matter, but as they sat before him and the warders there came to them now actual repulsion against him as one who had committed that act: killed. The fleeting resentment they had had in their early confusion refluxed, corrosive of what is known as natural feeling.

Another discovery. Each sensed it in the other, in conspiracy; it must not be revealed to the lawyer who believed he had all their confidences. Revulsion was their crime, committed against their own child and they were in it together. The seals of silences there had been between them were broken; they shut themselves up in the townhouse and talked, they drove out into the veld and tramped with the dog while they added, in step, each to the other's doubts they had about tendencies observed, and not spoken of at the time, in the child, the adolescent, the adult man. The charm the small boy had used to dominate his friends—all the games had to be his games, chosen and imposed by him, a tendency that doesn't end there; a lack of physical courage concealed by bragging: the only release in adult life for those who are afraid is to break out just once, at last, in violence? The young adult's uncertainty about a career: *what he wanted to be*? What do you want to be? So it was architecture, something on a large scale of ideas (which his doctor mother welcomed as a characteristic inherited from his cultured father, no ordinary businessman), and fortunately he turned out talented as he had been a charmer, cleverer than the colleague in the same firm who was his messenger, Verster. *What he wanted to be*. A mistake to take that, as it customarily was, as referring only to a career.

Apparently he did not know what he wanted to be.

Claudia understood her accomplice's observation to be about their son's sexuality. Even in this strange new form of intimacy that had come to replace the other (revitalized it in a way that shouldn't be examined), he could not tell her what really was coming back to him: '. . . the man is as he has wished to be, and as, until his last breath, he has never ceased to wish to be. He has revelled in slaying.'

The statements that seem to have been emptied of all meaning by endless repetition are the truest. Conventional wisdom is the most demonstrable. Life goes on. It did not stop dead that Friday night; that solution is not on offer. Ever. Neither from Harald's resource of God in His wisdom—he had to accept that refusal if not as His will, then as man's lot; nor from Claudia's rational experience that while some conditions appear terminal, some semblance of life persists. Hamilton said he was satisfied with the preparation of Heads of Argument and that he could come by and bring his clients up-to-date on his way home, why not, no inconvenience to him. So they put out the tray with glasses, the ice, soda, and bottles. Hamilton likes his tot of brandy. A few days before, Claudia, waiting at a traffic light, had unthinkingly beckoned to a prancing man holding up a candelabra of red lilies and bought flowers again, as she had used to on the way home from her surgery. They were under shaded lamplight. Hamilton entered the *mise en scène* of life going on as he did the equally well-appointed room in his chambers; as if every place were made ready for his presence. Something to drink was welcome; he tested the brandy, clucked his tongue, and got up from the chair he had chosen to serve himself a spurt of soda.

—My news is the date is set. A month from today.—

—It couldn't be sooner?—

—I know it seems long, but Duncan understands. And the judge is the one I had in mind. So.—

—What does Duncan understand, Hamilton?— Harald was not to be fobbed off with some assurance about delay. —We haven't much way of finding out from him. But you know that, we've gone through it with you over and over. Does he understand you're relying on getting the girl to show she was the one who drove him to some edge of madness from which he could do what he did? *She'll* do this, out of her own mouth. I mean, does he believe it: that *she* was what it was. That he was possessed—in some way. I don't see how your use of her can help Duncan if he won't accept this manoeuvring of the—this—I don't know what to call it—justification.—

—No no, not of the act; of the state of mind, the state of mind, Harald. This was not something premeditated. It was breaking-point—and she put him there, she did it! There on the sofa with Jespersen! It was her work!—

Motsamai was legs apart wide at the thighs, leaning out towards them in his body's emphasis, as he did from behind the desk in chambers, the gleam of day's efforts shone on the obsidian of his face, his blackness was the stamp of authority in the room. —He says he's guilty. That's all. I'm going to show why. I'm going to show who else is. How.—

—So he hates her now. Whether or not he's ready to blame her for himself and what he did. Hates her for what he found.— Claudia looked to Harald.

Motsamai answered them both, but taking his attention inward for a moment. —He doesn't speak about her. He doesn't want to think of her, that's my impression. I don't succeed, in that direction, with him. So I take it he leaves it to me. He knows I'm going to cross examine her.—

—Hates her now. Or he loves her.—

Claudia's laconic either/or is irrelevant to Motsamai.

—Of course he knows, too, that I'm calling Khulu Dladla. Ah-hêh.—

—For the adventure with Jespersen.—

—Oh indeed. Indeed I shall, Harald. Jespersen has—he had—his part in the state of mind, didn't he—ve-rr-y much so. He *and* the girl. Fatal combination. Isn't there good reason to believe that not content with throwing over his male lover, he got some kind of extra kick out of sleeping with the woman the ex-lover had taken up? Perhaps there was contempt or some sort of revenge, the lover has deserted the set in the house, so to speak, defecting to the female sex. Preferring women! Who really can follow these bisexual variations. They both were Duncan's lovers. Maybe each had some grievance against him, you know how such things are, even in ordinary love matters—my God, if you could hear some of the motives I come across in my briefs. Man! There could have been spite against Duncan the shameless pair were prepared to enjoy themselves with. Certainly they couldn't have thought of a better way to hurt and humiliate and push such a man to the point of self-destruction. A confession of guilt can be a kind of suicide. That's what I see here, and my task is to save my client from it. That's why I'm going to cross examine Miss Natalie James and I'm calling Mr Nkululeko Dladla.—

Suicide. But he didn't turn the gun on himself in the cottage, he threw it away.

Claudia and Harald are returned to that scene.

Suicide. The State may do it for you if you are convicted of murder. Harald speaks for them.

—We've never discussed the sentence. If the mitigation plea succeeds. Or if it does not.—

Hamilton Motsamai's face, the depth of bass in a long register of that intoning of his, the groaning, tender ah-hêhhêh . . . mmhê reached out to them in embrace. —I know what you're thinking. But the penalty hasn't been exacted for some time, there's been a moratorium, as you know, since 1990, when the scrapping of the old Constitution became inevitable. It's all about to go before the Constitutional Court now. The first case to be heard there, as a matter of fact, is the charge that it is illegal under the interim Constitution. The Death Penalty. I'm confident the Court will rule that it's unconstitutional. It will be abolished. Finished and done before we get sentence passed down. Ah-hêh. Only for the time being it's still on the Statute Book.—

As you know, Senior Counsel said. But what concern had it been of theirs, except in the general way of civilized people—privately uncertain whether crime could be deterred without the ultimate in retribution—dutifully supporting human rights and enlightened social policies where these had been violated in the country's past. There had been so much cruelty enacted in the name of that State they had lived in, so many fatal beatings, mortal interrogations, a dying man driven across a thousand kilometres naked in a police van; common-law criminals singing through the night before the morning of execution, hangings taking place in Pretoria while a second slice of bread pops up from the toaster—the penalty unknown individuals paid was not in question compared with state crime. None of it had anything to do with them. Murderers, child batterers and rapists; if Dr Lindgard once or twice had professional contact with their victims and related to her husband the damage that had been done, neither she nor he had in their orbit, even remotely, any likelihood of knowing the criminal perpetrators. (And perhaps, after all, they ought to be done away with for the general good?)

The Death Penalty. And now, too, it still had seemed to have nothing to do with them, with their son. They had been obsessively preoccupied with why he did what he did, how he, one like themselves, their own, could carry out an act of horror—they had been unable to think further, only abstractedly, confusedly now and then half-glanced at what a penalty could be, for him. The penalty had seemed to be the prison cell they had not seen, could not see, and the visitors' room which was the only place of his material existence, for them. Even Harald; who, in his religious faith, concerned himself with the act in relation to God's forgiveness, and committed the heresy of denying that this grace, for the perpetrator, exists: 'Not for me.' The Death Penalty: distilled at the bottom of the bottle pushed to the back of the cupboard.

Hamilton Motsamai has left them. Door closed behind him, footsteps became inaudible, car must have driven away through the security gates of the townhouse complex. He was all there was between them and the Death Penalty. Not only had he come from the Other Side; everything had come to them from the Other Side, the nakedness to the final disaster: powerlessness, helplessness, before the law. The queer sense Harald had had while he waited for Claudia in the secular cathedral of the courts' foyer, of being one among the fathers of thieves and murderers was now confirmed. The instinct to go and worship in the cathedral among people from the streets, which had seemed a way of avoiding the sympathy of his suburban peers, had been the taking of his rightful place with those most bowed to misfortune. The truth of all this was that he and his wife belonged, now, to the other side of privilege. Neither whiteness, nor observance of the teachings of Father and Son, nor the pious respectability of liberalism, nor money, that had kept them in safety—that other form of segregation—could change their status. In its way, that status was definitive as the forced removals of the old regime; no chance of remaining where they had been, surviving in themselves *as they were*. Even money;

that could buy for them only the best lawyer available. It could buy Motsamai. Motsamai's extenuating circumstances stood between them—Duncan, Harald, Claudia—and the decision of another court, a court whose decision would not be made on any circumstances in mitigation of the act of an individual, but on the collective morality of a nation which is the substance of a constitution—the right of an individual to life, even if that individual has taken another's life, and whether the State has the right itself to become a murderer, taking its victim's life by the neck, hanged in the early morning in Pretoria.

Death Penalty.

Motsamai is confident it will be abolished. 'Finished and done' (polylingual as he is, what was on his tongue and translated for their language preference was probably the more expressive Afrikaans-English slang, finished and *klaar*). But while the man killed on that sofa is under the ground, under the foundation of the townhouse and the prison, and Duncan is in a cell, it is on the Statute Book, it is the law's right, the State's right: to kill.

Just as it was the abstract larger question of a civilized nation's morality that was all that engaged Harald and Claudia when there was no question it could ever have any application to them and theirs, so this night the larger question had no place in the blinding immediacy: Duncan in a cell, awaiting the sentence to be passed down. They were two creatures caught in the headlights of catastrophe. Nothing between Duncan and the judge, passing sentence, but Motsamai and his confidence. The embrace of his confidence—wasn't it the expression of the man, rather than the lawyer, compassion that was on the Other Side, inner side, of his patronizing command, that shell of ego he had had to burnish to get where he was, granted as the best available for this case, among a choice of white Senior Counsel.

Neither could stop thinking about the repulsion they had felt, no escaping it, at the sight of, the situation of Duncan between two warders, this last time in the visitors' room, that place stripped bare of anything but confrontation. Prison, it was all confrontation, all—perpetrator and jailer, perpetrator turned victim of jailer, son become betrayer of the love parents had given him, parents become betrayers of the covenant made with him. The distaste they had felt suddenly that time, no, these last few times, before him in the visitors' room. It was revulsion that had brought them together. Revulsion against their child, their son, their man—no matter what he has done—who was brought into being by an old, first passion of mating. The sorrow that it was the shameful degeneracy, sickness of this conspiracy of rejection that had revitalized the marriage brought a collapse into grief. He lay with his arms around her, her back and the length of her legs against him, their feet touching like hands, what she used to like to call the stowed fork-and-spoon position, and they were dumb. Impossible to say it: sentenced to death. It was a long time, lying like that. At last she felt that he had fallen asleep, his hand on her body twitched in submerged distress, like the legs of the dog when it dreamt it was fleeing. Harald doesn't pray any more. Suddenly this came to her; and was terrible. She wept, careful not to wake him, her mouth open in a gasp, tears running into it.

Plan.

Duncan has a table, a T-square, an adjustable set-square, a scale rule, a circle template in the prison cell and while he is awaiting trial and sentence a month from now he draws a plan. Does he understand he may be going to die? Is this defiance—a plan, a future—because he understands that? Or is it that he has some crazed idea, inexpressible hope in despair, that he will walk out of that place back into his life. He will be free of what he has told, although he has told them, he killed a man. Time will reel backwards with the skitter of one of those tapes he and the girl must have played in bed at night—they were on the bamboo table with the journals and the notebook—and partying that Thursday will end no differently than it must have done many times.

A dead man, as Harald has said, is not present to receive grace; a dead man has no plan.

Everything is changed. So it is not incongruous to Harald that this old building commanding one of the ridges that drop away North from the highveld city, red-faced as the imperialist fathers who had it constructed with wide-flanked entrance and wood-valanced verandahs, has changed character. It is the old Fever Hospital facade he's looking along as he approaches but it is no longer a place of isolation for those who might spread disease down there among the population; it is the seat of the Constitutional Court. It will house the antithesis of the confusion and disorientation of the fevered mind: it is to be the venue of the furthest extension of measured justice that exists anywhere, a court where any citizen may bring any law that affects him or her to be tested against individual rights as entrenched in the new Constitution. The Constitutional Court, the Last Judgment, will be the final arbiter of human conduct down in the city, in the entire country. Its justice will be based on the morality of the State itself, land and shelter, freedom of expression, of movement, of labour—no doubt these will be the issues of some applications to the Court, but they are only components of the ultimate to which this kind of court is avowed as no other tribunal can be: the right to life. *The right to life*: it's engraved on the founding document of the State, it is the declared national ethos; there, in the Constitution.

Health not sickness, life not death is the venue.

The first application the Court will hear, convened for the first time, is that of two men in the cells in Pretoria awaiting execution. They exist under the moratorium. They do not know when or if the moratorium will end; the Death Penalty is still on the Statute Book. Neither has committed a capital crime for any cause larger than himself, a means to a political objective; each is what is known as a common criminal and he has been convicted of murder by due process in a court of law. He is not contesting his guilt. He is contesting the right of the State to murder him, in turn. The submission will be that the Death Penalty is in contravention of the Constitution. The right to life.

Harald has read this much in the newspapers. He comes, as if to a clandestine rendez-vous, to the old Fever Hospital. It is an assignation for him; he goes quickly up the steps, in the foyer does not know which carpeted area to follow, the place must have been totally refurbished, it has governmental status of elegance, not a whiff of disinfectant left, a bank of lifts before the inlaid floor's jigsaw of coloured stone, the potted palms. The atmosphere is less like the approach to Court B17 than the preparation for business seminars he attends in the conference centres of chain hotels. Men and women, minor functionaries, cross and recross with the unseeing eyes cultivated by waiters who do not want to be summoned. But a member of boards has a presence that is like a garment that can't be discarded although he himself feels that it hangs on him hollowly; a young woman recognizes it and consents to turn her attention to indicate the correct level and hall.

There is fuss and self-important to-and-fro in the destination he had found and where he is obviously early. He's shunted from one unfamiliar place to another these days: this is a well-appointed submarine, low ceiling lit over an elliptical dais where empty official chairs are ranged high-backed either side of an imposing presiding one. Behind the dais, stage curtains apparently disguise a private entrance. Facing all this is a well of polished panelling and tables with recording devices for scribes, and cordoned-off by a token wooden barrier (standard furnishings, he has learnt, of premises of the law) are rows of seats for the public who have come to hear final justice being done; or for other reasons, like himself.

The seats are empty but he is asked to move from the one he has chosen neither too near nor too far from the front because someone is dealing out 'Reserved' cards along that row. The pillars that hold up the ceiling are to be avoided; he hesitates before making a second choice, and now it's as if he is in some sort of theatre and must be able to follow the performance unhindered. A functionary brings water carafes to the curve of table before the official chairs; a tested microphone gargles and shrieks; the functionaries give one another chummy orders in a mixture of English and Afrikaans . . . the mind wanders . . . so at this level of the civil service (and of warders who stand at either side of the prisoner in the visitors' room) it is still the preserve of these white men and women, the once chosen people, old men wheezing out their days as janitors, the younger men and women belonging to the last generation whose employment by the State when they left school was a sinecure of whiteness. Back and forth they hasten, in front and behind Harald; the young women all seem to be wearing a uniform by tacit consent, some type of outfit varied according to fancy and enhancement of sexual attraction. Black-and-white, like the court-room figures in the reproductions of Daumier lithographs he and Claudia picked up along the bookstalls in Paris one year, they should give them to Hamilton, the right addition to the ikons of legal prestige in that room with its own shiny expanse—the desk—and the resuscitating cabinet from which brandy is dispensed with kindness at the right moment to a man drowning in what he has had revealed to him. Harald recalls himself; looking at his watch. And people are beginning to arrive and take up seats around him.

He does not know any of them, except to recognize one or two expressions from newspaper photographs or television debates—this is an audience come on principle, people who belong to human rights organizations or are politically involved in positions for or against issues such as the one about to be opened. He and his wife have never belonged in the public expression of private opinions, which he supposes is the transformation of opinions into convictions: here he is, among these men and women now. On his right there is suddenly the scent of lilies, a perfumed woman arranges herself with a polite glance of acknowledgment of a neighbour who is surely an ally of some kind, else why would he be present? She has long red hair of whose striking abundance she is aware, and keeps lifting it back from her nape with graceful gesture as she searches through a portfolio on her lap. On his other side a black man sits for a few minutes, alternately gazing down at crossed arms and lifting his head to look right and left, and when he gets up an elderly white man takes the seat and overflows it with girth and bulky clothing. Whether he is poor or whether the outsize jeans worn colourless over his knees and bulges, and the workman's checked shirt and scuffed leather waistcoat are the expression of a disregard for material things is something Harald, outside the milieu in which such a code of dress is significant, cannot know. He shifts a little, anyway, not to embarrass the man. This is how minutes pass; not to think, not to think why he, Harald, is here. He is intensely aware of the extraordinary presence he is, in his reason, unbeknown to all these people, for being among them.

He is alone as he never has been alone in his life.

And now they begin to file to the official chairs up there behind the shining arena, smiling and chattering softly to one another as they look for their allotted places—men and women who are to be the judges. Not all are judges in the sense of having been appointed to the bench in the ordinary courts, but all have the title for the purpose of this Court. It is impossible—because of the past, and even more because of the changes of the present—not to see them first as an impression of their colours. A black woman with the high cheek-bones and determined mouth of one of her race who has succeeded against odds, a black man with the heavy-set head in thick shoulders of traditional dignity turned academic (only he—Hamilton—has ceased to appear on the inner retina, of the mind, as black; dependency on him has taken his persona out of perception by colour). There is a brisk white woman with a homely Irish name who could be one of the feminist business executives who begin to appear on boards; a pale Indian with level eyes and sardonic curve to the lips associated with a critical mind. An old white judge from the bench emanates distinction, a patient face that has heard everything there is to be told by people in trouble; another who looks boyish, enquiring raised eyebrows as he rearranges his microphone and carafe, but he must be middle-aged, Harald's contemporary (but Harald has no contemporaries now). Others take their seats without capturing attention, except for one, a swarthy man (Italian or Jew?) with a scarred grin, and eyes, one dark-brilliant, one blurred blind, from whom radiant vitality comes impudently since he is gesticulating with a stump in place of one arm. They all wear green robes with black sashes and red-and-black bands on the sleeves—a sort of judo outfit with frilly white bib, which must have been designed to distinguish this court from any other. From the divide in the curtains the Judge President himself appears last, and he only is a connection with a past life, someone whom Harald has met or rather been present with on the eclectic guest list of a foreign consulate's reception. He is a man with one of those rare faces—easy to forget they exist—which present no projection of ego to impose upon others, upon the world. He seems to be handsome, but perhaps he is not; it is the calm without solemnity that harmonizes his features into that impression. He looks directly out at the public in acknowledgment that he is one of them. He does not smile but his eyes behind their panes have that expression, and further, a compassion—but perhaps it's the distancing of the thick glasses that gives Harald the idea that this is there, and touches him.

In one way, this is a strangely abstract hearing. Themba Makwanyane and Mvuso Mchunu—these are the names of the murderers—are not present. They are in the death cells. The application has been made jointly by lawyers representing them, and associations called Lawyers For Human Rights, the Society For The Abolition Of The Death Penalty, and even the Government itself; a government challenging the laws of the country—a paradox arising out of the hangover of statutes from the old regime.

Themba Makwanyane, Mvuso Mchunu—who are they? It doesn't matter to this tribunal, who they are, what they did, killers of four human beings; they are a test case for the most important moral tenet in human existence.

That ancient edict. Thou shalt not kill.

There is only one individual present in the concentration under the low ceiling for whom the proceedings are not on this higher plane of abstract justice. Yet the eloquence of the arguments sometimes draws Harald onto the higher plane, the atmosphere is that of a lively debate, with the abolitionists' lawyers basing their contention on sections of the Constitution's Bill of Rights, which they quote (in the aura of lilies the young woman at his right scribbles down what he side-glances to read: *Section 9 guarantees the right to life Section 10 protection of human dignity Section 11 outlaws cruel inhuman or degrading treatment or punishment*). The abolitionist Counsel's back, which is all that can be seen of him from the fifth row as he addresses the judges, sways with conviction as he gives his interpretation of Section 9: the first principle is the right not to be killed by the State. The retentionists' Counsel interprets the same section as the State's obligation to protect life by retaining the Death Penalty as the measure effective against violent crime that takes life. A letter from a member of the public is emotionally quoted: 'the only way to cleanse our land is capital punishment'. The judges interrupt, cross question wittily, and expound their own views; the case for retention of the Death Penalty seems to come up against the unanswerable when the judge who has lost an arm and an eye by an agent of the previous regime's attempt to murder him does not support an arm for an arm, an eye for an eye; does not express any wish to see the man hanged. Only the Judge President contains himself, reflectively, with perfect attention to all that is said, and sums up argument when this becomes too discursive. There is some clause in Section 33 which does allow for the limitation of constitutional rights—a questioning of the Last Judgment (she is scribbling again: *only to the extent that it is reasonable and justifiable in an open and democratic society based on freedom and equality*). The abolitionists' Counsel cuts through the discretionary clauses discourse and argues that even if there is a 'majoritarian' position in favour of retaining the Death Penalty this does not mean it necessarily is the right position: the Court is sharply reminded that the question faced by the Court is whether the Death Penalty is constitutional, not whether it is justified by popular demand.

The Court has risen for the lunch recess. Once the Judge President has slipped through the curtains an informality breaks out. Groups gather and block the way between the rows of public seats. One of the judges comes from wherever it is they are in retreat to take some document from a messenger, he smiles and lifts a hand to friends but when they make for him shakes his head and disappears: it is not proper for the judges to discuss the case with anyone. The scent of lilies sidles past along the row with a hasty apology, already mouthing across Harald to someone waiting for her, What a blood-thirsty bunch . . . People are asking whether there's anywhere in the building where one could get a cup of coffee, a handsome woman with an imperious head of white-streaked hair opens her picnic bag of mineral water and fruit for her companions and is amusedly rude to the official who tells her it is forbidden to eat or drink in court.

All this forms around Harald and eddies away.

They've gone in search of satisfying needs—toilets, food, drink—as at any intermission. Sitting on alone among emptied rows he is no longer disregarded; he is the focus of the shining arena, the vacated half-circle of official chairs up there identified now with the characteristics of the men and women to whom they were allotted. He gets up, walks down the stairs instead of taking the lift, goes out into the unreality of sunlight and the contrapuntal voices of black men working on a hole where some installation, water or electricity, is exposed for repair. Sun and *main d'oeuvre* —that is, has been the climate of the city, the human temporal taken along as eternal with the eternal. They will be here forever digging and singing. For a few moments dazzled by the sun, easy to have the illusion, nothing has changed. Those names, Themba Makwanyane, Mvuso Mchunu, two black criminals, are in the cells; the young architect is in his firm's offices somewhere down there in the living city, drawing plans.

The Death Penalty is a subject for dinner table discussion for those, the others, who will drift back into the Court as Harald will. Their concern, whether they want the State to murder or want to outlaw the State as a murderer, is objective, assumed by either side as a responsibility and a duty owed to society. Nothing personal. The Death Penalty is an issue; it will be decided in this Court, reversed under another constitution in some future time, under some other government, God knows, God only knows how man has twisted and interpreted, reinterpreted, his Word, thou shalt not kill. For these men and women strolling back to the building from the coffee bars they have found down in the streets, their concern is the issue, a dispassionate value above his; he knows, and the God he has been responsible to all his life knows this. Like him, like Claudia and him, it is unthinkable that the issue would ever enter the lives of these men and women—who is there among them or theirs who would be so uncivilized as to kill as a solution to anger, pain, jealousy, despair? The retentionists fear death at the hands of others; the abolitionists abhor the right to repeat the crime by killing the killer; neither conceive they themselves could commit murder.

The only people with whom he would have common cause would be the parents of whoever Themba Makwanyane and Mvuso Mchunu might be, those to whom what is the subject of learned argument is not an issue but at home with them, forced entry there by sons who murdered four people, and by the son who put a bullet into the head of the man on the sofa. It was unlikely these parents would be among the crowd in court, almost certainly they are poor and illiterate, afraid to think of exposing themselves to authority in a process incomprehensible any other way than as whether or not a son was going to be hanged one daybreak in Pretoria.

He stood a while after everyone else had re-entered the building. The flash of sunlight on the metal of cars signalled activity unceasing in the city, its chorus was muted into murmurs of what was always left half-unsaid down there; it was reaching him in waves of impulse.

Death is the penalty of life. Fifty. He is fifty; easy to recall the figure, but at this moment in this place he is experiencing what that means, his age. In twenty years the life-span will be reached. He accepts that in obedience to his faith, although many contrive with drugs and implants, Claudia's domain, an extension. A long time ahead, for him. Fifty, but he still wakes with an erection every morning, alive. Fifty. That the penalty could be paid at twenty-seven—that is what is being laid bare for him, argument by argument, in the guise of an issue. He goes back to the Court to hear what nobody else hears.

Judgment was reserved at the end of the second day of the hearing. With a razor blade Harald cut reports of the proceedings out of the newspapers and added these to his own account, for Claudia. He did not need to confess his assignation; since Hamilton's carefully off-hand admittance of what was still on the Statute Book both accepted that each was seized in preoccupation with means of dealing with this in his and her own mind; the conspiracy buried its shame, transformed to another end: how to do everything, anything, employ any means to evade for Duncan any possibility of what was still on the Statute Book. Inform themselves. A newspaper published selected surveys of the activities of and views expressed by the judges in the past; inferring that they came to the Constitutional Court already decided in favour of the abolition of the Death Penalty; the verdict was a foregone conclusion. Speculation based on personal background and hearsay which, of course, was most likely the source of Hamilton's wager disguised as reassurance. But Harald had heard passionate testimony quoting the petition for restoration of the Death Penalty whose number of signatories was growing even while the Court sat; read every day of the robberies, rapes, hijacks—murders—that would bring more and more names to such petitions—imprisonment doesn't deter, life sentences are always commuted, 'good behaviour' in prison releases criminals to kill again: only a life for a life is protection, is justice. He told Claudia of this. Fell silent. Suddenly:

Where do people with infectious diseases go now?

Very slowly, she smiled, for him. Most of those epidemics don't exist any more. So no more Fever Hospital. People are inoculated as children. What we have to worry about medically is only communicated intimately, as you know; so it wouldn't be right to isolate the carriers from ordinary contacts, moving about among us. Yet that's another thing people fear.

There is a labyrinth of violence not counter to the city but a form of communication within the city itself. They no longer were unaware of it, behind security gates. It claimed them. There is a terrible defiance to be drawn upon in the fact that, no matter how desperately you struggle to reject this, Duncan is contained in that labyrinth along with the men who robbed and knifed a man and flung his body from a sixth-floor window—today's news; tomorrow, as yesterday, there will be someone else, one who has strangled his wife or incinerated a family asleep inside a hut. Violence; a reading of its varying density could be taken if a device like that which measures air pollution were to register this daily. The context into which their own context, Duncan, Harald, Claudia fits, it's natural. It is in the closed air of a living-room at three a.m. with dry breath of wool from a carpet, the whiff of coffee dregs and the creak of wood under atmospheric pressures. The difference between Harald and Claudia as what they used to be, watching the sunset, and what they are now is that they are within the labyrinth through intimate contact with a carrier of a nature other than the ones Claudia cited. Harald, once again, comes upon his text. It is there one night when he has quietly left the bed not to disturb her, taking up a book he has read before but doesn't remember. '. . . the transition from any value system to a new one must pass through that zero-point of atomic dissolution, must take its way through a generation destitute of any connection with either the old or the new system, a generation whose very detachment, whose almost insane indifference to the suffering of others, whose state of denudation of values proves an ethical and so an historical justification for the ruthless rejection, in times of revolution, of all that is humane . . . And perhaps it must be so, since only such a generation is able to endure the sight of the Absolute and the rising glare of freedom, the light that flares out over the deepest darkness, and only over the deepest darkness . . .'

Without rejection of all that is humane, in the times only just become the past a human being could not have endured the inhumanity of the old regime's assault upon body and mind, its beatings and interrogations, maimings and assassinations, or his own need to plant bombs in the cities and kill in guerrilla ambushes. Is that what this text is saying to Harald? What happens, afterwards, to this rejection of all that is human that has been learnt through so much pain, so lacerating and passionate a desperation, a deliberate cultivation of cruel unfeeling, whether to endure blows inflicted upon oneself, or to inflict them on others? Is that what is living on beyond its time, blindly roving; not only the hut burnings and assassinations of atavistic political rivalry in one part of the country, but also the hijackers who take life as well as the keys of the vehicle, the taxi drivers who kill rivals for the patronage of fares, and gives licence to a young man to pick up a gun that's to hand and shoot in the head a lover (lover of a lover, in God's name, who can say)—a young man who was not even subject to the fearsome necessities of that revolution, neither suffering blows inflicted upon himself, nor inflicting suffering upon others, as with the connivance of his parents he never was thrust further into conflict than the training camps where his target was a dummy. Violence desecrates freedom, that's what the text is saying. That is what the country is doing to itself; he knows himself as part of it, not as a claim that what his white son has done can be excused in a collective phenomenon, an aberration passed on by those in whom it mutated out of suffering, but because violence is the common hell of all who are associated with it.

Get him off.

The crude expression from the jargon of the criminal fraternity was the apt one for the determination they were committed to now. Some way, hook or by crook—yes, the old metaphor openly accepted, expected deviousness. Since Harald read out to Claudia the judgments reported in court cases they never would have glanced at, before, having had no taste for vicarious sensations, they were aware of how interstices of the law, abstruse interpretations of the word of the law saved accused who in all other respects were unmistakably guilty. Got them off.

Where Claudia had gone reluctantly in summons to Counsel's chambers, she and Harald together now badgered Hamilton Motsamai for his time. What they wanted from him was wiliness, a special kind of shrewd ability a lay individual could not have and that people whose generalized prejudices they used to find distasteful attributed to lawyers who belonged to certain races. Jewish or Indian lawyers, those were the ones. Would a black lawyer have the same secret resources? Was it a sharpened edge that could be acquired in legal practice and training? Or was it in the making of a racial stereotype brought about originally by the necessity of those certain races to find ways of defeating laws that discriminated against them? In which case, why shouldn't Hamilton have developed every natural instinct of life-saving wiliness and shrewdness, who better? Why should he be presumed to have forgone it forever in exchange for the lofty professional rectitude of an Aryan member of the Bar who had never lived on the Other Side? Was it there in his chambers, slyly, under the gaze of the framed photographs of his presence among distinguished Gray's Inn colleagues in London? Harald thought it was; the whole approach to the girl, the prying into her motivation in the relationship with their son, was to him an indication. But Claudia, in conflict with the trust she had come to place in the man, wondered whether one of the others, spoken of by people whose admiration was also denigration, would not be the right advocate for any means, any means whatever, that could be found to defend their son. A Jew, an Indian. Though she did not say so, her husband understood; many compromises with stereotype attitudes easily rejected in their old safe life were coming about now that the other values of that time had been broken with. Once there has been killing, what else matters? Only what might save another. The townhouse ethics of doctor, board member, are trivial.

Hamilton responded with zest to the new attitude he sensed in them. As if he had been coaxing it all along, ah-hêh, ah-hêh, nice decent white couple from their unworld. He did not see, or pretended not to see, that they thought they were making some challenging disguised demand for him to do something, anything unethical (as they saw it) in defence of their son. The ignorance of educated people, white and black, of the conventions of the law was endlessly surprising, probably she would have the same thing to say about people and the practice of medicine. They still did not understand the scope to be claimed by a leading Counsel in defence tactics. How else could one take on representation of a self-confessed murderer?

—Couldn't you use what's the man's name—Julian—the one

who told us, the one Duncan called right away, that night? I have the feeling he dislikes the girl, he's been present at scenes she made that shocked him, when she behaved—I don't know—wildly, provocative towards Duncan in the way you've said will be important.—

—My Heads of Argument, yes.— He encourages Claudia.

—Things you can get out of him. Although he strikes me as being reluctant to talk because he's got some idea of the confidentiality of friendship and all that. Loyalty to what went on in that house, maybe he's afraid of others reproaching him . . .—

—Oh you are right. I've been working on him. Withdrawn fellow. But the point is, what you say about the house, those who frequent it or live there—true, he likes to have found favour with them, but he's really attached to Duncan, Duncan's the one who matters to him. But I doubt if he's worth calling as a witness.—

Harald keeps in pursuit of the other, Khulu. —Isn't he more impressive? If I were a judge I'd give more weight to what he might be prepared to say. And he actually is a member of that household, he's not someone who happens to work with Duncan, a colleague from outside, a friend who wasn't always around to observe what went on. Whereas Khulu.—

—And Khulu is gay. Ah-hêh. He knows the kind of morals, whatever you like to call it, what's done and not done, in the way they arrange their lives, settle things between them.—

I mean

Could it

Not that

Ah-hêh

I mean

Just a moment

But if

Let me explain

They become animated, it's both a consultation and a contest. Blessedly for his clients in trouble, Duncan has become an issue, not there, present among them in his prison cell as he usually is when the parents are in chambers.

The plumber's assistant-cum-gardener: is he worth calling?

—With what purpose? The State can have him!— Motsamai is suddenly very attractive when he laughs, some persona he keeps for other occasions breaks out of protocol, whether it comes from his place, distinguished by the African cut of his beard-wisp, in a coterie of ancient aristocracy, or whether it is his mastery of the other, the legal fraternity's bonhomie in chambers' dining-room.

The vulgar street term isn't used here: get him off. But it is mutually understood in its limitations. What his clients are asking, they and their Counsel know cannot set Duncan free; free of what he says he has done, free of what contains him as he was once in his mother's womb, unseen. Punished he must be, whether by the will of his father's God or the man-made laws his mother lives by. The term can serve only as the means, all and every means, to set him out of reach of what is still on the Statute Book. His life for a life.

—And I'm going to need more from you two. You realize that. Ah-hêh . . . much more. In that area (a spread of the raised hand in the air) we haven't talked enough. Not nearly enough. What was he like, growing up. Really like. Any problems you might have seen then. What might have affected his reactions later, conflicts and so forth. Some of the things you've forgotten, you think over and done with.—

It was as if blinds rattled up from the accord in that room, shadowless clarity fell upon them.

There never were any.

He was a happy boy.

But this was not spoken.

PART TWO

•

Why is Duncan not in the story? He is a vortex from which, flung away, around, are all: Harald, Claudia, Motsamai, Khulu, the girl, and the dead man.

His act has made him a vacuum; a vacuum is the antithesis of life. If they cannot understand how he could do what he did, neither does he. Except the girl; she might, she would. She was prepared to kill; herself. That's the nearest you could get to the act upon another. The act itself, not the meaning. He does not remember the act itself; the lawyer believes him or wants to, needs to believe him, but the prosecutor, the judge and the assessors, whoever it is who will be told this will not believe him. He did not, in the words of the lawyer's question, 'premeditate' what he did. It was *enacted* so quickly, a climax that is over, the unbearable emotion out of grasp, gone. He can follow the sight of the gun lying there, but that is the night before, some idiot was talking of buying one and had asked to be shown how to use the thing. The house gun. It was always somewhere about, no use having it for protection if when the time came no-one would remember where it was safely stashed away. He can see it put down, forgotten, on the table among the bottles and glasses, the night before. And when they—Jespersen, Natalie, the two of them—washed the dishes, cleared up, made love on the sofa, they left it there. The time came. They left it there for him.

He doesn't see it when he follows how he found them. Exactly how he found them is clear in every detail. They're both dressed (that's the way she likes it), only their genitals offered each to the other, her skirt bunched out of the way and his backside still half-covered by his pants as he's busy inside her. They egg each other on with the sounds that are, he can't stop himself hearing, familiar to him from both of them, and at the very moment they realize someone has come upon them they are seized by what they can't stop, it's happening in front of him, it seems to him that's what it's always like, if you could see yourself, a contortion, an epileptic fit. He fled from it. He thought he heard her laughing and crying. He sat in the dark in the cottage waiting for her to feel her way in and say, That's all there is to it, so! But this time it's not all there is to it.

How many nights in their terrible hours after their good hours, middle of the night had she stood over him shaking her head of flying hair, a Fury (oh yes, put me on a pillar or something in your Greek classical post-post-modern whateveritis architecture) laughing and crying—they're the same to her—and bending to him as if he were deaf: 'You faggot! Why don't you go back to one of your boys! Go on, go over to the house if I don't suit you, you want to make me over, Mr Godalmighty.' She, to whom everything was permissible, would not hesitate to abuse him for what she actually regarded as of no account. In confidence in the freedom of experience, of emotions, she professed and practised, he had done what he never should have—told her of the incident, no, be honest, it was more than that: the time with Jespersen. Given her a weapon to whirl above his head, hold at his throat, and when she saw in him the reaction she wanted, whip away as a big joke.

The awful torrent of her ranting came back to torture him in the cell. She had him cornered there. The most articulate being he had ever known, a kind of curse in her. You dragged me back you made me puke my death out of my lungs you revived me after the madhouse of psychopath doctors you plan you planned to *save* me in the missionary position not only on my back good taste married your babies because I gave mine away like the bitch who eats the puppy she's whelped develop 'careers' you invent for me because that's what a woman you've saved should have you took away from me my death for *that* for what *you* decide I live for said I must stop punishing myself but here's news for you if I stay with you it's because *I* choose I choose the worst punishment I can find for myself I revel in it do you know that

It does not end there. It flows from all the nights they talked until three in the morning, high on her words, they hardly needed anything else. And all the time while she enraged and flayed him—he heard again what he had thrown at her in place of a blow of his hand against her mouth, one violence resisted only for another: I should have let you die. I wish I had let you die—he had been aware in the most intense sorrow of lines she had written for him in one of her poems 'I'm a candle flame that sways/in currents of air you can't see./You need to be the one/who steadies me to burn.' He had not done this for her; he was not the one.

I should have let you die.

Does this mean he wanted to kill her. Look back on his Eurydice he had brought from the Shades, so that she could follow him no more. Rid of her and loving her so much; choosing her disastrously as she said she chose him.

That would have been premeditated. How many times had he stayed the hand that was to go out against her mouth. She was right when she taunted him about his middle-class background; what's it all about but docility, she laughed. Your parents—a pair of self-righteous prigs. Your father took you to church, he's a confessing Christian but real Christians are rebels they've gone to prison for what they see is wrong instead of taking their piddling little sins to the priest behind the curtain pretending to stand in for God up in heaven. Your mama's a good liberal, which means she deplored, oh yes, what went on in this country in the old days and let other people risk themselves to change it.

And you (had he said it to her) you think you are an anarchist, and anarchy has no form, it's chaos you are, and it's what I've left my drawing board for.

All day in the cottage waiting for her to come back and she did not. Other times when there'd been an affair, she disappearing for a few days somewhere, she had reappeared with the little carryall that was provision enough for a weekend with a lover, she had been unapologetic (she was a free being) but calm, obviously pleased to see him. Once she even brought him a souvenir she had collected, a fossil fragment. She could get away with such improbable gestures. There had followed a night of talk. He desired her strongly all through it but did not want to be so soon where another man had been. After a day or two they made love again, and for her it was as if nothing had intervened. That's all there is to it.

At last, in the late afternoon he got up from their bed where he had lain all day and went over to the house. But first, the strange ordinary movements gone through, he opened a can of pet food, placed it in a bowl outside the door; the dog prancing and leaping about him in anticipation, the simple joy of appetite, existence. He went to the house. He didn't want to speak to anyone but he heard himself in silent monologue and this time the words were not to be in the middle of the night and not with her. He did not know what he was saying, going to say. He was aggrieved right to the back of his throat, stopped up there. If he had any purpose at all it was to know what whoever was listening to his silence would say. It was Jespersen. Jespersen was lying on the same sofa.

So he came upon him again.

The man lifted his head and smiled, opening his eyes wide under cocked brows and pulling down the corners of his mouth, his familiar attractive representation of culpability in the style of an accomplished mime. What he said was: Oh dear. I'm sorry, *Bra*. The form of address picked up from the black frequenters of the communal house came in handy to assert between the two of them overall brotherhood which would absorb any transgressions.

It was exactly the manner, the words, with which the man had announced the end of the months they had lived as lovers.

Bewilderment exploded; he had not had in mind anything but her, she was what was filling him right up to the source of speech, she was what he was carrying before him in accusation, the corpse of his emotions. With the enactment of those words, that facial gesture there came the stun of that previous blow, he felt again, saw lying there relaxed in one of those remembered Japanese cotton gowns and flexing the toes of a muscular foot in favoured sandals, the torn bereavement of that rejection which he had long thought of as a forgotten phase in the evolvement that living is, as the passions and frustrations of adolescence dwindle to their minor proportions. It was Jespersen who was lost; lost in the body of the girl. Jespersen too, was the corpse of life. This man had himself destroyed it all, everything, the meaning of himself and the meaning of the girl, in the contortions, the hideous fit of their coupling.

Talk. Jespersen with his sing-song Norwegian English talked reason that was obvious. We are not children. We don't own each other. We want to live freely don't we. We shouldn't stifle impulses that bring people together, whether it's going to be sex or taking a long walk, never mind, eh. The walk is over, the sex is over, it was a nice time, that's it, isn't it. Just unfortunate we were a bit too impulsive. I mean, she's a girl who usually arranges things more privately, doesn't she. All of us know it . . . you know it, my Bra. It hasn't changed things with you and her before. You see, you should never follow anyone around, never, that's a mistake, that's for the people who make a prison out of what they feel and lock someone up inside. If it hadn't turned out the way you made it turn out, she's a great girl you've got, she would never have given it another thought and me too, for me no claims just part of the good evening we had, the drinks, the laughs she and I had cleaning up together. Why don't you help yourself to a drink.

Talk.

All through the talk there was another babble going on inside him as if the tuning knob of a transistor were racing from frequency to frequency, snatches and blarings of the past, of the night, other nights, despair, self-hatred, inexpressible tenderness, raw disgust, insupportable rage for which there was no means of order. The communications of the brain were blown. He could not know what it was he thought, felt under the talk, talk, talk. It was the grand apocalypse of all the talk through all the nights until three in the morning. It was that he must have put an end to when he picked up the house gun left lying in his peripheral vision and shot their lover, his and hers, in the head.

That's all there is to it.

Of course he would never do such a thing. So that is why there is nothing to explain to those poor two when they come to sit with him in the visitors' room. What there was, is, in himself he did not know about, they certainly did not, cannot know. The clever lawyer must make up an explanation. We are now in your hands, Bra. It was the lawyer who told him the post-mortem confirmed that Carl, Carl Jespersen, was dead of a gunshot in the head. That was how he came to believe it. He had not seen Carl bleed. He had not waited to see what picking up the house gun had done. He had fled as he fled into the garden when he overturned and broke a lamp in his mother's bedroom as a child. If the death sentence is to be carried out perhaps the brain should go to research; maybe there is an explanation to be found there that might be useful. To society. All he can do for the two in the visitors' room is hope that society won't subject them to much publicity when the trial begins. *He* has status as a big-business target for the journalists in one sector, *she* has status as a target in the sector of good works for humanity; people will like to see what press photographers can show of people of status whose son has done what he never could do. But perhaps it will go unnoticed, what is an indoor killing (homeground in the suburbs), lovers' obscure quarrel, gays' domestic jealousy, something of that kind, in comparison with the spectacular public violence where you can film or photograph people shot dead on the streets in crossfire of the new hit-squads, hired by taxi drivers and drug dealers who have learnt their tactics from the state hit-squads of the old regime with its range of methods of 'permanently removing' political opponents, from blowing them up with car and parcel bombs to knifing their bodies again and again to make bloodily sure bullets have done their work.

If something could be found in the lobes of the brain to explain how all, all these, like himself, could do these things; continue to wound and savage and, final achievement of it all, kill.

A house gun. If it hadn't been there how could you defend yourself, in this city, against losing your hi-fi equipment, your television set and computer, your watch and rings, against being gagged, raped, knifed. If it hadn't been there the man on the sofa would not be under the ground of the city.

He was a happy boy. Wasn't he. Claudia did not have to ask Harald that question. Of course he was. What did they have to recall from what—the lawyer attributed to them—they 'thought over and done with'. As if there were to be something hidden; from him; from themselves. What did Duncan want of them. What did he need of them.

Have you still got the letter?

One of those box files in the old cupboard we brought when we moved. But there's only the first page.

Yes, he remembered; they had thought of it, unavoidable, in all their confusion after that Friday night. *A terrible thing happened* the boy wrote. They had accused each other over who was or was not responsible to tell their son *we're always there for you. Always*.

I was thinking it might be something for Hamilton. But I suppose not. It didn't show any particular shock, the boy seemed to have dealt pretty well with whatever the business of that child hanging himself meant to him. *We* were the ones who were so disturbed.

That he didn't write that way doesn't mean he didn't feel it. Upset, afraid.

But he couldn't write it to us. Yes. Why.

Children don't say things outright. They offer some version for grownups to interpret. I know that from when I'm trying to diagnose a child.

Harald lifted his head and his gaze wandered the room, in denial, seeking. One of them—Claudia, himself, that silly self-justifying argument they'd had—both of them had made the covenant with the boy, There's nothing you cannot tell us. Nothing. But he had not been able to tell them anything that was leading him towards that Friday night when something terrible happened to him. He had not told them that he loved a man, or at least desired him, explored that emotion, although he had been taught to give expression to his emotions, nonsense that boys don't cry. He had not told them that he had brought a girl from the water, lived with her in conflict with her embrace of death. He introduced young women for a drink on the terrace of the town-house; an hour of talk about public events in the city, holidays, politics maybe, exchange of anecdotes and laughter, of opinions of a book both he and his father had read—and they might or might not see the woman again. This one whom he had taken in apparently permanently they had not seen much more of; he would walk in alone, you are always at home to your own son, and sit down to eat with them. Then there would be an old form of intimacy, a recognition between the three of them, you might call it, they would talk together in that privacy of family matters, their experiences in the different worlds of their work, he would tell his mother it concerned him that she worked such long hours and discuss with his father the possibility that he might hive off from the firm in which he was employed and start his own architectural practice more in accordance with his aesthetic directions. Once Harald had asked, You're in love with this girl, and he had seemed to welcome the admittance coming from without. —I suppose I am.—

But to say that was to be saying love was difficult; there were difficulties. Harald, Claudia should have read that. But there was freedom, his right to his own privacy: their form of love for him.

The covenant meant nothing.

It had been the most important commitment in their lives. Without it all the people whose old age she eased and the men, women and children whose wounds of many kinds she tended, were nothing, and without it all Harald's love of God was nothing. And if *he* could have, no, would have come to them, would they have been able to stop in time, what happened? At what stage in the disorder that was taking over his life could that have been done? What—when—was the point *before no return*; when the girl was resuscitated—the basic form of 'saved'—could he have been prevented, protected, from taking on to 'save' her in the final sense, in reconciliation to life? While it was obviously the self-destruction that was her dynamo, the very energy itself that attracted him to her?

Or was there a point earlier, predating the girl. They thought —all this often surfaced and was spoken between them—about the homosexual episode. If it was that: an episode. Was that something at which a halt should have been called, was it to be seen, diagnosed, as a beginning of disintegration of a personality—and wasn't theirs a heterosexual judgment of homosexuality as a 'disintegration'! If he had told them of that attraction would it have been the right thing to counsel him in a worldly way, suggest that for him it was a matter of the ambience in that house, a fashion, the beguilement of male bonding in a period—his adulthood— and a place where social groupings were in transition. In that house, as the saying goes: no problem, black and white, brothers in bed together.

There could have been that.

But then Harald thought about it alone, at night, and came back to bed to find her awake. Perhaps if we had had a chance, if he could have come to us then—it would have been a mistake to see the Jespersen thing as an episode. Maybe that was the stability for him.

You mean the life in that house. That way.

Yes. Saving the girl: it was an attempt to make himself something he's not. Someone like us. I don't know what it's like to feel yourself wanting to make love to a man. I don't know whether I would have been wanting to run away from myself. Coming from our sort of background. Maybe he should have stayed with men. That was really for him. If not Jespersen, there would have been someone else and they might have had a better life together in the cottage than the sordid mess he committed himself to with a woman.

She got up out of their bed.

What're you doing?

Over at the window, she drew back the curtains, it was a night shiny-black as wet coal and a plane making for the airport trailed its own constellation of landing lights up along the stars. The world was witnessing. D'you think that's what he would have wanted from us?

Get back to bed.

They were closer, coming upon discoveries in one another's being, than they had been since first they had met, when they were young and in the novelty of perilous human intimacy.

The Constitutional Court has gone into deliberation on the verdict and Harald and Claudia have no information as to how long this may take.

For them, their son has been already on trial—this trial in a court other than the one in which he will appear—and is awaiting a Last Judgment above any that may be within the jurisdiction to be handed down when his own case is heard. Motsamai is sympathetically condescending, reiterating reassurance. —I know you don't believe me. Ah-hêh . . . I know what you think: what can I know if the whole question has been argued before the highest authority we have except the President of the country and God Himself, and those judges haven't been able to come up with a verdict? But it may take them many weeks. My concern for my client does not include any fears about the outcome. What will emerge will be the end of the Death Penalty. My concern is to demonstrate without any doubt that this young man was driven by circumstances to act totally against his own nature. This woman, and the individual who was once more than his friend— the pair betrayed him out of his mind!—

There were other people in trouble waiting to be received by him. He ushered these two to the door of chambers. —Look, I want you to meet my wife, and my son—we've applied for medical school for him, I don't know if he's got the aptitude, you could give us some good advice, Claudia? What about this Friday evening? I hope you'll get a good dinner. I'll be coming back from the Appeal Court in Bloemfontein, so let's say around eight-thirty, something like that.—

The aplomb glossed urbanely over the sensitivity to their situation; he knew how it was, they would be in retreat from the company of friends whose sympathetic faces served only to set them apart from the basis of old friendship, common circumstances no longer shared. It was not always necessary or desirable to keep the relationship with clients formal. Taking on a brief means establishing the confidence of human feeling, some sort of give-and-take, with the family of the life to be defended, even while retaining professional objectivity. This white couple didn't have the resilience that blacks have acquired in all their generations of being people in trouble by the nature of their skins. He knows how to handle these two: they'll feel they're able to do something for him; that aside about wanting advice on a career for an ambitious son.

When they are in the visitors' room neither lets surface their preoccupation with the unknown deliberations of the Constitutional Court. It was not the first time they had had to employ this tact; there are so many subjects and reactions that are inappropriate to display to someone living unimaginably, exposed there before you only for a half-hour between two prison warders. The prisoner is a stranger who should not be confronted with what can be dealt with only in the familiarity of freedom. Certainly Duncan knew of the subject of the first sitting of the Constitutional Court; he had access to newspapers but he—also out of tact, it's a two-way process if it's to make these visits possible—he does not speak of it either. Or perhaps it is because they could not even begin to comprehend what the proceedings of that Court must have meant to him as he followed reports. A man who declares himself guilty, is he declaring himself ready to die? Or does he, as only he can, know himself in the death cells with Makwanyane and Mchunu, asserting the right to life no matter what he has done?

They ask him instead if he's able to make progress with the plans he's drawing and he says yes he is, he is, the work is going well enough.

—It's pretty remarkable you manage all that.— Harald is admiring; admiration is a form of encouragement that's admissible.

—The only problem is I don't get a chance to discuss any difficulty that comes up. With the others at the office, as we generally do. So this really will be all my own work . . . a bit eccentrically so, who knows.—

—Maybe someone from the firm could come and talk about it with you. Why not.— Harald is prepared to ask the senior partners for this service (if his junior colleague Verster had been the right person Duncan surely would have mentioned him); prison is not a disease, there's nothing infectious to keep clear of, in this visitors' room.

—Not worth the trouble. When I've finished the draft plan Motsamai will take it out and someone'll look at it.—

What is really being said here is that he understands that if the Last Judgment is going to be in his favour and will ensure that his life will not end now, it still has to be endured: back to the drawing board. But what that means to him, having once sacrificed the life of order for chaos, is something that cannot be conveyed.

When they retreat down the corridors behind the riding buttocks of the usual warder, Claudia—and maybe Harald—envies a woman taking the same route who humbly tries to hide her face in a scarf as she brays aloud, like a beast of burden, in tears.

Claudia supposed they couldn't very well refuse. They preferred to be at home together, these days. Best off like that. Recently Harald had taken tickets for a chamber music concert, his favourite César Franck on the programme, but the paths music takes are so vital, unlike the perceptions that divert in a film or a play—it drove them even deeper into their isolation.

He means well. Harald was familiar with the combination of business interests and a certain trace of personal liking come about, of course, that prompted such invitations.

Harald and Claudia had never been to a black man's home before. This kind of gesture on both sides—the black man asking, the white man accepting—was that of the Left-wing circles to which they had not belonged during the old regime, and of the circles of hastily-formed new liberals of whose conversion they were sceptical. If they themselves in the past had not had the courage to act against the daily horrors of the time as the Left Wing did beyond dinner parties, risking their professions and lives, at least neither he nor she sought to disguise this lack (of guts: Harald faced it for himself, as he now did other soft moral options taken) by dining and wining it away. Black fellow members on the Board; well, they were no longer content to be names listed on letterheads; they were raising issues and influencing decisions; recognizing this—that at least had some meaning? And Claudia—she had something remote from anything he had, familiarity with the feel and touch of blacks' flesh, knowing it to be like her own, always had known—an accusation, too, for all she failed to do further, in the past, but a qualification for the present; she didn't need any gesture of passing the salt across a dinner table.

The address Motsamai's secretary handed on his card was in a suburb that had been built in the Thirties and Forties by white businessmen of the second generation of money. Their fathers had immigrated in the years when gold-mining was growing from the panning by adventurers to an industry making profit for shareholders and creating a city of consumers; they were pedlars and shopkeepers who became processors of maize the millions of blacks who had lost the land they grew their food on couldn't subsist without, manufacturers of building materials, clothing, furniture, importers of cigars, radios, jewellery, carpets. Their educated sons had the means of their fathers' success to indulge in the erection of houses they believed to express the distinction of old money; dwellings like the ones the fathers might have looked on from their cottages and izbas in another country: the counts' mansions, the squires' manors. Architects they employed interpreted these ideas in accordance with their own conception of prestige and substance, the plantation-house pillars of the Deep South and the solid flounced balconies from which in Italy fascists of the period were making speeches. In the gardens, standard equipment, were swimming pools and tennis courts.

Some of the fortunes had declined so that portions of the grounds had been sold, some of the sons had emigrated again, to Canada or Australia this time. Some grandsons had reacted against materialism, as third generations can afford to, and left the suburb to live and work in accordance with a social conscience. There was a hiatus during which the houses were inappropriate to the taste of the time; they were regarded as relics of the *nouveau riche*, while newer money favoured country estates with stables, outside the city: the houses would be demolished and the suburb become the site of multinational company complexes.

But it looked as if it might be saved by the unpredicted solution of desegregation. A new generation of still newer money arrived, and these were no immigrants from another country. They were those who had always belonged, but only looked on the pillars and balconies from the hovels and township yards they were confined to. It was one of these houses that Motsamai had bought. Whether or not he admired the architecture (the parents did not have their son's criteria for determining the worth or otherwise of people's taste) it provided a comfortable space for a successful man and his family and was now supplied with current standard equipment, electrically-controlled gates for their security against those who remained in township yards and city squatter camps.

The enthusiastic chatter of the television set was part of the company, its changing levels of brightness another face among them. They were gathered in one area by a natural response to the oversize of the living-room where islands of armchairs and spindly tables were grouped. Hamilton Motsamai had discarded his jacket as he shed the persona of his day spent flying back and forth to plead in the Appeal Court at Bloemfontein. —Make yourself at home, Harald!—

A domestic bar that must have been part of the original equipment of the house was stocked with the best brands, a young man who seemed slight in contrast with the confident ebullience of his father was chivvied to offer drinks between Motsamai's introductions to various others summoned—a brother-in-law, someone's sister, someone else's friend; unclear whether these were all guests or more or less living in the house. Motsamai switched angrily to his mother tongue to reproach several youngsters who were lying stomach-down on the carpet, paddling their legs in glee at the pop group performing on television, and had not risen to greet the guests.

The wife and a daughter—so many introductions at once—
had entered with bowls of potato crisps and peanuts. Motsamai's
wife was a beauty in the outmoded style, broad-bosomed, her hair
straightened and re-curled in European matronly fashion, but the
daughter was tall and slender, nature's old dutiful emphasis on the
source of nourishment, the breasts, mutated into insignificance under loose clothing, her long dreadlocks drawn away from a Nefertiti
profile, the worldly-wise eyes of her father emerging in slanting
assertion under painted lids, and the delicate jut of her jaw a rejection of everything that would have determined her life in the
past.

Motsamai's wife—Lenali, that's right—was animatedly embar-
rassed by the behaviour of the children.

—Never mind, they're enjoying themselves, let's not interrupt
them.— Hadn't she, Claudia—oh long ago—had the same parental reaction when her own son had ignored the boring conventions
of the adult world.

—These kids are terrible. You can believe me. I don't know
what they learn at school. No respect. If you've had a boy, of
course you know how it is, the mother can't do anything with
them and the father—well, he's got important things on his mind,
isn't it . . . always! Hamilton only complains to me! I don't know
if you found it like that!—

This woman doesn't know what happened to the boy Claudia
'found like that'; or rather, if she does (surely Hamilton has told
her something of the story of the clients he's brought home) she
doesn't draw attention to their plight by the pretence that their
son doesn't exist, that what he says he has done has nullified everything he once was, the way old friends feel they must do. Duncan
is not taboo, tonight, here. —I used to think it was because ours
is an only child, and he was too much among grownups, he showed
this the only way he could, just ignoring them. Wouldn't kiss the
aunts who patted his head and asked what he wanted to be when
he was big . . . he'd disappear to his room.—

—Oh I find the teenage is the worst! In our culture, I mean, you don't kiss your auntie, but you must greet her in the proper way we've always done.—

Harald, under his conversation with others heard; Claudia was laughing, talking about Duncan.

—You're in the legal game, with Hamilton?— The brother-in-law, or was it some other relative.

—No, no, insurance.—

—That's also a good game to be in. You pay, pay all your life and if you live a long time before you die the insurance people have had more of your money than they're going to give out, isn't it.—

There was head-thrown-back laughter.

—That's the law of diminishing returns.—

The different levels of education and sophistication at ease in the gathering were something that didn't exist in the social life Harald had known; there, if you had a brother-in-law who was a meat packer at a wholesale butchery (the first man had announced his métier) you would not invite him on the same occasion when you expected compatibility with a client from the corporate business world, and an academic introduced as Professor Seakhoa who would drily produce an axiom in ironic correction of naïve humour. Hamilton put a hand on either shoulder, Harald's and the meat packer's. —Beki, my friend here doesn't come knocking on your door selling funeral policies, he's a director who sits away up on the fifteenth floor of one of those corporate headquarters where bonds for millions are being negotiated for industries and housing down there below—the big development stuff.—

—Well, that must be an even better game, nê. More bucks. Because the government's got to pay up.—

New faces appeared with the movement in and out, about the room. Some young friends of the adolescents, their voices in the higher register. The academic, whose belly wobbled in appreciation of his own wit, turned to tease them. Claudia—where was Claudia—Harald kept antennae out for her—she was talking to the son, no doubt about the prospects of a career in medicine, he had been captured by his father and delivered to her. A glimpse of her face as she was distracted for a moment to the offer of *samoosas*: Claudia's expression with her generous frown of energy; probably about to suggest that the boy come to her clinic, put on a white coat, lend a hand where it could be useful and try out for himself what the practice of medicine should mean in service to the people and the country. She laughed again, apparently in encouragement of something the boy was saying.

A tiny, light-coloured old man had already scented substantial food and sat with a heaped plate on his knees eating a chicken leg warily as a cat that has stolen from the table. Everyone sauntered, talking, colliding amiably, to another room almost as large as the one they had left, where meat, chicken and potatoes, *putu* and salads, bowls of dessert decorated with swirling scripts of whipped cream were set out. Harald found his way to her. —We didn't expect a party.— But she only smiled as if she were still talking to another guest. —Oh I don't think it's really that. Just the way the family gets together for the weekend.—

He had the curious feeling she wanted to move away from him, away among others choosing their food, among them, these strangers not only of this night, but of all her life outside the encounters in her profession, the dissection of their being into body parts. Here, among closely mingled lives that had no connection with hers and his—even the connection that Hamilton had in his chambers was closed off by an entry to his privacy—if she lost herself among these others she escaped from what held the two of them bound more tightly than love, than marriage, a bag tied over their heads, unable to breathe any air but that of something terrible that had happened on another Friday night. There was the hiss of beer cans being opened all around but Hamilton, who had filled his clients' gin-and-tonic glasses several times, brought out wine. His own glass in hand, he went about offering one bottle after another; Harald didn't refuse, as he customarily would, to mix drinks—anything that would maintain the level of equanimity attained would do. A man holding his plate of food carefully balanced before him came dancing up with intricate footwork as if with a gift; not of food, but with an unspoken invitation to partake—of the evening, the company, the short-term consolations. A man who had overheard that Harald was in the business of financing loans was taking the opportunity to corner him for advice, with heckling interruptions from others.

—It's no win, man, without the collateral you can't get the kind of money you're dreaming about. Ask him. Ask him. Am I right? If you want to build a little house for yourself somewhere, that's a different thing, then go to one of the government agencies, housing whatyoucallit, you get your little cents for bricks and windows—

—A casino! And where'll you find a licence for that—

—Oh licence is nothing. Don't you know the new laws coming in about gambling? He'll get that. But if he finds the property, the piece of land and maybe there's something on it he wants to convert, or maybe it's empty—then the trouble begins. Oh just wait, man. Objections. Objections from the people in the neighbourhood, applications to the city council—you don't know what hit you, it can drag on for months. And still you won't win. I know, I know. Freedom. Freedom to object, object.—

—That's how whites see it. Live anywhere you like but not next door to me.—

—Let him answer Matsepa—

—We don't have capital. What is this 'collateral' but capital? For generations we've never had a chance to create capital, tonight's Friday, every Friday people have had their pay packet and that's what they ate until the next pay day. Finish. No bucks. Collateral is property, a good *position*, not just a job. We couldn't have it—not our grandfathers, not our fathers, and now we're supposed to have this *collateral* after two years of our government. Two years!—

—But let Matsepa ask, man!—

—The people your company gives money to for projects, where is their collateral? Where do they get it?—

—Look—the route to take is by consortium. That's how it is done. We are talking of sizeable projects which require development funds; yes.— Harald hears his Board Room vocabulary in his own voice coming on as at the accidental touch of some remote control: who is that holding forth? —It's a matter of the individual who has the vision, the idea . . . project . . . finding others who will come in . . . most have studied . . . the project requires . . . criteria laid down . . . our co-operation with the National Development Council . . . viable economically . . . benefit to the population . . . employment . . . production of commodity . . . The man may have the brains—and the empty pockets; he has to link up with people whose position in some trustworthy way . . . — He was being heard by a young man, a son, lying in a cell looking up at a barred window.

—So I must look for another Dr Motlana or Don Ncube?—

—Man, they've got all the ideas already, they don't need you, Matsepa.—

—I'm coming to see you, anyway, Mr . . . Lindgard, that right? I'll contact your secretary, she can call me when you've got free time. I move around a lot but at least I've got a cell phone, there's my collateral.—

Hamilton came by. —Gentlemen, no free consultations. We're here to relax. My people, Harald . . . I can't get out of my car in town without someone blocking my way and wanting to know what they must do about some shop that's repossessed their furniture or their wife who's run away with their savings.—

Harald's neighbour turned to his ear against the volume of laughter and music. —But you don't know how he takes everyone's troubles, doesn't forget them. I'm telling you the truth. Although he's a big man today. Helps many who don't pay him. We were kids together in Alex.—

The professor was holding the beauty, Motsamai's daughter, by the elbow. —Did you meet this niece of mine, Motshiditsi?—

She laughed as with long-suffering indulgence. —*Ntate*, who can pronounce that mouthful. I'm Tshidi, that's enough. But Mr Lindgard and I have already met.—

—She's my protégée. I saw her potential when she was this high and asking questions we dignified savants in the family couldn't answer.—

He says what's expected of him. —And she's fulfilled what you saw.—

—Well, let me tell you she started off shrewdly by being born at the right time, growing up at the right time. That's the aleatory factor that counts most for us! Her father and I belong to the generation that was educated at missionary school, St. Peter's, no less . . . Fort Hare. So we were equipped ahead of our time to take our place eventually in the new South Africa that needs us. Then came the generation subjected to that system euphemistically called education, 'Bantu education'. They were equipped to be messengers, cleaners and nannies. Her generation came next— some of them could have admission to private schools, to universities, study overseas; they completed a real education equipped just in time to take up planning, administering our country. That's the story. She's going to outshine even her father.—

—You're a lawyer, too.—

—I'm an agricultural economist at the Land Bank.—

—Oh that's interesting . . . there are things that are unclear to me, in the process of providing loans for housing—although our field is urban, of course, the same kind of problems in principle must come up in the transformation I understand is taking place at the Bank.—

This young woman is too confident to feel a need to make him acknowledge any further her competence to answer, he's passed the test, he's placed himself on the receiving end of their exchange.

—In principle, yes. But the agricultural sector was not only integrated broadly into the financial establishment, through apartheid marketing structures, the Maize Board and so on—in fact in many ways it could afford to be independent of it—the Land Bank was there for them, essentially a politically-based resource for the underwriting of white farmers. The government, through the Bank, provided loans which were never expected to be paid back. The agricultural community, by definition white, because blacks were not allowed to own land, they weren't even statistics in the deal —the white farmers were expected to make good only in terms of political loyalty coming from an important constituency.—

—And now this is changing.—

—Changing!—

—How d'you see it's going to happen?—

He has only half her attention for a moment—she has caught the eye of, and makes a discreet signal with a red-nailed hand graceful as a wing to, someone across the room.

—By making it happen. New criteria for raising loans. Small grants to broaden the base of the sector, instead of huge grants to the few: all those who didn't really have to worry whether their crops grew or not. You could always be bailed out by the Land Bank.—

—No more automatic compensation if the crop fails?—

—Fails? That means there's been poor farming.—

—Natural disaster? Floods, drought?—

—Ah, failure may be compensated for; it won't be rewarded.— She laughs with him at her own brusqueness.

—Excuse me—someone's calling for me. We must talk about these things again, Mr Lindgard. The housing aspect, from you . . .— She has her father's beguiling flash of warmth; the *dop* of brandy.

Motsamai's children—at last, they too have professions; economists, prospective doctors, and lawyers and architects, God knows, there are other children of his in the room. Their grandfathers and fathers having survived so much, does this mean they're safe; these will not bring down upon themselves something terrible.

Where was Claudia?

Claudia was dancing. Someone had replaced the children's rock and rap with music of the Sixties, changing the rhythm of the room, and he followed the familiar, forgotten twists and pauses of her body, the skilful angles of her feet in response to her partner's as if the arms and thighs and feet of the man were his own. Where is the past. Obliterated by the present; able to obliterate the present. What brought Claudia out among the dancers, was it a heavy, downcast woman who had been sitting alone, who now danced by herself in self-possession, stomping out on swollen legs the burdens within her? Or was it the music that was the metronome beat of student days when she boasted to her friends with excitement and bravado that she was pregnant, his happy wild love-making with her had evaded the precautions of the know-all young doctor-to-be. Or was it Hamilton's libations. Or all these at once. Claudia had been found by a man who came from a different experience in every other way but this one: the music, its expression in body and feet, of the Sixties, it didn't matter where he had performed its rituals in shebeens and yards, and she had carried them out in student union halls, they assumed the form of an assertion of life that was hidden in each. The impromptu straggle of dancers wove about in relation to one another with the unconscious volition of atoms; she disappeared and reappeared with her man—or was this a new partner—and passing near, lifted a hand in a small flutter of greeting. When they drove home she did not say, Why didn't you dance with me, although he was asking it himself. He had had only to go over and take her hand, his body, too, knew that music which did not, like César Franck, reach into the wrong places. Remarks surfaced here and there, between them—Hamilton's family connections: who was what?—impressions of the house, whom might it have belonged to originally; giggles at what the first owners would think of how it was inherited outside their dynasty now; at home, they shed clothes and were asleep in mid-sentence.

In the morning Claudia stood, dressed, in the doorway. You know I was drunk last night.

I knew. God bless Hamilton.

It wasn't a manner of speaking; coming from Harald.

When the girl failed to arrive on the appointed day on two occasions, Senior Counsel Motsamai took over the telephone call
made by his secretary for the third one and made clear to Ms
Natalie James that she was expected without fail. This time she
came, and sat herself down on one of the chairs facing the broad
and deep moat of desk without waiting for the formality of his
inviting her to do so. She was in charge: he read. For his taste,
he did not regard her as beautiful, but he could feel how her
manner of confrontation, distancing and beckoning at the same
time—those yellow-streaked dark eyes with the pin-point gaze
of creatures of prey which fix on you steadily without deigning to
see you—was a strong attraction: male reaction to which was, *Here
I am.*

Here he was; but *he* was in charge, in the chambers of the law.
He had his notes before him. He went over with her once more
the events of the Thursday evening in January. She had the ability,
unusual in his experience of witnesses, of repeating exactly, word
for word, the replies she had given before. There were no interstices to be taken advantage of in the text of testimony she had

edited for herself. She and Duncan had not quarrelled—not that day, though they often did.

—So there was no particular provocation that perhaps led to your behaviour that night?—

She paused, slight movements of her head and twitch of lips in puzzled innocence. Her reactions, calculated or not, were inexplicably contradicted by her words, as if someone else spoke out of her. —I don't do what I do because someone provokes me.—

It was while they were continuing in this way, the rally of his questions and her answers that he was enduring with the undeflected patience of professionalism, sure of her faltering to his advantage in the end, that she simply let drop the subject of the exchange, and made a remark as if reminded of something that might not be of interest to him.

—By the way, I'm pregnant.—

If she expected some sudden reaction she should have known better. Counsel conceals all irritation and anger in court—a discipline that serves to control the reception of any unforeseen statement. The art is to be quick in deciding how to use it. He nudged his back against the support of his chair. Ah-hêh. And simply asked another question.

—Is the child Duncan's?—

She smiled at the accusation behind the question.

—It doesn't matter.—

—Natalie . . . why doesn't it matter?— He tries the fatherly approach.

—Because then they won't be able to make any claim. It could be from that night, couldn't it. They won't claim.—

—What d'you mean, they won't claim?—

—They'd want something of him. If something terrible happens to him.—

—The Death Penalty is going to be abolished, my dear. Duncan will go to prison and he will come out. Surely, for yourself, it must matter whose child it is you're going to have. You must know, don't you? You do know.—

—We made love—Duncan—that morning before we went to work, it was all in the same twenty-four hours. So who can say. It doesn't matter.—

—No? You don't care?—

Oh she is in charge, she is in charge. —I do care; it's going to be my child, that's who it is, mine.—

It was Counsel's task—everything was his task, no wonder his wife complained that he had little attention to give at home in the fine house he had provided—his task to tell his client and the parents what might or might not be a new element in their life as people in trouble.

On their next half-hour in the visitors' room Harald referred to it as a fact, without mention of any circumstances the girl related. —Hamilton has told us Natalie James is expecting a baby.—

Duncan faced them kindly, as if looking back at something from afar. —That's good for her.—

Do you love her.

I suppose so.

And now.

Change the subject.

Claudia is talking to him of other things, she's telling him what a nice boy Sechaba Motsamai is to have around helping at the clinic on Wednesdays, Claudia is able to feel herself close to her son, these last days before the trial, she looks forward to the visitors' room, now, they've found the communication is there, all along, in just seeing each other between the barriers of the unspeakable.

Harald hears their voices and does not follow.

I suppose so.

He and Claudia will never know what it was that happened. What happened to their son.

Claudia wanted to go to the visitors' room the day before the trial began. During the morning Harald abruptly left his office, passed his secretary's careful absorption at her computer (she knows, she knows, there's something that emanates from people when they are about the business of their trouble); down in the lift where employees whose names they're aware he does not recall greet the executive member of the Board as a sign of loyalty to the firm that feeds them; is saluted in the building's basement car-park by the security guard in paramilitary uniform, and arrives unannounced at chambers. Hamilton Motsamai is in conference with another client but when his secretary—she knows, she knows the trial starts tomorrow—informs him on the intercom he excuses himself to the client and comes to Harald. Nobody's need is greater than Harald's; Motsamai's hand is outstretched, his mouth still is parted with the words he was speaking when he left his office, the switch of attention from one set of people in trouble to another is in his face as a slide projector flicks one transparency away for another to drop into view. Motsamai's face has been formed by this succession; whatever his clients pay him for, however high his fees, they leave, like initials scratched into the living bark of a tree, their anguish on the surface of his facial expression; his strength, confidence and pride wear it as a palimpsest upon him. He and Harald go into an anteroom full of files and boxes. Motsamai's tongue moves back and forth along the teeth of his lower jaw, bulging under the membrane of the lip, his wisp of beard lifts, as he listens to Harald: no, no. —Much better if you stay away. I'll see him, I'll be with him this afternoon. He's prepared himself, nothing should be allowed to disturb that. His mother, no—you know, that can only get him thinking how he's got to face you from the dock again tomorrow. He'll be all right. He's fine, he's in control.—

Harald sits in his car. The key is in the ignition. A beggar sprawled against a shopfront is clawing bread from a half-loaf and stuffing it into his mouth. Mama traders call and argue among pyramids of tomatoes and onions. Rotting cabbage leaves adrift in the gutter; life pullulating in one way or another. People cross the windscreen as darkness overtaking light. Is Duncan afraid, the day before the trial?

Duncan is not afraid. Nothing could be more terrifying than that Friday night.

There is a face at the window. It's the familiar face, the city's face of a street boy: Harald has forgotten to give him his handout for having whistled and gestured the availability of this parking-bay when he arrived. He lowers the window. The boy has his glue-sniffer's plastic bottle half-stuffed under the neck of the garment he's wearing, his black skin is yellowed, like a sick plant. What's left of his intelligence darts quickly at the coin, his survival is to see at a glance if it is enough.

The exaltation of putting a face to everything denied me.

By both of them joined like rutting dogs on the sofa. The exaltation—so that is what violence is, street violence. I know it, I am *of it*, now. How it comes to you because there is nothing else.

It comes back to me through the hours with the two psychiatrists with their carefully arranged patient faces—how difficult for us humans to concoct an expression empty of judgment: that's idiocy, or arrogance, superhuman—but they couldn't get it out of me. Comprehend. Not Motsamai, either. And the court will not. No-one.

That face. His face. Bra.

Only *she* knows why I could do it. It was something made possible in me by her.

The courtroom is a present so intense it is eternity; all that has passed since that Friday night is made one in it, there is nothing conceivable after it.

There are many to bear witness. Not in the empty stand in the well of the court; all around Harald and Claudia. A murder trial, out of the common criminal class, with a privileged son in the professions accused of murder has provided the Sunday papers with a story of a 'love triangle' calling up not only readers' concupiscence but also some shallow-buried prejudices: the milieu is described as a 'commune', 'a pad' where blacks and whites, 'gay and straight', live together, and there have been photographs somehow got hold of—large ones of Natalie James and the reproduction of an itinerant photographer's nightclub group in which Carl Jespersen appears with Khulu. All around: the curious, who may or may not be able to identify the parents. Within the whispering, shuffle and creak, they are not obvious among strangers; as for themselves, theirs is a single identity they now have that years of marriage never achieved. There is only this court, this time, this existence, mother/father.

Not all in the visitors' seats are voyeurs. There are Duncan's friends. Some unexpected friends they did not know; what a secretive person he was—with them, his parents. A mother and daughter—women with a lot of hair who look like two versions of the same woman some years apart. Jewish probably. Duncan had Jewish and black friends Harald and Claudia did not have; he had moved on. The two women came up and gave their names. The younger version was saying, For me it's as if it's happening to my brother, but the elder's voice elbowed hers out of the way, speaking in French, *Nous sommes tous créatures mêlées d'amour et du mal. Tous.*

Claudia thanked them for coming; there is a form for everything, it occurs to you unbidden.

What was that.

Claudia fingered distractedly back through school French. Something like us being creatures mixed of love and evil, all of us. I don't quite see what she was getting at.

But Harald did.

Others approached, shook the parents' hands, but none knew what to say as that foreign woman had, whoever she was: a messenger. And the other messenger was there. He stood distressed, forever guilty as the one who had brought, a curse he could not discard like a gun, on the way, the news that Friday evening that something terrible had happened.

Now what Hamilton had prepared them for was being enacted. Duncan was in the well of the court wearing a wide-striped shirt and red tie with grey pants and one of those outsize linen jackets young men choose these days—the nearest Motsamai will have been able to get him to wear a suit like Motsamai's elegant own, Duncan probably didn't own a suit. An appearance consistent with the moral world the judge and his chosen assessors occupy—the accused's mother and father paid close attention to the outfit and what it implied about the gaunt man on his throne. An urbane judge—Hamilton had said in the hinting tone of satisfaction. Up there, the only distinguishing feature of the man in his crimson robe was round ears standing out alertly from his skull. Was the convention of dress Duncan presented something acceptable to a worldly judge who would not associate moral standards with a suit; did it matter what a man wore when whatever his clothes might say about him, he killed. The voice of a functionary—the judge's clerk—confirms Duncan's identity in this place, for this reason.

—Are you Duncan Peter Lindgard?—

—Yes.—

—You are charged with a crime of murder, in that you wrongfully and maliciously killed, on January 19th, 1996, Carl Jespersen. How do you plead?—

As on that Friday night in the townhouse when the messenger made his pronouncement, everything has come to a stop; held by Duncan's profile, his presence. But the moment is broken into by Hamilton Motsamai, Senior Counsel for the Defence. He has swiftly risen. —M'Lord, in view of the nature of the accused's defence, would M'Lord allow me to enter a plea on my client's behalf? The plea is not guilty. The nature of the defence, M'Lord, will become apparent during my cross examination of the Prosecution's first witness, whom my Learned Friend for the State has identified to me.—

The judge has nodded assent.

All about was the movement of people shifting closer to make place for more to be seated, but by now everyone has realized which couple is the parents; no-one presses up against them in the row where they sit.

The girl materializes; the one. She was the one on the sofa with her pants down, who may be seen: the other is out of reach of anyone's gaze, underground along with all the others who are knifed or strangled or shot in the violence that is the city's, the way of death. Three more were killed in rivalry between minibus taxi owners at a rank round the corner this morning. But Duncan, when he was awaiting trial, had been wrong when he thought that what happened to him would be lost in random violence and of no public interest. It is the street killings that are of no interest, happening every day.

There she is. The one. There are women who have days when they are ugly and days when they are beautiful. It may have something to do with a number of things: digestion, stage of biological cycle, and the mood of the way they wish to present themselves. She has on her a beautiful day. Claudia was not surprised at the aspect presented; she knew, from her medical practice, how the neurotic personality likes an audience, any audience, even one that can picture her with her legs apart on the sofa. Harald saw her for the first time as Duncan must always have seen her, his definitive image, even on her ugly days; the lovely soft skin indented, the twist of a chisel on a statue, to the curl of the lip at either side of the mouth, the rosy-buffed high forehead under stringy wisps of fringe, the lazy, intense pupils of eyes within a disguise of childish turn-down at the outer corners where the thicket of lashes met, the clothes that hid and suggested her body, modest flowing skirt that slid back and forth across the divide of her buttocks as she walked to the witness stand, cossack blouse whose gauzy amplitude fell from the Modigliani shoulders and touched upon the points of meagre breasts. She is not a beauty but she has beauty at her command. And to be looking at her is to see that the design of her face is one that can transform into something menacing. Ugly days. When she entered the well of the court it was difficult to make out whether she avoided finding Duncan; suddenly—Harald saw—from the stand she was looking straight at Duncan, perfectly still and concentrated; and would Duncan reply for her, as she drew it from him: *Here I am*. Would he! Harald could not see, could not see Duncan's eyes and, wildly agitated, scarcely knew how to contain this—imagined—male empathy with his son.

He felt an animus towards the Prosecutor the moment the man rose. It was a physical sense along his skin. The Prosecutor had the lugubrious high-arched brows and the elliptical wide mouth of the comedian that also may become the glaring face of the samurai. Wearing the endearing version of his features, he led his evidence in chief.

—You lived, as lovers, with Duncan Lindgard?—

—Yes.—

—How long had this relationship existed?—

—About a year and a half.—

—Were you happy together?—

She smiled, bunched lips and made an odd gesture that was the only sign of nerves evident in her—passed bent fingers lightly down the skin of her throat, as if to claw at herself. —Hardly that. Well, occasionally. Between all the other times.—

—Why was the relationship you both had chosen not a happy one?—

—Choose. I didn't choose.—

—How was that?—

—He owned my life because he took me to a hospital.—

—Could you explain to the court what that means?—

—I had drowned and would have been dead if he hadn't done it.—

—You had got into difficulties while going for a swim?—

—I walked out into the sea.—

—It was your intention to drown.—

—That's right.—

The assembly is thrilled by this grand laconic recklessness towards the precious possession of life itself. Harald and Claudia can feel that the people around them already have fallen in love with this girl, their faces turned on her are capitulating: *Here I am*.

—Weren't you glad to be alive, after all?—

—He wanted me to be. That was nice.—

—So why were you not happy, grateful?—

—He wanted me to be glad his way, to forget why I had made my decision that time, everything I hadn't been able to deal with, as if it had disappeared. Pumped out of my lungs with the seawater, *basta*, a new Natalie. According to plan. He's an architect, that's all he knows—making plans, a plan for somebody's life according to his specifications. Not mine. He found careers I ought to have, even attitudes. Nothing was mine.—

—What was your reaction?—

—I wanted to get myself back from him.—

—He saved you and then he proceeded to undermine you, is that it? He undermined your return to confidence? Why did you continue to cohabit in the cottage with him?—

How is it she can be a vulnerable woman, soft-fleshed creature with those eyes whose shape has not changed with the rest of her, stayed with the innocence of childhood, and say the things she does: —I thought—I was fascinated—if I could go on living like that with him—then that was the worst thing that could ever happen to me. I'd have tested it out, and if I could survive . . . well, a kind of dare. I've had so many failures.—

—So you were desperate. You had already attempted suicide and now once again you were desperate.—

—I suppose you'd call it that.—

—Did he understand your desperation?—

—Oh yes. That was why he was always trying to find *his* solution for me. What he'll never understand, doesn't want to understand is that I can't use someone else's solutions hanging like a chain round my neck. He could only strangle me.—

—In what some might see as his well-meaning, would you say he was possessive? Jealous?—

—Possessive . . . every thought I have, every trivial action, he pored over, took to pieces.—

—Jealous of other men—their interest in you?—

—He was jealous of the air I breathe.—

—What were your relations with the men at the house?—

—They were his friends and they became mine as well. Thank heaven for them, because they didn't take life too seriously, they were not like him and me, we could all let our hair down and have fun together. He kept me away from friends I might make for myself. They were always the wrong people for me—*he* decided. It wasn't worth quarrelling about, in the end.—

—You knew he had a homosexual affair with one of the men in the house?—

—Oh yes, he told me everything about himself. But everyone had forgotten about it.—

—On the night of January 18th, did you have sexual intercourse with one of the men? Carl Jespersen?—

—Yes. It happened.—

—How did it come about?—

—Carl was someone you could talk to about anything. And he knew what Duncan was like. I used to go to him when Duncan and I had quarrelled and he had a way of, well, putting things in perspective. It's not the end of the world.—

—Did you have an intimate relationship with Carl Jespersen previous to that night?—

—Good God, no. He was gay; he and David were together. He found this job for me where he worked, and that was a *solution* Duncan approved for me. Duncan was reassured that Carl would keep an eye on me so that I wouldn't have anything to do with other men there. Duncan was always afraid that I'd leave. It had happened to him before; he closes his hand so tightly on what he wants that he kills it.—

The Prosecutor paused to let her mere figure of speech find its resonance in the charge before the court: murder.

—So the accused had no reason to be jealous of Carl Jespersen?—

—No reason. But that's to say—he is jealous of everything, he broods on everything connected with me, even when he himself has chosen the solution. Carl and I got along well together, we worked together every day, he could have cooked up something in his mind even over the fact that Carl was the one who smoothed things between him—Duncan—and me. Reconciled us to each other. I mean, to what Duncan is, what Duncan was doing to me.—

—Why did your relationship as a friend with Carl Jespersen change, that night?—

—A party developed at the house and I was enjoying myself. But Duncan again wouldn't have it, he was sure I wouldn't get up in time for work next morning. I didn't know whether I really was in my place in an advertising agency but Duncan was always worried that I wouldn't take it seriously. He wanted me to go back to the cottage with him. In front of other people he was pleading and arguing—humiliating me. I'd had enough that day.—

—What had occurred that distressed you?—

—We'd talked half the night before, started again, quarrelled when we woke up in the morning, it ended the usual way. I'd had enough.—

—Was that the reason why you did not go back to the cottage with the accused when the party ended?—

—Yes.—

—You were afraid that the hostility of the accused would subject you to another night of abuse.—

—I stayed on to help Carl clean up and to get the whole scene off my chest, talking to him about it. I couldn't bear to go back to the cottage and be reproached all over again, *for my own good*. I should have taken my car and driven off, right then—anywhere—as I've done many other times.—

—Was violence part of the accused's reproaches to you, did he strike you?—

—No. It didn't come to that.—

—But he threatened you?—

—Often I knew it. Not in what he said. But in the way he was; the way he looked. He was wanting to kill me. Sometimes it came out of him like a light.—

—You were sure he had the capacity of violence. You were afraid?—

—I knew he couldn't kill me, because I was the one he had taken out of the water.—

—But you had to take refuge from him that night?—

—I just needed something without chains. Carl made me laugh instead of crying and he comforted me. Then what we did was natural. Part of it. I have never had any comfort from Duncan. I don't know what he brought me back to life for.—

Again, why is Duncan not in the story?

He is the vortex from which, flung away, around, is the court. If he cannot understand why he did what he did, there will be the explanations of others. Versions. And there is this version of what he saw from the doorway; the first time, that is. She is on trial, not he. This is the way it was for her; natural. Part of it. A mating dance for three, first he with one and the other, then those two together. She was 'enjoying herself', the wildness he knew so well, that was her means of exploding the self that tormented her, that ended in the water, or with the pills she was able to charm out of doctors and pharmacists. When she said he took me to a hospital, she didn't say how many times. Enjoying herself and he was the rescue service again, needing to take her back to the cottage and give her love, loving, no matter what she did (what other comfort is there). Not drunk, no. She doesn't need alcohol to stimulate her, going on the attack with words is all the stimulant she needs, it can keep up her excitation through the nights. So this time she doesn't want to be 'saved' as she puts it, in advance. It's his turn to be victim.

If he could free himself (his companions the police are beside him) and walk across the well of the court to her, what is it that he would want to say?

How could you think of something so exquisitely (Motsamai's adverb) appropriate to destroy me? The two of you; both so clever, knowing me so well.

You've told it to them your way: you didn't tell them that it was in you, it was in your head, it was you who put it in me, so that was what you saw in me: you said to me more than once at three, four in the morning—there were birds beginning to call in the garden where I dropped that thing—you said, one day you'll want to kill me, that's what you want more than anything, to kill me to get what you want, save me and yourself.

But she's saved herself. She got into her car and drove away from us, Carl and me. The dead and the accused. There she is up on that stand and we'll never talk until we hear the birds, again.

—**M**s James, are you pregnant?—

At once the judge stops Motsamai; but the flourish with which Motsamai has opened his cross examination has cut through the air.

—Mr Motsamai, what has this invasion of the witness's privacy to do with the case—I order it withdrawn.—

—With respect, M'Lord, it is most pertinent to the relationship of the witness with the accused, and the tragic consequences of that relationship. May I have your permission to proceed?—

—Your claim to pertinence better be good, Mr Motsamai, and promptly evidenced.—

The two understand one another; both know the judge had to make the objection, both knew he would rescind it. Senior Counsel doesn't ask questions merely to create a sensation, although the immediate effect of this one, on the temperature of the public, is just that. There are stirrings and stifled exclamations. *Shame*. Not shame for her antics on the sofa, which they relish the opportunity to review, but *shame*, poor good-looker, for having what happens to women brought out before them all by the nasty prying of a lawyer and—one of those old, officially outlawed reactions comes back—a white girl, spoken to like this by this black man with his lined face drawn tight and demanding by the years when his kind couldn't have asked any question at all of her, a white.

In the moment the question was put to her, to the whole court, the public, her amazement swiftly had become a reluctant, ironic recognition of this wily enemy: she should never have told him, in passing, so to speak, to dramatize herself in his chambers!

Motsamai repeats the question softly; she's heard it once.

—Yes.—

Watching her, Harald understood that the girl had not given the Prosecutor this information when he was preparing her as State witness. And Hamilton—he must have made a shrewd guess that this would be so; the Prosecutor's moral climate, to be met by her, was one in which she knew he would want to think the best of her.

—Is Duncan Lindgard the father of the child you expect?—

She answered, no need to whisper. —I can't say.—

—Could it be the child of Carl Jespersen?—

—Possibly.—

—You took no precautions against such an eventuality, in your impulsiveness that night after the party?—

—That's so.—

—Is that why you can't say whether the child is Duncan Lindgard's, the man with whom you were cohabiting, or Carl Jespersen's, the man with whom you were intimate that night?—

—Yes.—

—Doesn't the date of conception, of which you must be more or less aware from your doctor's confirmation of your pregnancy, rule out one of the two men as father?—

—It doesn't.—

—How is that?—

—You know. I told you when you asked me in your office. Duncan made love to me in the early morning, the same day, it was the way bad nights ended.—

—Are you not worried, does it trouble you that you don't know who is the father of the child you're going to give birth to?—

Natalie turns her head away, first this side then that, away from them all, she escapes the court borne by the will of the public: *shame*. Then she comes back to answer them all. —It's my child.—

Duncan wants to thrust the policemen against the walls and rush to hold her poor head, face, mouthing foul words at him, silenced against his chest, cradling her for the child she abandoned, Natalie/Nastasya, the death she submerged herself for and lost— but Motsamai can't be restrained, the process can't be halted. Ever since he, Duncan, stood in the doorway something was started that can't be stopped.

—Doesn't it disturb you to think of the distress this news will cause the accused, who has given you his faithful love and support, and which you have accepted from him, despite all your accusations against him, for several years?—

—Nobody's business but mine.—

—Is that your answer to the question of whatever effect, however painful, your news will have on him?—

It is as if, for her, Motsamai and his pursuit of her don't exist. She repeats—Nobody's business but mine.—

—You don't care. Very well. Ms James, I believe you are something of a writer, poems and so on, you're familiar with many expressions. Do you know the meaning of *in flagrante delicto*?—

—I don't need any explanation.—

—You don't need any explanation. Were you found *in flagrante delicto* with Carl Jespersen on the sofa in the living-room where the party was held, the lights on and the doors open, anyone could have walked in, on the night of Thursday 18th of January? Was it the accused, the man who saved your life and with whom you had been cohabiting as lovers, who walked in and found you there?—

—Yes.— And the monosyllable spreads through the keen receptivity of the public: yes   yes   yes.

—You admit that you performed, before his eyes, the sexual

act with his intimate friend. Have you not thought of the renewed anguish this latest news is going to bring him in addition to the shock and pain you caused him when he was confronted with the sight of you and Jespersen that night? You admit to intercourse with both men within the period of twenty-four hours. *The child is yours*. What does this mean? There is no child without a father. Are you proclaiming a miracle, Ms James? Your immaculate conception?—

Objection from the Prosecutor, upheld; Motsamai withdraws the question and proceeds with a wave of the hand.

—You have two putative fathers for your child. *It doesn't matter to you*. M'Lord, I put it to the court: this callous, careless, yes, *uncaring* attitude is surely abhorrent to any responsible person who has due concern for the feelings of another. How is the accused supposed to accept that the woman he loves doesn't care whether the child she is going to bear is or is not his? Isn't this cynical coda the final, cruel afterword to the dance she led him, which evidence we shall place before this court describes as a life of hell. Finally, there was the extreme, the unendurable provocation she subjected him to on the night of January 18th, so that the attitude of her partner to that exhibition of the sexual act, when next day the accused found the man at ease on the same sofa on which it was committed, culminated in the accused as a blankout in which he committed a tragic act. The witness's share in responsibility for that tragedy has just been *confirmed out of her own mouth*. It has been confirmed once and for all by the sentiments she has now openly expressed in total indifference to the abuse of the accused she commits *yet again*, this time taking no account of his feelings that she may be bearing his child.—

—Have you concluded, Mr Motsamai?—

Yes, like an opera singer breaking off on the top note, he knows the pitch at which to stop. The public is fickle, led by whoever has the gift to sway them, or they are such a community of voyeurs, now, that there are even factions which have developed among them. It's the judge's adjournment for tea, and as Harald and Claudia move out with them someone manoeuvres close and says, claiming hissing intimacy, *She's* the one who ought to be up for it. Khulu has joined Harald and Claudia and he uses the tilt of his broad shoulders to make way for them in protection.

The State's psychiatrist is a woman, while the Defence's choice is a man. For some reason, Defence Counsel is pleased about this; Hamilton explains: a woman, even in the moral climate of an urbane judge, will be likely to be perceived as soft on the character of the woman in the case, vis-à-vis the issue of provocation, a male is likely to be accepted as more professionally objective. Claudia smiles behind a fist held at her mouth.

—That's the fact of it, my dear doctor.— Hamilton gives a short briefing in the echoing corridors, just before the court sitting resumes. Voices, the dialogues of other people in trouble rebound hollow against the high ceilings but Harald and Claudia hear only their own exchanges with the man who has them in his hands. His confidence is like the *dop* of brandy he offers in chambers, a warmth that quickly fades from the blood.

The Prosecutor continues his case, calling the State psychiatrist and leading her evidence. She exudes competence from the freckled flesh of breasts tightly twinned like displaced plump thighs in the neckline of her dress as she testifies that the accused's intellect is within high limits, his judgment sound.

—In your opinion, would such a level of intellect and sound judgment operate in conscious responsibility for actions, even in stressful situations?—

—Yes. The accused was not entirely unprepared for what he saw on that night after the party. I believe, from my consultations with him, that he was suspicious of the situation before he came upon the couple in the sexual act. He had made himself custodian of his partner's morals, this was a constant source of quarrels and conflict between them. There is deep subconscious animosity present within his passionate possessiveness towards her. He would not face the reality of her personality, although she was frank with him, and he prides himself on being an advocate of personal freedom, including sexual freedom. He constantly suspected her of infidelity, whether on occasions when this was justified, or not. He had an obsessional, evangelical attachment to her which manifested itself in rational, precisely practical direction of every aspect of her life.—

—Was his day of inaction after the discovery of the couple consistent with this rationality?—

—In my opinion it was.—

—A day of inaction, contemplation, followed by action—is this also consistent with purposeful behaviour?—

—Yes. His is the personality of a brooder. He does not act on the spur of the moment. He plans. He planned the young woman's whole life without her volition or consent.—

—Do you believe, then, that he could have shot Jespersen 'on the spur of the moment', almost *twenty-four hours later* than he had discovered the compromised couple?—

—No. If he were to have acted in an irrational state, unable to appreciate the wrongfulness of his behaviour, he would have attacked Jespersen at once, in the shock of his suspicions proved by what he came upon.—

—In what state of mind, then, would you say, with what intentions, would you say, he went to the house next day?—

—He went to the house with the conscious intentions of jealousy built up during his solitude.—

—In a rational state of mind?—

—Yes.—

—He went to the house intending to kill Jespersen?—

She would not be able to say to what extreme his intentions might carry him. But she was not convinced of the amnesia of the accused in respect of what happened at the house after Jespersen told him to pour himself a drink.

—The fact is that after forming those intentions in his hours in the cottage, he murdered Jespersen. Was he in full awareness of what he was doing?—

—He is an individual in whom self-control has been strongly established since childhood. It is an axiom of his middle-class background. He is not led by emotion to act on impulse, he's deliberate in every course of action he takes, whatever that might turn out to be.—

The Prosecutor's gesture was of complete satisfaction with his expert's testimony: no more questions necessary.

Motsamai rose with arms away from the body, elbows and hands curved open before him as if to take up something offered him. —Doctor, what is a state of shock?—

—It's a mental phenomenon that affects different people in different ways. Some people cry, some burst into anger, some run.—

—But in general—not the variety of reaction, but the effect on cognition, the sudden disorder of mental processes?—

—There is the effect of mental confusion. Yes. And as I have explained, it manifests itself in different ways.—

—Including the impulse to run away and hide?—

—Yes.—

—In your experience, Doctor, is a profound shock something that is quickly over, the individual concerned regains emotional balance, with the self-control this implies, just like that? Indeed, among your patients there surely have been some for whom a profound shock has had extremely long-term consequences—from what I have learnt, it haunts them to such an extent that in order to regain emotional balance they seek out your skills . . .—

Harald is alert to a stir of disapproval under the judge's robe, but this passes without an objection to the jibe.

—Is it not feasible that when the accused fled in shock from the sexual exhibition of Ms James and Jespersen and hid himself in the cottage, he spent the hours there not in instant recovery to his rationality and capability of deliberate intentions, but in the state of mental confusion that you have identified as the effect of shock?—

—It is possible.—

—You would agree that his was profound shock?—

—Yes.—

—In the case of profound shock, would you say that it may increase, rather than decrease, mental and emotional confusion in the process you term brooding? (A tendency to which you have diagnosed in the accused.) Is it not true that the impact of what has caused the shock gathers force as all the implications of the painful situation mount in a growing mental and emotional confusion? Mind-blowing. So that the individual cannot, as we say, think straight; think at all.—

—Shock could have extended effects of mental confusion. Again, this depends on the personality of the individual. In my opinion, Mr Lindgard is one whose long experience of emotional stress has equipped him to regain mental equilibrium and rationality rapidly, in accordance with his nature.—

—So you confirm that the accused had had a long experience of emotional stress, with Natalie James.—

—Yes. He brought it upon himself.—

—Both you and your learned colleague, Dr Basil Reed, a psychiatrist with twenty-three years experience in your field, have had the opportunity to assess the personality and mental state of the accused during a period of twenty-eight days?—

—Yes.—

—How long have you been in practice as a psychiatrist, Dr Albrecht?—

—Seven years.—

—Your senior colleague's, Dr Reed's opinion, as set out in his report to the court, is that the accused's long experience of emotional stress, *to which you yourself attest*, is of a nature that far from finding resolution in rational thought and intention, culminated in unbearable emotional stress in which the accused was precipitated into a state of dissociation from reason and reality. Is it true that such a state, as a result of prolonged stress compounded by profound shock, is a state recognized by your profession?—

—It is recognized. As one among other reactions to trauma.—

—It is recognized.— Motsamai's palms come slowly, measuredly together. —No further questions, M'Lord.—

His gesture claims the State's case is closed, although the Prosecutor has still to declare this. Harald and Claudia watch the Prosecutor intently and hear his words without interpreting meaning; where is their son, what happened to their son, in these statements that turn him about as some lay figure, he is this, no, he's that? Motsamai will have the hermeneutics according with the legal moral climate; he'll explain.

The Prosecutor wears his down-turned samurai mouth and his eyebrows are furled together; he does not require any other, particular vehemence and he has not Motsamai's range; a prosecutor knows he's not the star the constellation of the Bar needed, its black diamond. —The sum of evidence is that the accused is a highly intelligent man, in full possession of the faculties of conscience, who shot dead, in cold blood, a man lying defenceless on a sofa. The issue before the court is plain: it is that of capability. Criminal capability; did the accused or did he not have this. Whatever conflicting expert opinions may emerge, it is clear that he did not act when it would seem natural, even excusable, for him to do so. He did not tackle the deceased immediately, when he found the man taking his place, performing sexual intimacy with the individual he believed he owned, body and soul. If he had done so, it would not be necessary to seek expert opinion to know that that attack would have been made when he was out of his mind, so to speak, overcome by emotion. But no; he turned his back on the scene, went away to spend a whole day examining his feelings and the options open to satisfy them; his sexual defeat, his male pride, the pride of a totally domineering male (which we have heard testimony was his unfortunate nature). He could have thrown the girl out of the cottage, severed relations with her as his creation—he brought her back to life, remember—turned ingrate. He could have scorned to have anything further to do with her, Jespersen, and the house where such things could happen. These were options. But in full possession of his rightful senses, after plenty of time to consider his course of action, he went to the house, knowing Jespersen would be there at that time of the evening, and made use of the gun he knew was kept in the house, to kill Jespersen. These are the indisputable facts. The accused was criminally capable of the act of murder he performed and I submit, Your Lordship, that the court deal with him in cognizance of this, if justice is to be done to his victim and to the moral code of our society: Thou shalt not kill.—

For some reason that is not explained it is announced at what would have been the adjournment for lunch that the court will not sit in the afternoon; the case will continue at 9 a.m. tomorrow. The judge is not obliged to give account of what may be some urgent commitment elsewhere; or perhaps an aching tooth for which a visit to the dentist is his priority. People make the claims of these commonplace ills against matters of life and death. To hell with them. But a judge cannot be consigned in this way, by Harald, or anybody else.

The tension Hamilton Motsamai meets in their faces, concentrated on him, must surely irk him. No, he is impervious but not indifferent; he has his interpretation of the process so far, ready for them. It is all going as expected, he tells. There are no surprises. Nothing to worry about.

And tomorrow?

You can't ask him about tomorrow. Tomorrow he will have Duncan on the witness stand. Not even to Harald and Claudia will he reveal his strategy, one can only try to infer some idea, from the angle of his approach with State witnesses today, how he will conduct his case tomorrow: Duncan in those hands.

They are right. All of them. It is so: he and she cannot distinguish which Duncan is being described in truth by the Prosecutor, the psychiatrist, by Motsamai. Perhaps he himself, back in his cell, knows. Perhaps they will know, tomorrow.

—**A**lthough Natalie James, with whom you were cohabiting, worked in the same advertising offices with Carl Jespersen, where he had obtained a position for her, and she was travelling to-and-fro to work with him, spending her lunch hours with him daily, you were not concerned that an attachment might be forming between them?—

At last, Duncan is about to speak. To speak for himself.

—No.—

—Why?—

Motsamai's question is a cue in a dialogue everyone knows is of his devising, rehearsed. But Duncan's replies are not lines learnt. Harald and Claudia hear his voice coming as if Duncan is talking to himself. To them; they are overhearing their son.

—Because Carl was not interested in women. Except as friends.—

—Why were you sure of this?—

—He was gay. A homosexual.—

—How did you know?—

Ah, but the banal question had a lawyerly purpose, Motsamai has the flair to build his scene carefully for his client.

—He lived as a homosexual. Everyone who shared the house was homosexual.—

—You lived on the same property. Did you share the same inclinations?—

—At one time I had a relationship—with a man.—

—One of the men in the house?—

—Yes.—

—With whom?—

—With Carl.—

—With Carl Jespersen. So it was this experience that led you to believe that there could be nothing between Natalie James and Jespersen. Were you in love with Natalie James?—

As it touches on his nerve-ends, Harald and Claudia shrink from the question, with him.

—We were close.—

—It was a love relationship, a sexual relationship between a man and a woman?—

—Yes.—

—Ah-hêh. If you could have a homoerotic affair, and then fall in love with a woman, enjoy a heterosexual relationship, how could you be sure that Carl Jespersen would not have sexual designs on your lover, Natalie?—

It is difficult to trust Hamilton as he shows himself now. Harald sees Motsamai is enjoying himself, Duncan's life is material for a professional performance. The man who brings from the Other Side the understanding of people in trouble, the man in whose hands there is the succouring glass of brandy, is left behind in chambers.

—Because he wasn't attracted to women. Sexually. Anatomically, he told me often, he found them repulsive. I can't go into —repeat—some of the things he liked to say. I can only put it— their genitals—he felt disgust for women.—

—Did he say these things to you in an attempt to dissuade you from heterosexual relations?—

—I suppose so. At one time.—

—So you were absolutely confident that he could have no erotic intentions towards your woman lover?—

—Yes, quite sure.—

—Although you yourself had had homosexual relations with him, and then fell in love and entered into a close relationship with a woman, it did not occur to you that he might be capable of the same instincts?—

—No. It was out of the question. I am not homosexual, not any more than any adult human being has some erotic ambivalence that may or may not—come out—in certain circumstances. I had only that one attachment. He was actively homosexual, he'd been so, he often told me, from the age of twelve.—

—So you had absolutely no idea that he was having an affair —Natalie was having an affair with Jespersen?—

Across the well, in the rapt, prurient silence of the court, from the target that was the witness stand there came distinctly the sharp small sound of Duncan's tongue pressed and released against his palate. The air of the spectators tingled; they had been waiting before a cage for the creature to cry out: —There was no affair.—

—You are completely convinced of that?—

—I know. Carl was David's lover, Carl was heavily involved with him.—

—Can you describe what happened on the night of the 18th January: there was a party at the house?—

—It was not really a party. The house is a place where people just turn up. And often Natalie and I would join the men at the house and we'd eat together at night. I suppose we were a sort of family. Better than a nuclear family, a lot of friendship and trust between us.—

—That night you had a meal together.—

—Some other friends of David and Khulu came in for drinks

and then as it got late, stayed on to eat with us. So I suppose you could say it became a spontaneous kind of party. David had done quite a lot of drinking and he went to bed when the others had gone. Khulu left with one of them—some rendez-vous of his own. Natalie had been keeping the party going with her anecdotes about experiences as a cruise hostess, she's a devastating mimic, and she hadn't been much help in the kitchen so she offered to stay behind and clean up with Carl. She'll make that sort of gesture. When she's been particularly flamboyant. Just because she hates—never does domestic chores. I know it's necessary for the sense she has of herself, so I left her to it and went to our cottage—to bed.—

The judge lifted his head as if he had at last found something that intrigued him. —Natalie James, in her testimony yesterday, gave a rather different version of the events. Was there not an argument between you, didn't you try to make her return with you to the cottage?—

—You cannot persuade Natalie when she is in that sort of state.—

—Are you saying that there was no altercation with her before the others present?—

—She was in the mood. So if she wouldn't come home and give herself some rest, it was better for me to leave.—

The judge's glance gives Motsamai the signal to continue.

—What time was that?—

—About one o'clock.—

—You expected she would follow?—

—Naturally.—

—Did she?—

—No.—

Motsamai is patient against resistance; Harald, Claudia have the sense of Duncan fleeing, fleeing, out of the cell he has occupied, out of the closed institution for the mentally incapacitated, out of the court, out of the gallery of faces whose prey he is—out of himself.

Motsamai is in pursuit.

—What happened then?—

—I woke up. She wasn't there. I saw it was half-past two. I was worried. About her crossing the garden so late in the dark, there are intruders all over the suburb.—

—And then?—

Now he tells it by rote; it is something he has been told happened to him. By another self; the lawyer becomes the accused's other self once he has absorbed, appropriated the facts.

—I went out, through the garden, to the house. The lights were on and the verandah door was open. I went into the living-room and she was under him on the sofa. Carl.—

—They were making love?—

—They were finishing. They couldn't stop. So I saw it.—

In the minds and memories of all, strangers, bodies side by side in the public gathering, there is the shared moment before the orgasm. They are a collective of the flesh. They know. Does the judge partake, does he recall, does he too know that moment, made love last night, so that he truly understands what it was that the accused could not help seeing, that couldn't stop? Not even for the one standing in the doorway.

What did they do, those two discovered, and what did he do, Motsamai is asking. The answer is Duncan doesn't know, he left what he saw as Natalie was suddenly aware of him and Carl's face appeared for a moment with the rise and fall of the bodies, he turned back to the dark.

Duncan fled, flight was possible that time, as it is not now.

For Motsamai is developing that part of the progression which is easily comprehensible: what Natalie James did was drive away, she did not return to the cottage that night or next day. Duncan did not sleep during what was left of the night. He did not go to his work at the drawing board in the morning. It was Friday. Friday, January 19th.

—What did you do? You spent the day in the cottage?—

—Just thinking.—

—Were you thinking what you might do about the situation.—

—No. No. I was looking for an explanation. A reason. Trying to work out why.—

—Why such a thing could happen?—

—Yes. Whether what I saw.—

—Were you thinking of confronting Natalie? Of seeking out your friend Carl, to confront him?—

—I didn't want to see them. *I had seen them*. I was looking for the explanation, in myself. That's all I thought of, all day. I'm used to facing crises of one kind or another with her; I can depend on myself in dealing with them.—

—Have you done this successfully, that is to say with no ill consequences, before?—

—Many times.—

—So you had no thought of revenge of any kind, towards either of them?—

—Revenge for what. I don't own either of them, they are free to do as they like.—

—You had no thought at all of any kind of revengeful accusation, let alone action for how their 'doing as they like' affected you? Your life? Your love relationship with Natalie?—

—No.—

—Your former relationship with Carl Jespersen?—

Surely what he said now was not in Motsamai's rehearsed script.

—No. All I could remember—about seeing them there like that—was disgust, a disintegration of everything, disgust with myself, everyone.—

—Yes?— Motsamai's is a conductor's gesture from the podium.

—This was what I was trying to explain, so that I could put— things—together again, understand myself.—

—Were you thinking about the future of your relationship with Natalie? Did you think it could continue, after what you saw— her particular use of her freedom, her reward of your love and care for her?—

—How do I know. It had continued after so many occasions that could have put an end to it.—

—You stayed in the cottage all that day, lying on the bed? Alone?—

—Yes. With the dog.—

—When did you get up, what prompted you?—

—The dog, he was hungry, restless. I got dressed and gave him his dish of food.—

Motsamai drew a tide of deep breath, his black gown rose over his breast, he took time, for the two of them, Duncan and himself. —And then?—

—Outside. He eats outside. So I was in the garden.—

—What time was this?—

—I hadn't looked at a watch, it must have been the time we usually fed him, about half-past six, or seven.—

—You were in the garden; did you return to the cottage?—

—No.—

—Why?—

—I just (the gesture fell back half-way; it was the first time he had used his hands, those attributes of defence given up along with admittance of guilt) I just walked over to the house.—

—What was your purpose?—

—I found myself in the garden. Instead of going back into the cottage, I walked over.—

—Did you hope to see anyone at the house, talk to someone there? One of the other friends?—

—I didn't want to talk to anyone.—

—Then you mean to tell the court, you had no reason to go there?— Which one of the carefully chosen assessors, one white, one sufficiently tinctured to pass as black, was it who was speaking—both sat, either side of the judge, silent henchmen. The voice was slow and clumsy. Harald had the strange sense that it came from a medium through whose mouth the public, the people filling the court, spoke.

—I found myself in the garden, I think then I had to find myself standing again where I stood in the doorway.—

Motsamai leaves no moment of silence before he takes up affirmation: —So you crossed the garden to the house to stand once again from where you saw the pair, your former male lover and the woman, your present lover, coupling on the sofa. And when you reached the same doorway, what then?—

Claudia could smell her own sweat, there is no cosmetic that can suppress anguish that only the body, primitive mute that it is, can express, hygiene is a polite convention that covers the animal powers in suburban life. Is Harald praying—is that the other kind of emanation, that comes from him; let them mingle, the brutish and the spiritual, if they can produce the solidarity promised long ago in covenant with their son.

Duncan is now speaking by rote again. As if there is something switched off, a power cut in some part of the brain.

—Jespersen was lying on the sofa.—

—What was his reaction when he saw you?—

—Smiled.—

—He smiled. Did he speak?—

—Carl said, *Oh dear. I'm sorry, Bra.*—

The judge addresses his question as if it may be answered either by the accused or his counsel. —'Bra', what does that signify, 'bra'?—

—It's a fraternal diminutive used between us black men, M'Lord, and also extended to white men with whom blacks share fraternal bonds now, in a united country. It means you claim the person thus addressed as your brother.— And Motsamai switched in perfect timing from judge to accused: —So—he claimed you as still a brother.—

—He did.—

—What was your response?—

—I thought then, it was him I had come to.—

—Did you confront him for an explanation of his behaviour,

did you think a casual 'I'm sorry', the kind of apology a man makes when he bumps against someone in the street, was sufficient?—

—He talked. We are not children, didn't we both of us have the same credo, we don't own each other, we want to live freely, don't we, whether it's going to be sex or something like taking a long walk. Never mind, he said, the walk is over the sex is over, it was a nice time, that's it, isn't it. Hadn't that always been understood between him and me. Just unfortunate, he said, he and Natalie had been a bit too impulsive, she's usually a girl who arranges things more carefully, privately. He had his good-natured laugh. He told me, all of us know it—he said—I knew it, and it hadn't changed things with Natalie and me before. He told me: he said to me, I shouldn't ever follow anyone around, come to look for them in their lives, that's for people who make a prison out of what they feel and lock someone up inside. He said she was a great girl and she'd never give it another thought. And as for him, I knew his tastes—no claims, God no—he said it was just a little crazy nightcap, that's what he called it, part of the good evening we'd all had, the drinks, the laughs he and she had, cleaning up together.—

—What did you say to him?—

—I don't know. He was talking talking talking, he was laughing, it was one of the times we had talked like this about adventures we'd had—that's what it was. He couldn't stop, I couldn't stop him.—

—And then what happened?—

—He wanted me to drink with him as we used to.—

—And then?—

A necessity to present the precise formulation.

—'Why don't you pour yourself a drink.' Those words I heard out of a babble I couldn't follow any more. The last thing I heard him say to me. I suddenly picked up the gun on the table. And then he was quiet. The noise stopped. I had shot him.—

Duncan's head has tipped slowly back. His eyes close against them all, Motsamai, the judge, assessors, Prosecutor, clerks, the public where some woman gasped a theatrical sob, mother and father. Harald and Claudia cannot be there for him, where he is, alone with the man shot dead in the head with a gun that was handy.

Harald felt not fear but certainty. This man, the Prosecutor, is set to trap their son into confessing that he wished to do harm to Carl Jespersen and went to the house with that intention. And maybe, to stop the questions, stop the noise, the voice directed only at him of all the throng filling this closed space, Duncan might say yes, yes—he has already confessed to killing, what more do they want of him? And this man, the Prosecutor, is only doing his job, it's nothing to him that Jespersen is dead, that Duncan is destroyed by himself; this is this man's performance. To do his job he must get the conviction he wants, that's all, as a measure of his competence, one of the daily steps in the furtherance of a career. Like climbing the corporate ladder.

—You lay in the cottage all day on that Friday, 19th of January, brooding over the event of the night before?—

—Thinking.—

—Isn't that the same thing, going over and over in your mind the injury done to you. What you desired to do about it. Wasn't that it?—

—Not that. Because there was nothing to be done about it.—

—Yet later in the day you went over to the house. Was that not doing something about it? It was between six and seven o'clock in the evening, there was every likelihood that Jespersen would be home from work. You knew that, didn't you?—

—I found myself in the garden, I didn't think about who would be in the house.—

—You 'found yourself in the garden' and I put it to you that it was then that you also were aware that the time was right for you to carry out what you had been thinking, planning all day— to find Jespersen, take your revenge for the wrong you felt he had done you, although he was not the first man with whom your live-in lover had been unfaithful to you. I put it to you that your thinking, all day, was the brooding of jealousy, and you went to the house in a consequent aggressive mood with the intention of confronting Jespersen violently.—

The task of the Prosecutor is to make out an accused to be a liar: that is how Harald and Claudia see his process. Claudia shifts in her seat as if unable to sit there any longer, and he crushes her knuckles a moment, comfort that comes from his own resentment.

But if they knew—perhaps they partly know; Duncan is not sure what they have learnt, are learning about him—he is a liar. A liar by omission. Because the Prosecutor cannot know, is not being told—there is no telling of the staggering conflict of his feelings towards Carl Jespersen, towards Natalie, his confusion of their betrayals, a revulsion in sorrow; that was his thinking, in the cottage. Revenge: if Natalie had come back that day, why not have thought of killing her? But she—oh Natalie—she has taken enough revenge upon herself for being herself.

The gun is in court. It has become Exhibit 1. A draught of curiosity bends the companions in the public forward to try and catch a glimpse of it.

It's nothing but a piece of fashioned metal; Harald and Claudia don't need to see it. The fingerprints of the accused's left hand, the Prosecutor says, were discovered upon it by forensic tests, his fingerprints unique to him in all humanity, as he is unique to them as their only son.

—You know this handgun?—

—Yes.—

—Do you own it?—

—No.—

—Who does?—

—I don't know in whose name it was licensed. It was the gun kept in the house so that if someone was attacked, intruders broke in, whoever it was could defend himself. Everyone.—

—Did you know where it was kept?—

—Yes. Usually in a drawer in the room David and Carl shared.—

—You lived in the cottage, not the house; how did you know this?—

—We all knew. We live—lived in the same grounds together. If the others were out, and I heard something suspicious, I'd be the one who would need it.—

—You knew how to handle a gun.—

—This one. It was the only one I'd ever touched. In the army, privates were trained on rifles. David demonstrated, when it was bought.—

—On the night of January 18th the gun was brought into the living-room and shown to one of the guests who was about to acquire one for himself. Did you show it to him, handle it?—

—No. I don't remember who did—probably David.—

—Were you aware that the gun wasn't put away—back in the drawer in another room where it customarily was kept?—

—No. I left while the others were tidying up.—

—But you saw the gun lying about before you left? On the table near the sofa?—

—I didn't notice the gun.—

—How was that?—

—There were glasses and plates all over the place, I suppose it was somewhere mixed up.—

—So when you entered the room the next evening you saw for the first time that the gun had been left out, lying on the table?—

—I didn't see it.—

—How was that?—

—I wasn't looking anywhere, only saw Carl.—

—And at what point did you see the gun?—

—I can't say when.—

—Was it before he said 'Why don't you pour yourself a drink' as if this was just a drinking session between mates?—

—I suppose so. I don't know.—

—Did you know if the gun was loaded?—

—I didn't know.—

—But weren't you present when the use of the gun was being shown to the guest? And wasn't he shown how—wasn't it loaded for him?—

—I didn't see. I suppose so. I was talking to other people.—

—So when you entered the living-room the next evening you saw the gun lying there, you had every reason to know it was loaded, and you made the decision to take the opportunity perhaps to threaten Carl Jespersen with it?—

—I didn't threaten him, I didn't make any decision.—

—So you didn't give him any chance? Any warning?—

—I was hearing him, I didn't threaten—

—No. You picked up the gun and shot him in the head. A shot you knew, because you know how to handle a gun, almost certain to be fatal. In this way you satisfied the thoughts of revenge you had been occupied with all day, and that you had gone over to the house in intention of pursuing, one way or another. The gun to hand was an opportunity presented to you, so that you didn't have to grapple with the man fist to fist, you didn't have to plan any other way of eliminating him as a rival in your life, your desire to do so reached fulfilment of your intentions.—

Motsamai was signalling; there is a procedure for everything in this ritual: I object M'Lord. But the judge is urbane and democratic, let everyone have his say. Objection over-ruled.

A stir along the row, people making way for someone to pass, an appearance on the witness stand singling him out like a celebrity. Khulu Dladla came and sat beside them after he had given his evidence for the Defence.

Khulu; behinds shifted to make place for him next to Claudia. She lifted her hand, it sank towards her lap then lifted again, a tendril reaching out, found and pressed a moment the large warm back of his hand.

Yes, I can say I know him well, very well, he said when Motsamai led his testimony. And the young woman? Yes, Natalie too. Since she joined our place. But Duncan, before that. In the well of the court, where no signs of recognition are exchanged, Khulu smiled directly at Duncan as if he had just walked into his presence in an ordinary room somewhere. Hi, Duncan. It was because of this that Claudia wanted to touch him.

—Before Natalie joined the friends—what were relations like between those living in the house?—

—Oh very nice. We got on well, that's why we got together, nê?—

—You, David Baker, Carl Jespersen and Duncan Lindgard. You were all homosexuals?—

—I don't know about Duncan, really. He didn't live in the house. Anyway, then he brought a woman along . . . but the rest of us, yes, we are men. Gay.—

—Some of you were intimate with one another?—

—Yes.—

—Were you aware that Duncan had a relationship of this nature?—

—Yes.—

—And who was the man?—

—Jespersen. Carl was the kind who when he takes a fancy to someone, that person can't escape him. He seemed to get a kick out of making it with Duncan, I don't think Duncan had had our kind of experience before, I mean, that a man could feel that way about him, Jespersen could be such a charmer. He could make you feel like you were missing something great in life if you passed up on him. He was from overseas and all that, he thought he was special. Like some kind of food or drink from there. Something we hadn't tried.—

—So you observed that Jespersen was having an affair with Duncan. Surely this wasn't surprising, in your set-up?—

—No, it was. Because Duncan was straight, we knew that. There are a lot of straight people among our friends. He took the cottage and sort of shared the house not because he was one of us, gay, but because we got on well in other ways. He's an interesting guy. I'd call him a real artist in his designs of buildings. You can work out ideas with him, politics, art, music, God—no frontiers.—

—Was Natalie James the cause of the break-up of the affair?—

—No way. It happened before she came on the scene. Jespersen got tired of it. Quickly. He was like that with everything. That's why he'd moved around in so many countries. He broke off with Duncan.—

—What was Duncan's reaction? Did he take the same casual attitude?—

—Not at all. He was upset. Couldn't understand why he'd been so involved, you know, emotionally, and then just thrown over.—

—How did you know all this? From observation only?—

Khulu was looking at Duncan again, as if Duncan would join him in confirmation. —He talked to me. I didn't know how to get him to understand . . . he was in a bad way . . . his ideas, some of them were different from ours, certainly from Carl's.—

—Did you succeed in consoling him?—

—I think I got him to see that his reaction was, how shall I say, a bit—inappropriate, that was it, to make a fuss, a drama, was spoiling all the good things about our kind of life on the property, that he liked so much.—

—So the incident, as it seemed to you, was smoothed over?—

—Oh he calmed down.—

—He and Carl Jespersen continued to live in the group, as friends?—

—That's right. And when he brought the girl along and set her up with him in the cottage, that looked fine, the right thing for him. At first.—

—Why 'at first'? What happened after? Didn't the men at the house like her?—

—We all got on with Natalie. Though Carl when he was in a bad mood would carry on with all his usual stuff about women— make fun behind Duncan's back, sometimes, of what he said was going on in the cottage with Duncan and her—thoughts about women in general, but at the same time he and she and Duncan, well, they went along together, were good friends. We really forgot all about that business between Duncan and him. He was the one who found her that job at his advertising firm and Duncan was pleased she at last had work that might interest her, something in her line, she writes, you know.—

—So what was it that no longer looked fine, for Duncan?—

—She's a strange person. Well, he knew that—she'd tried to

kill herself, there was that business of the child—she'd be the life of the party one minute and all over him, and the next she'd be jeering at him, attacking him for what she would say was 'he wanted her to be like that'.—

—Be like what exactly?—

—Happy. 'Performing her life for him'—that's exactly what she always said. That's why I remember the words.—

—Did he tell you about this or was this type of scene taking place in the house, in front of you others?—

—Oh we were all there, around to see, to hear.—

—What was Duncan's reaction when she taunted him in front of their friends?—

—He was so patient with her. Like with a sick person. Although she gave him hell. You could tell, it was hell. He would go about next day very depressed. But he didn't talk to me or any of us about it—not the way he talked to me over the fling with Jespersen, for instance.—

—So the relationship between Natalie James and Duncan was not happy?—

—She tortured him. Really. She even tried again to commit suicide, it was with pills, and he seemed to think it was his fault. But you could see, he always tried again, to get her right. You couldn't understand how he could keep on.—

—He loved her?—

Now this witness looked to the judge, who was impervious to the feel of eyes upon him. Khulu appealed to him, to all who judge, human or divine. —Who of us can say what it means to love.—

In the person of the samurai, the Prosecutor turned that face to the public in moments of solicitation during his cross examination of Dladla.

—'Who can say what it means to love.' Indeed, we can say that it is common knowledge that it means to be jealous. Jealousy is the passion that arises from love and is stronger than love itself, as it ruthlessly abandons all respect for the right to life of the cause of the jealousy, the man who has taken the lover's place in the arms of the loved one. You describe the way the accused was devoted to the care of Natalie James, over-protecting her to the point when, as she has testified, this was offensive to her dignity, you have recounted his slavish attachment and behaviour. Do you not think that, with this background to the relationship, having come upon Carl Jespersen in the act with the loved one, his reaction must inevitably be jealousy? Violent jealousy. The shock that he has described—wasn't that the extreme impact of jealousy? When he went back to the cottage that night, when he waited in vain for her to return, when he spent the day alone there, wasn't it jealousy that he was brooding on?—

—I don't know.—

—Wouldn't you say he was extremely possessive about her, on the evidence of his general behaviour?—

—He felt responsible for her.—

—That may be another way of putting it. Why do you think your friend killed Carl Jespersen if it wasn't out of premeditated jealous revenge for making love to Natalie James?—

—Killing a person.—

All around, the public is stilled with anticipation. How will he go on? It excites this audience, admitted for free, to think that the samurai has this victim cornered.

—I know Duncan; so well. He doesn't have a gun. Nothing. He was not sitting there planning to go and kill Jespersen. It is not in his nature. Never. I swear on my own life. It couldn't ever have happened like that: that he was going to look for Carl to kill him. I don't know how it happened—but not that. God knows how. I don't understand killing.—

Motsamai's man, the Defence psychiatrist—in the blur of becoming aware of who comes and goes in the witness stand the appearance only of some irrelevance notes itself—wore an elaborate watch like a weapon, flash of light off his raised hand reaching Harald and Claudia. He addressed himself directly to the judge rather than the Defence Counsel. To emphasize objectivity? Or because they are equally of authority: the judge decides who is guilty, the psychiatrist decides who is mad. Motsamai has asked his opinion of the accused's mental state in relation to the events in the house on January the 18th and 19th.

—In psychiatry we look at 'life events' as precipitating abnormal behaviour, but we also see this as consciously or subconsciously reflecting any distortion of social norms. In a society where violence is prevalent the moral taboos against violence are devalued. Where it has become, for whatever historical reasons, the way to deal with frustration, despair or injury, natural abhorrence of violence is suspended. Everyone becomes accustomed to the solution of violence, whether as victim, perpetrator or observer. You live with it. In considering abnormal behaviour, the act must take into account the general climate of behaviour in which it has taken place.—

The judge responds to this private exchange.

—All very interesting, Doctor, but what the court expects to hear is a report on the mental state of the accused, not that of the city.—

—With respect, the act that the accused has admitted he committed did not take place in a vacuum. Just as there may be the unconscious restraint which comes from the moral climate, there may be the unconscious sanction of violence, in its general use, general resort to it. This can overcome the protective inhibitions of the individual's conscious morality in which such an act would be abhorrent. It is necessary to keep in mind this context in which events which led to the act, and the act itself, took place.—

—Are you proposing, Doctor, that hijacks, muggings and so on sanction murder as a solution to personal conflict?—

The judge's sarcasm does not disturb the man; Motsamai would not have chosen anyone easily outsmarted in urbanity.

—No such immoral proposal, Your Lordship . . . Simply a duty to inform the court of the methodology followed in psychiatric examination.—

There has been a rise of attention among the public, even a policeman shifts from one foot to another like a dray-horse standing by. The public is enjoying the exchange between two men who are so sure of their superiority. This free show is getting better all the time, good as a talk-show at the television studios. But Harald and Claudia are clenched to attention in a different way, they are instantly analyzing every word. This man is theirs, Duncan's, they are sure. What he will have confirmed in their son can only be his salvation.

He found the accused to have been precipitated into a state of dissociation from what he was doing on the evening of January 19th, unable to exert proper control over his actions, which culminated in the death of Carl Jespersen.

Motsamai has his attention. —Doctor, when would you say this state began?—

In the doctor's opinion it was the accused's condition before he left the cottage and entered the house. Psychiatric examination found no evidence to doubt that the accused was telling the truth when he said he went to the house to stand where he stood the previous night; his disbelief of what he had seen from there would be part of a state of dissociation from reality. Nor was there any indication that he was not truthful in telling of confusion, lack of recollection of detailed sequence of his actions when he found himself in the house and Jespersen was lying on the sofa. The accused suffers from a genuine amnesia in regard to certain events of that evening.

The judge attracts attention by moving his shoulders. Whenever he gave this signal, the court hung in balance between what had been said and what would now tip it. This time he thrust his chin forward and cocked his head. —The accused gave a detailed and coherent account of what the deceased said to him. How is it he remembers this?—

—A tremendous emotional blow is as forceful as any external blow to the head. When Jespersen said 'Why don't you pour yourself a drink' the callousness of this attitude constituted a second such blow. He was confused before; he cannot remember what he said, if anything, to Jespersen. With the impact of these last words he recalls Jespersen saying, he would have entered a state of automatism in which inhibitions disintegrated.—

—How could he have used a gun? If he was in this state of dissociation, diminished awareness? He's testified he could not know whether or not the gun was loaded. Would he not have had to release the safety catch, if it was—and it was—loaded, and would not that have been a fully conscious act, a rational act?—

—It would be an automatic reaction, without cognition, in anyone who has ever handled a gun. Like getting on a bicycle for anyone who knows how to ride.—

With M'Lord's permission, Motsamai has questions to lead.

—Doctor, in your experience of such states of diminished or total lack of capacity, what caused, what made the accused *able* to pick up and use the gun?—

—Cumulative provocation reaching its climax in the subject's total loss of control.—

—Could you explain—the morphology, the case history, so to speak, of this cumulation?—

—Lindgard is a man with a bisexual nature. That in itself is a source of personality conflict. He had suffered emotional distress when he followed his homoerotic instincts and had a love affair which his partner, Jespersen, did not take seriously and broke off at whim. He overcame the unhappiness of the rejection and turned to the other, and probably dominant side of his nature, a heterosexual alliance for which, again, he took on serious responsibility. Even more so, since the alliance was with an obviously neurotic personality with complex self-destructive tendencies for which, when crossed in what she saw as her right to pursue them, she punished him with denigration and mental aggression. When he saw her in the sexual act with his former male lover, he felt himself emasculated by them both.—

This is the model of their son put together, as a human being is comprised in X-ray plates and scans lit on a screen, by the dialectic method of a court and the knowledge of experts in the mystery of what is felt and thought and acted by the model. Duncan, led away for the judge's lunch break is the *doppelgänger*. How can they ask him, is this you, my son?

When they left the court building a man was capering about on his hunkers before them, a tame ape aiming a camera. The photograph that appeared in an evening paper was also something which put them together, each of them, from a kit of conceptions: mother and father of a murderer.

The Prosecutor's questions to Motsamai's man, their man, the Defence psychiatrist, became their self-questioning. His comments ran together as the desperate narrative of their own. Was the court to believe the day of inaction in the cottage was a vacuum? The accused testifies he was merely 'thinking'. Can you think about *nothing*? Was it not clear that the day in the cottage was consistent with only one interpretation, rational premeditation of jealous intention to confront the victim in revenge—an intention duly carried out? The accused 'found himself in the garden'; couldn't he have gone over to the house to look again at the sofa, the scene of the previous night's event, at any time during the day? Why did he choose instead to do so at an hour when the victim would have returned from work? As for the use of the gun, the accused said in evidence that he was not familiar with handguns; it was the only one he had held. How, then, could he have used it with such efficiency, ensuring that it was loaded and cocked, if he were to have been in a state of automatism? Did he not have to perform rational, deliberate actions in order to take advantage of the proximity of a weapon that would carry out his deadly intention?

What was the man saying, what were they themselves, what was the court being led to think? That the Defence had damned itself out of its own psychiatrist's mouth?

They could not ask Motsamai for an interpretation of this inference—a sign ominous, or a disguised defeat; he was in his place in the well of the court preparing to close his case.

Claudia saw Harald slide a hand into his jacket pocket and bring out a notebook when Motsamai rose to address the court. It was the small hard-backed one schoolchildren use, not the embossed leather kind with attached gilt ballpoint that lay open for him at Board meetings. It belonged to the pared, humbled other life he and she lived now, he must have gone himself to a stationer's to buy it: the sort of errand run by his secretary. Claudia had the delicacy not to give in to the distraction of covertly glancing at what he was writing while Motsamai spoke; she felt a loving empathy with him like a gentle tide, there and subsided, beneath the intent with which she was following every syllable that came from Motsamai. Not only was it Motsamai's turn to engage attention; he was, he made himself, the focus of the court. His presence asserted that the court was for him, this short man with the dry-lined face like a dark worn glove, that seemed hardly to contain eyes hard as glass, bright against black; from all the years he had been shut out on the Other Side of the law he claimed the right to arrogant bearing of its dignity.

—A person is said to be criminally responsible, that is to say, to have criminal capacity, when he is able to appreciate the wrongfulness of his act at the time of committing it. To assess this criminal capacity one must be in full cognizance of the events and the consequent state of mind of such a person before the act was committed. What were the events and the state of mind in the case of Duncan Lindgard?

The previous night, towards the early hours of the morning, he is concerned for the safety of the woman he loves because she has not returned to the cottage where she lives with him in an intimate relationship. Now I want to go back a little into certain aspects of this relationship because it is significant to the character, the consistent caring nature, the sense of human responsibility of Lindgard. Natalie James attempted suicide, to take her own life, and Duncan Lindgard saved her life. It was due to his desperate efforts that she was resuscitated. He had no emotional attachment, no sexual relation with her at the time; scarcely knew her. After that, a relationship developed and he took her in. They cohabited in the cottage in the grounds of a house where three friends of Lindgard lived, and occupied the property, as the accused has described to the court, as something like a family—not mother, father, children and so forth, but adults in loyal friendship, in harmony, the three homosexual members and the heterosexual couple. Lindgard not only brought Natalie James physically back to life; as a member of the so-called family has testified, out of love for her he took on the self-appointed burden of reconciling her to the problems of her stormy past—the child she had borne and given to adoption, and other personality problems—and devoted himself to try to help her develop her positive side, the potential he saw in her that was constantly threatened by irresponsible self-destructive tendencies. In the two years or so they had cohabited as lovers there is no evidence that he responded to her mental aggression and her various transgressions threatening the relationship, with anything but patient endurance and a willingness to help her. No provocation from her brought him ever to act violently during that period.— Motsamai flashed a look to the public for a second, holding their attention ready, then was back to the judge. —With respect, M'Lord, I am not blackening this young woman's character, I wish only to give the actual background to the accused's concern for her in the early hours of the morning, when she failed to appear.—

It is difficult for Claudia, for Harald writing with his fist shielding the page, to keep conscious of the judge's presence; he is, as she knows Harald believes God to be, there, even though one is not aware of this.

Motsamai's reminder has not lost his hold on the public.

—Duncan Lindgard crosses to the house, anxious that she may have been attacked by an intruder in the dark garden. What does he find? An open door, all the lights on, and on the sofa, Natalie James and Carl Jespersen in the throes of the sexual act. With respect, M'Lord, they are so engaged that they do not even spring apart at Lindgard's presence. Ah-hêh. What does Lindgard do? The blow is so terrible, so unbelievable, that he flees. Now why was what he came upon so devastating? To any man, any woman, the sight of his or her partner performing the sexual act with another is a painful shock. No question about that. But what Duncan Lindgard was struck with was a double betrayal of an appalling nature. For what he saw on that sofa was not only the unfaithfulness of the woman he loved, but the fact that *the man performing the sexual act with her was the very man with whom he himself had had a brief homosexual affair*, and who had caused him pain, at that past time, by abruptly breaking off the affair. He knew only too well that Jespersen did not desire women—he has told the court how Jespersen talked distastefully, even disgustingly, about their sexual characteristics, their genital organs. That Jespersen should *overcome* this revulsion specifically to perform the act with Lindgard's woman could mean only one of two things, equally horrifying: either Jespersen took some pleasure in the idea of humiliating once again the man he had already rejected, or there was an added kick to that idea in aiding Natalie in some impulse she had to take advantage of this—*exquisitely*—cruel way to humiliate and wound the lover to whom she felt some perverse resentment for owing him so much: her life. What Duncan saw was an act so *sickening* in its implications that, as he has said in his evidence of how he spent the next day thinking in the cottage, nothing could be done about it. No considered course of action would be adequate to deal with it.

He spent the next day alone in the cottage in a state of shock inconsistent with any resolution of intent. He was incapable of formulating any feelings towards either Natalie James or Carl Jespersen. As a highly-experienced psychiatrist reports, there was a sense of amnesiac unreality, in regard to them. He was not capable, as my Learned Friend has suggested he was, of any intention to take revenge. And as he himself said in response to my Learned Friend, the Prosecutor's question: revenge for what? Her betrayal? Carl Jespersen's betrayal? The betrayal of James and Jespersen in collusion?

He had lain in the cottage all day, incapacitated. If the dog had not roused him because it was hungry, if he had not gone through the motions of feeding the dog outside, would he not have stayed on in his isolation until, maybe, someone had come to seek him out? Would he have found himself in the garden, across which he had fled in anguish the night before, if he hadn't gone out to feed the dog? He found himself in the garden, yes; and there was the house where what was unbelievable happened. He went over to that place to stand where he had seen it, to make it believable to his confused state.—

The lines in Motsamai's face became deep slashes. He drew a long breath in pretext for his calculated pause. He seemed himself to be witnessing what he was about to describe.

—What does he see? The man, Carl Jespersen, is lounging at his ease on that same sofa. He has mixed himself his favourite drink. He smiles. He hails Duncan Lindgard, the friend, the former lover whose woman he has seduced before his eyes—he hails him as *Bra, brother*. Then he goes into a monologue, the tone is kidding along, sophisticated man-talk. That, he assumes, is the context in which the 'incident', the coupling that couldn't stop, that concluded brazenly in Lindgard's presence, must be received, shared, by Lindgard. Pour yourself a drink, he says. Yes, let's drink on it, brother. The whole event of the night before is *nothing*. A grotesque joke!

Is this shock any less than that of the coupling itself?

The spectacle now before Lindgard comes as the culmination of total emotional stress. There is a gun lying on the table. It offers itself. He does not know whether it is loaded or not. He picks it up and fires at the source from which the tirade aimed at himself keeps coming. What he has described as 'the noise' stops. That is the way he becomes aware that he has shot Carl Jespersen.

I repeat, M'Lord, with your permission, the definition of criminal responsibility. A person is said to be criminally responsible, to have criminal capacity to perform an act, when he is able to appreciate the wrongfulness of his act at the time of committing it. Lack of criminal capacity, as a result neither of insanity nor youth, is recognized in our law in principle in regard to, among other things, provocation—M'Lord will see in my Heads of Argument I cite State versus Campher, 1987—and severe emotional stress—I refer the court to State versus Arnold, 1985.

Everything in the accused's attested general behaviour as an adult, his sense of moral responsibility, Christian and humanist, as inculcated since childhood by his parents, is against the performance of any violent act. Was he not provoked beyond rational endurance to loss of control when he saw a gun to hand and picked it up? In a word, did the accused know what he was doing? Did Duncan Lindgard have criminal capacity?

I submit, M'Lord, that he did not, could not.—

The voice of the judge, a private murmur, has nevertheless the authority to stop Motsamai rather than interrupt. —Mr Motsamai, are you pleading insanity?—

—No, M'Lord. I am not.—

—Temporary insanity?—

—No. The accused is a man of sound mind whose lack of criminal capacity was overcome by a brain-storm of emotional stress during which he could not be aware of the wrongfulness of his act because he was not aware of any intention to commit it.—

—What is the difference between that and temporary insanity?—

Your son is not mad.

But for Harald and Claudia, the judge may be right; insanity, perhaps that sorrow might be the explanation they have never had from their son. Not even what he has said in court has given them what they want—it seems to replay, as if Motsamai's voice with its emphases from the rhythms of his African language is a broadcast overlaid: Duncan's presence interrupts, *it was not that, it was not exactly like that*. Nobody here knows. Perhaps there really is a frequency, coming from him where he is seated, turned away from them in the well of the court.

—Loss of self-control as inability to act in appreciation of wrongfulness, M'Lord, as against delusions confusing right and wrong. That is the difference.—

Harald felt Claudia's head disturb the space between them, stirring in denial; yes, the response seemed not to be Motsamai at his best. And perhaps he was wrong; temporary insanity, something in Duncan's brain that had been there always, the mystery that is the other individual, even the one you have created out of your own flesh? Claudia made as if to whisper something but Harald put up the hand holding a pen; dismay was wordless, it was as if the heating up of air in the crowded space was generated between Harald, Claudia and their son, overcoming everyone.

—Duncan Lindgard had no intention whatever to kill Jespersen. There was no premeditation. He had, he has, no criminal capacity to commit such an act. Brought about by provocation under severe emotional stress, it was done in lack of criminal capacity. His confession, his past history, his testimony are indisputable proof of that.—

—Have you concluded, Mr Motsamai?—

—Thank you, M'Lord. The case for the Defence is closed.—

The judge rose, the court was adjourned. There was a coming to life among the public like that at the end of the act in any theatre; they would be back. In the corridors, Motsamai become Hamilton put a hand on the forearm each of Harald and Claudia, drawing them together with him. He had the abstracted animation he showed when he came to chambers from a lunch. It's gone well enough, he said to his confidants, leaving his attorney, Philip the good friend, standing by with an arm-load of documents. They did not ask him about the insanity aspect, the question—what could they term it?

In his hands.

We're neither of us going to call any further witnesses, he told them, with a that-suits-me pause and shrug. We? He was in a hurry to consult with his attorney. As he left them they saw him greet his opponent, the Prosecutor; the two gowned men paused, Motsamai's arm resting briefly on the other's shoulder, shaking their heads over something, laughed together, swept past one another.

So it was all a performance, for them, for the judge, the assessors, the Prosecutor, even Motsamai. Justice is a performance.

As he and Claudia wandered the corridors, Harald slid something back into his pocket. It was the notebook he had found and taken from the table beside the bed, in the cottage.

Tomorrow it will be over. There will be the verdict.

We. Motsamai and the Prosecutor—each has decided not to call further evidence, either in indictment or mitigation. In agreement; over their tea: Harald is ready to believe. This kind of thinking was to be reduced to the lowest point in himself.

For him, here is another kind of evidence: the lack of any integrity, in the two opposing counsel, to the principled attacks they make upon one another's submissions in court. Claudia does not find surprising their professional camaraderie outside the referee's authority of the judge; she knows that to do your work well you concentrate on the process, uninvolved with personal feelings. In a café with Khulu, they talk about this quietly, between long pauses, while he has gone off to buy a newspaper.

I think a judge would be irritated by a lawyer who showed emotional attachment to a client. Maybe even inclined to be sceptical of the argument of someone suspected of going further than his professional commitment to defend. After all, they have to defend anybody. It's anyone's right to be defended, isn't it. We know that.

So Hamilton doesn't care what happens to Duncan. Apart from winning his case. Tomorrow he and the Prosecutor shake hands across the net, no matter who's won.

She refilled his cup, they, too, deal with the question of Duncan's life in the interim over a pot of tea. After a while, seeing Khulu coming back to them, she spoke quickly.

He cares. Hamilton cares, all right. You must believe that? Harald? Surely he's shown it. To us. But the court's not the place, not there.

Khulu held up the paper in acknowledgment of his return. She was watching him making his way through lanes of tables.

And that's the other one who does. Who would have thought he'd be the one who'd know we need someone with us every day, and it turns out we'd want nobody but him.

Claudia prescribed a sleeping pill for herself and went to bed.

Harald alone in the living-room took out the notebook and added, in reflection, details of the trial. He did not know what the purpose of these notes was. The question was put to himself as his attention wandered and came to rest on dead flowers in a vase; the only answer was the man, Khulu's. *I don't understand killing.* He tried to find a practical purpose for the notes; if there were to be an appeal against sentence, he would want to be able to refer to the impressions he had of how evidence that led to sentence (Duncan hasn't waited for judgment, there's only the degree of guilt, this play on words with culpability that Hamilton Motsamai's counting on) was received by the laconic judge, the silent assessors, the lawyers, even the clerks, your Indian and Afrikaner girls entered into a male domain, and those mannequins of the law, the policemen standing by without emanating human presence. Even the bodies pressed about Claudia and him—their reactions. Because all there are old hands, familiars of which way things are going in a trial and must know signs he and Claudia miss or cannot read.

Or maybe what he is recording simply belongs along with what

Duncan had written there and that he, Harald, has read in transgression of his own codes of behaviour. Probably it will go to the box in the cupboard where that letter the boy wrote from school has lain so long.

The word *performance* keeps rising. He sees he wrote down his nadir reached: Justice is a performance. Scribbled what he has described as Hamilton's self-promoting 'performance'; and then Khulu Dladla's quote from the girl—that Duncan wanted her to be 'performing her life' for him. He turned on the television to keep himself from going to bed unable to sleep (he refuses Claudia's prescription of a tranquillizer or sleeping pill, she thinks—privately—that he is one of those fortunately disciplined individuals who have the subconscious instinct that there is in them something that would lead to addiction) but what was offered was just another performance, a rock group contest on one channel and a sitcom in a language he didn't understand, on another.

He sat on, the notebook under his hand, and turned to the radio. He had come upon the middle of one of the phone-in programmes on subjects of public preoccupation, from abortion to supermarket prices and the culling of elephants, which are the circuses provided by democracy so that those who have bread but are aware that it is not true that anybody can (as opposed to 'may') become president have the opportunity and recognition at least of hearing his or her own voicing of opinions and frustrations aloud to the populace. The callers are, however meandering and inarticulate (he usually switches off at once), sometimes calling up deep impulses that lie beneath conformation to the ethos of their time and place. The Death Penalty: this was what talk-show democracy was open about to these eager citizens, this night. But the Death Penalty will be abolished! In-the-know Motsamai is certain of it. It will be proved a violation of the Constitution; there is no possibility, now, that Duncan—God forbid, and He has—could have sentence of death passed on him for what he has done, whyever he did it?

This is a civilized country now, and the State does not commit murder. But as Harald sits with his gaze fixed on the flowers that should have been thrown away he hears them, those callers for the death cell and the rope, early mornings with the hangman in Pretoria. They want, they still want, they are ready to demand over the air, for everyone, the President, the Minister of Justice, the Constitutional Court to hear—they want a corpse for a corpse, a murderer for a murderer. And they stumble indignantly through what can't be denied: the satisfaction they feel, the only reconciliation there is for them, lies in the death of one whose act took one of their own, or whose example threatens other lives. Their voices relayed over the telephone to the studio, the patronizing check on their verbosity by the presenter—for them the Death Penalty cannot be abolished. They—the people clamouring out there beyond the townhouse complex and the prison where Duncan awaits the verdict of his trial—they will condemn him to death in their minds no matter what sentence the judge passes down upon him, no matter how many assurances of mitigation Motsamai, out of his knowledge, his cleverness, his experience gives. In the air of the country, they are calling for a referendum; they, not the Constitutional Court will have the Last Judgment on murderers like Duncan. And referendum or not, Harald hears and knows, his son and sleeping Claudia's shall have this will to his death surrounding him as long as he lives. The malediction is upon him even if the law does not exact it.

No performance; this is reality.

She turned in her sleep and was awakened by the sense of emptiness beside her; felt for her watch. The luminous message: past two o'clock. She got up as Duncan had done and went to find the missing one. The door to the bathroom that was what the townhouse complex's brochure called *en suite* with the bedroom was ajar; no-one there. The living-room was dark and mum. She went cautiously down the passage as if she thought to meet an intruder. In the second bathroom Harald was lying, asleep in the tub, his head supported on the rim but his body, to Claudia, that of a drowned man.

Motsamai has assured his client, the accused, as well: tomorrow it will be over. And it has gone very encouragingly: he is confident. Colleagues who have been following the case say ten years, and of course there's always remission. But he, Motsamai, he thinks he has succeeded in a manner that has a good chance of seven. And then, with remission . . . The best way to talk to Duncan, he knows, is to do so as if Duncan were a fellow lawyer and they were considering someone else's case in which both were interested. That is the way, he is sensitive to, this young man in deep trouble can best manage himself; but he cannot resist repeating, indeed, as if to a colleague—Extremely well, particularly the cross examination with her.—

They've all gone away to await tomorrow when it will be over for them: his mother, his father, Khulu their proxy son he sees sits beside them where he cannot be, Motsamai, the judge, the girl clerks with their hair falling over their arms as they touch the keyboards of their word-processors, the faces of the spectators of his life; gone home. Alone. His parents, his friend Khulu (he hadn't realized, until now, how that one in the house really was his friend among the others) feel bad about leaving him behind, particularly this time, he knows, but he is relieved to have them gone.

So Motsamai, playing father when father cannot, has saved him at the cost of her. Natalie/Nastasya. He has opened her up and exposed her, dissected her womb with a baby in it, held out for all to see her mind and motives and body whose force and contradictions a lover knew only too well. Who will put Natalie together again; no-one. Motsamai is confident; this time she has saved him.

During the night, he did not dream in his cell but lived a fantasy while wakeful. Ten years, with remission, whatever spell of time has gone by, he comes out blinking into the sun, the city. Someone points to a child. Is it a girl, it looks like Natalie/Nastasya. No, it's a boy, it looks like us, Carl and Duncan.

Motsamai is wearing a particularly well-cut suit and the close coir of his hair has been shaped, the 19th-century African chief's wisp of chin-beard is combed to assert its mobile emphasis when he's speaking; this is the care Harald's business colleagues will take with their appearance on the day an important meeting is scheduled.

Motsamai was waiting for them in the corridors where echoes of everything they have heard in court in the past days is trapped under the high ceilings. He walked them along with calm tread through the skitter of clerks and messengers and the wandering of people looking for this court or that. When he found a little space for them he stopped. —You're all right, Claudia? I hope you had a night's rest, Harald. Me? Oh I always sleep, when I finally do get to bed if I'm preparing myself . . . Ah-hêh. Today. Now look, I've got the Prosecutor to agree that you can see Duncan at the lunch break. You know—it'll be after everything's concluded this morning, I don't expect the verdict and so forth until the afternoon. So you'll see him. Before it's handed down.—

When you find yourself confronted—can't look away, no evasion of propriety, class or privilege possible—with justice, you understand: the defenders and the prosecutors come to a reasonable settlement on the price of a murder. For Harald—that's what's been agreed. Motsamai's Learned Friend, for the State, is satisfied he's exacted all he can get. Motsamai himself—he actually makes a balancing gesture, his two hands are the scales: let well alone. —Judges are touchy people. Ah-hêh. You know? They get tired like us—when you keep on going after they've made up their minds. There's a stage at which . . . You follow me? He sits with his assessors and the verdict is there. More evidence—that's not going to affect it. We've made our impression with our witnesses, our cross examination. I don't want to disturb this with over-kill. With regard to sentence—that's something else. (He's using the phrase as one of the *double entendre* expressions in his voguish sophistication, implying not only another matter but also something exceptional.) I'll be applying myself to that this afternoon.—

They sit with Khulu through the summings-up. The Prosecutor and the Senior Counsel for the Defence each review with succinct force and conviction what they have already submitted on the evidence in chief, elicited, each according to his own purpose and skill, from accused and witnesses during that process and in cross examination.

Duncan is a fanatically possessive man who jealously premeditated revenging himself, harming Carl Jespersen who had sexual intercourse with his lover, Natalie James, and, in full awareness of the situation, in purposeful behaviour, in full capability, with criminal capacity, took advantage of the availability of a gun and deliberately shot the man where he knew it would be fatal, in the head.

Harald and Claudia and Khulu follow in common comprehension only these key terms in what comes from the samurai face the Prosecutor is wearing: criminal capacity, purposeful behaviour, full awareness. The combinations of phrases ignite as words in a column of newspaper set alight run together in flame. In a single attention, they scarcely hear the connecting sequence, the sense of the Prosecutor's long discourse. These legalistic terms, set down in the books of reference both Defence Counsel and Prosecutor have on their tables, are what will pronounce judgment of Duncan. When it is Hamilton's, Motsamai's turn, the three become separate attentions again, each listening with a different silent accompaniment, out of different ideas of what Duncan is, to every word, detail, nuance in what Motsamai is saying.

Duncan is a man totally without violent instincts, as his record of behaviour and caring for a mentally aggressive partner shows. As he well knew, there was no love affair possible between his former homosexual lover and the woman to whom he himself devoted such loving care. Therefore there was no jealous premeditation of violence or any other form of action towards the man. What he was suddenly confronted with on the night of January 18th was a shameless spectacle of crude sexual exhibitionism performed by these two people. Would not any violent man have attacked Jespersen at once? He certainly would. Duncan Lindgard did not attack Jespersen then and there, as any violent instincts undoubtedly would have led him to. All next day the shock and pain incapacitated him, he could not go to work. Scarcely believing he had seen what he had seen, he went back to the house only to look again at where it happened. Jespersen's unexpected presence on the very sofa where the degrading spectacle had taken place, Jespersen's incredible lack of shame, his assumption that it could just be brushed aside between men who were *brothers*, once even been lovers, over a drink together—this was a second terrible shock on top of the first. Equalling the force of a blow to the head, psychiatric evidence bears out, such shock has the effect of producing blankout.

An interruption from one of the two presences, the Greek chorus of the assessors forgotten round the judge deity: the white one asks, What is that? You used that word before. You mean a blackout?

—What is a blankout? A blankout is not a blackout, a state

when the individual loses consciousness. A blankout is the state
in which the individual suffers loss of self-control, a loss in which
there is inability to act in accordance with appreciation of wrongfulness, a state of criminal incapacity. It was in this state that, as
a result of provocation and severe emotional stress, Duncan Lindgard picked up the gun that was lying there and silenced his tor-
mentor with a shot.—

No-one—Harald, Claudia, Khulu—Duncan?—what was Duncan looking for in him—no-one could have any idea of the judge's
reactions from the face inclined slightly over the papers apparently
being ordered under his precise hands. Perhaps (this is what Harald
believes) he has, as Motsamai suggests, made up his mind on the
verdict much earlier; or perhaps he is going with his two assessors
who ramble behind him for the lunch adjournment like compan-
ionable dogs, to decide with them what it was that Duncan really
did when he shot a man in the head. For it becomes clear to those
who witness a trial that there is no such act as the simple act of
murder. To kill is only the definitive act arising out of many others
surrounding it, acts of spilled words, presumptions, sexual congress,
and, all around these, muggings in the streets.

Motsamai offers no experienced observations he may have
made of the judge's reception of his summing-up and that of the
Prosecutor, and Harald and Claudia don't have the sense that it
is right to ask him. It would be like questioning his effectiveness;
making him feel the weight of them, finally, in his hands. His
demeanour is Senior Counsel Motsamai rather than Hamilton as
he leads them, at last, to what they have never seen, a cell. It is
not quite the cell where Duncan has been led back to as they left
him after the visitors' room, but a cell under the well of the court
where prisoners are kept during the intervals of their trials.

Corridors and steps and doors for which warders have bracelets
of keys. It's a cellar-like place and in a corner behind a knee-high
wall there's a lavatory bowl. Some wooden chairs with numbers
chalked on them. There is a plate of food on the seat of one.
Duncan, their son, is standing with a glass of water in his hand,

he feels for somewhere to put it down, it wobbles against the plate. He embraces his mother, a hug as he always used to when he came for a meal, and then presses his father to him, the touch of his beard against Harald's cheek and ear something unfamiliar to them both.

Motsamai had left them alone; the presence of warders, policemen, has long ceased to count, with them. —He's confident about this afternoon.— Claudia is the first to speak. But what does that mean, confident? Duncan's gentle smile: it says he does not need the judge to tell him he did what he did.

—The circumstances.— Harald can't quite bring himself to make full reference to everything that has been done to Duncan and everything Duncan has done, but he wants to take the three of them to the safety of the concession by justice—extenuating circumstances; salvation has come down to this practical compromise from its place on High.

—Anyway. I'm glad it will be over for you two soon. Time for you to get back to work, I'm sure. Take things up.—

Harald doesn't want to be pictured sitting in a board room, he's here, for his son in a cell. —How did you feel about Motsamai, the way he handled it, was it what you expected? I couldn't see at all what was going on with you.—

—I left it all to him. Except when I was on the stand myself. I said what I had to say, that's all. The rest is his work, his decisions.—

—It's a good thing you trusted him. There's so much it's difficult for people like us to understand—about the process, I mean.—

He can't ask their son about the real subject they can't help circling, Motsamai's cross examination of the girl. What might be crucial for the verdict, what Motsamai did to that girl—how does he feel about Motsamai using like this Natalie whom he loved—loves? She stayed with him because he was 'more dreadful than the water', it's in the notebook—only Harald and his son know it, Harald thought from time to time in Motsamai's chambers he ought to show him the notebook but, unknown to his son that he had stolen it, he kept it between him and his son. Now the son has had to stand by between warders and watch her destruction by a lawyer because he has, yes, done something more dreadful, far worse than her choice to drown herself, taken a life not his own to take. Because of what he came upon on the sofa that night, did he rejoice to see her subjected to Motsamai's tactics? *I left it all to him.* Was there now a new solitariness, a new suffering to add to all the others that had assailed him, now it is bitterness against the man who has destroyed Natalie/Nastasya, a turning against the man in whose hands he was, no-one else can do anything for him, not even the parents who made a covenant always to be there for him? Inside Harald there cried out in anger to his God, is there no end to what my son has to bear?

—Has Motsamai said anything to you about what you might expect?— Claudia says this because she can't believe there really will be a verdict this afternoon and then a sentence passed next morning, the judge and his assessors will settle themselves into their chairs again and she will hear it.

—Yes, we've talked. I hope he has, to you and Dad as well.— Harald answered. —He has. But of course, it's only what he thinks, I mean from some precedent. All the time, no sign of what the judge was concluding about anything, even when he interrupted, asked something, or objected to something—I tried to make out whether he was impressed, disbelieving, whatever. But they're past masters at the neutral voice and the expressionless face.—

—Like the deadpan of a tough negotiator you're used to in the Board Room, Dad.—

He forces them to smile.

—Khulu sends his greetings—a message. You have it, Harald?—

Harald has written, at Khulu's dictation, on a page torn from the back of the notebook: UNGEKE UDLIWE UMZWANGEDWA SISEKHONA. He gives the piece of paper to Duncan.

—Do you understand?—

—The gist. I've picked up a bit of Zulu from him.—

—What does it mean? You know he's been with us nearly all the time.—

He doesn't answer his mother at once, not because he is unsure of the translation but because what it is, is hard to speak out in this hour, between the three of them.

—Something like, you will never be alone because we are alone without you.—

It's been said for them, the parents, there is nothing more to be said. They clung to the rest of their precious time with their son, talking a surface made of matters meaningless to all three, which could at least hold above sheer fall.

When it was time for the judge to convene the afternoon sitting of the court, one of the warders, a young Afrikaner, led them, and turned to regard Duncan. —He should eat something, lady. It's no good on an empty stummick. Your mother wants you to eat something, man.—

There has been, there is, no silence like the silence in a court when the judge lifts his head to hand down judgment. All other communication, within and without, is stilled; all is ended.

This is the last word.

She sits with hands trapped under her thighs as if in recognition of the irritation he has endured in being aware, in this place, the past days, of her beside him constantly turning the nail of her thumb under the rim of each nail. Khulu is with them. Khulu sits at her other side.

And darkness fell upon the land.

Each of the three is in the state of intense concentration that, as he, her husband, once tried to explain to her, was Simone Weil's definition of prayer. He doesn't know if he's praying; there is doubt about everything for him. What is habit praying for now—twelve years could be the maximum, ten likely, Hamilton says seven, eight is the leniency expected—it's implied—as the triumph of the Defence.

He/she. They don't look at their son now. There is no gaze able to reach him; the well of the court is not only the measure that sets him apart, in this enclosure within what everyone else experiences of the world—his progenitors, friends, the messenger Verster, the woman who knows we are all creatures of love and evil, are among them. Even Motsamai has done with him; whatever the bond was, the succour nobody, nobody else could give, it soon shall belong to the next client.

A judge takes his time. There must be nothing precipitate about the law. Twelve years, if it is to be twelve years, there is no hurry to decide a verdict on what will take so long to serve.

Does a sentence begin from the moment the verdict is pronounced, like the striking of a clock that signals a new hour to commence—My Lord Jesus Christ!—how demeaning it has been, all along, to be content to be an ignoramus, apparently immune from contact with the secular processes of crime and punishment! Only to have understood sins to be absolved by one of Your servants, mornings at confession. With great effort, he touches her arm and her hand comes out from suppression beneath the weight of her body so that he takes it. She has released the other hand, too. He is aware of Khulu's slight side-glance on him, on her. He sees Khulu's hand take this other hand.

The judge is feeling for something in the recesses of his robes; it was a handkerchief. The judge blows his nose, working the cloth up into one nostril, wipes the corners of his lips, replaces the handkerchief.

The judge looks out once, over the assembly, and then begins to address himself.

—The accused, Duncan Peter Lindgard, is charged with murder, arising out of the killing of Carl Jespersen, a fellow resident on a communally-occupied property. The accused's plea of not guilty is based on the defence of lack of criminal capacity, defined as temporary non-pathological incapacity.—

Our son is not mad.

—An accused person who submits non-pathological causes in support of a defence of criminal incapacity is required to lay a factual foundation sufficient for the court to decide the issue of the accused's criminal responsibility for his actions having regard to the expert evidence and to all the facts of the case, including the nature of the accused's actions during the period relevant to the alleged crime.

The defence to the charges is that owing to extreme stress and provocation he had been unable to form the intention required to commit the alleged crime; unable to appreciate the wrongfulness of his actions or act in accordance with such appreciation, and unable to engage in any purposeful conduct.—

There is something salutary, necessary, for Harald and Claudia, perhaps even for their son himself, in this plain setting out of facts that, within themselves, have been so overgrown by emotion and entangled out of comprehension by distress.

—The main events of the night of Thursday, January 18th, 1996, have been proved by evidence which is either common cause or not seriously disputed. A party took place with the arrival of friends of the occupants of the main house on the property, David Baker, Nkululeko Dladla, Carl Jespersen, and the occupants of the cottage on the property, Natalie James and the accused. The accused and Natalie cohabited as heterosexual lovers, the three men in the house were homosexuals, with Baker and Jespersen as a couple. Before his relationship with Natalie, the accused had had a homosexual relationship with Jespersen, but this does not appear to have affected the close friendship, the amicable sharing of what was virtually a single household by the five individuals.—

And as he delivers the next statement the judge looks up, head lifted, straight out to the public assembly, for the first time.

—They even owned and knew how to use, a gun, in common.—

It is also a first hint of any personal attitude to the case. The context of the case. He has allowed himself the show of a brief ironic comment for those, like the father of the accused, who are sophisticated enough to interpret it as a shrug of disapproval of the household he has, dispassionately, and without prejudice on sexual mores, described. The significance of the shared gun ('they even') as a symbol of the shared interchangeable relations there distracts Harald as something he should have gone into, wanted to all along but that can't be attended to now, no no, because every phrase that comes from this man is selective progress in the discourse of judgment, you must keep up with him, read between the lines (read his lips, of their intent) at the same time as you miss no single word. Harald wants to convey to Claudia and Khulu this attitude he sees purposely let slip by the judge, but there's no time even to alert them with a glance.

—When the party broke up that night and guests left, accompanied by Nkululeko Dladla, David Baker retired to bed in the house and the accused went to the cottage after an altercation with Natalie, who stayed behind, volunteering to assist Jespersen to tidy up and wash dishes.—

He has his audience now. For all those others round the parents and their surrogate son Khulu, here is a drama addressed directly to them. They've seen in the flesh some of the characters; up there, on the witness stand. They are invited to share the right of familiarity the judge takes to himself, referring to one of the leading characters in the affair not as he does the men, by their surnames, but simply as 'Natalie', because she's only a woman. If Claudia reads the lips of the man up there on the bench, his patronage is an aside unimportant to her today; or maybe for her it is all the respect from anyone this bitch should expect.

—Some two hours later, the accused wakened in the cottage and found that Natalie had not returned. Concerned for her safety crossing the garden so late, he went to the house, where he came upon Natalie and Jespersen *in flagrante delicto*, engaged in the sexual act on the sofa in the living-room. They became aware of his presence but he did not confront them. He went back to the cottage. Natalie did not come to the cottage; she took her car and drove away.—

With the daring matter-of-fact of this account his attention has left his audience. His eyes are on his text again; let them contemplate the salacious scene he has just presented.

—The accused, an architect, did not go to work on Friday, January 19th. He stayed in the cottage, alone, all day. Some time between 6.30 and 7 p.m.—he does not recall looking at his watch, and a gardener, the only witness that he went to the house, since he saw him return, does not own a watch—during that period the accused emerged from the cottage, fed his dog, and walked through the garden to the house. There, with the door open to the garden as it had been the night before, Jespersen was lying on the sofa drinking a sundowner. He made light of the incident of the previous night, claiming a shared brotherly context of the sexual mores of the communal household, and suggested that the accused join him with a drink.—

No, no he didn't feed the dog *on the way to the house*, that's the way it's been phrased to sound but it was to feed the dog, not to go to the house, that he left the cottage! This isn't just a detail! It may be vital! The judge has let them down, deviated from the trust warily granted him. Claudia and Khulu are aware of a sudden surge of agitation in Harald but do not know its particular source. Claudia turns to Khulu, and he draws his face into planes of troubled assurance: it may be that Harald is momentarily overcome by the totality of where they are, what is actually taking place this day. The gun, that's what the judge is bringing up now. He, Khulu, has held that gun, flipped it over in his hand, once or twice, yes.

—The house gun, which had been produced as a demonstration model for one of the guests of the previous night who intended to acquire one, had been left lying on a table. With it, the accused shot Jespersen in the head where he lay. The shot was fatal. On his way back to the cottage the accused dropped the gun in the garden, where he was observed by Petrus Ntuli, a plumber's assistant who worked as a part-time gardener on the property in exchange for accommodation in an outhouse. David Baker and Nkululeko Dladla came home shortly after and found the deceased's body. They ran to the cottage to tell the accused but there was no response to their calls or knocking on the door, so they presumed he was not there. They called the police who in the course of searching the garden came upon Petrus Ntuli who told them the accused was in the cottage and that he, Ntuli, had seen him drop something on his way to the cottage from the house. The police found the gun, effected entry to the cottage, arrested the accused and took him to the police station for questioning. He was charged with murder. The gun, Exhibit 1, bears his fingerprints.—

These are the facts—but what about the reasons for coming out of the cottage, what about the *intention*, the dog! The dog!

—None of the facts has been disputed by the Defence. This granted, what the assessors and I have had to decide in handing down judgment is the validity of the claim of temporary nonpathological criminal incapacity submitted by the Defence on behalf of the accused. I cite, exceptionally, 'on behalf of' although it goes without saying that any counsel's chosen defence is proxy for an accused, because in this case the accused has not taken the right to defend himself vociferously.

He denies that he spent Friday in the cottage brooding on revenge against the deceased. He said in evidence 'Revenge for what. I don't own either of them, they are free to do as they like'—thus *indirectly* defending himself against premeditation of his crime, but he does not emphasize the responsibility the couple bore in gross violation of his feelings; he describes his reactions that night as something generated within, by himself, without attribution of blame to them. In reply as to whether he thought of any revengeful accusation, let alone action, against the couple, he said 'All I could remember—about seeing them there like that—was . . . a disintegration of everything, disgust with myself, everyone . . .'

Similarly, he makes no *categorical* denial, forcefully expressed, of the suggestion that when he walked across the garden to the house on Friday evening, he had the intention of confronting Jespersen. All he offered the court was the oblique statement 'I found myself in the garden . . . I didn't want to talk to anyone . . . I think then I had to find myself standing again where I stood in the doorway.' He is referring to the previous night, when he came upon the couple. The Defence has interpreted this statement as standing for his disbelief—that is to say, what he saw in the house that night could not have happened; he had to go back, as if to verify the *mise en scène*. We unanimously find this interpretation acceptable. The State's allegation that the accused spent the day of Friday, 19th January, premeditating revenge on the deceased is borne out neither by the content of the accused's evidence nor the manner of his delivery, which, to those like myself and the assessors, accustomed to the tenor and timbre of lying, have the characteristics of truth.—

A new tension—hope—holds the three. Harald and Claudia stiffen, recklessly afraid to let go, in any contact. It is so unexpected, this show of understanding by one who is judging Duncan, nothing contradictory to be read from the lips—is it at all usual for such empathy with an accused to be expressed in the course of a judgment? How can they know? Can't ask the one who would: Motsamai, he's unreachable in the well of the court beside his client. Harald hears Claudia's fast breathing from a thumping heart. Their son is not mad and he is not a liar. What he says (and his body doesn't contradict it) has the characteristics of truth. If Motsamai, Hamilton, could relay some answer?—does the truth count? Can the truth save you?

And while these questions take height, they suddenly plummet again. What is the judge delivering himself of now? Motsamai, *Hamilton!*—is judgment a one-man game in which the player challenges himself, enjoys shifting conclusions to weigh down first one side of the famous scales, then the other?

—Absence of premeditation, however, does not imply subsequent criminal incapacity in the actual perpetration of a crime, the series of actions by which a crime is committed *at the time*. If it is accepted that the accused went from the cottage to the house to convince himself that what he saw on the sofa in the living-room the previous night actually happened, only to look once again at the scene (the judge seems to lose concentration for a moment, preoccupied wearisomely with some matter surfacing in him from his own life, but perhaps he's paused for effect, he's a pro, they're all pros, his assessors, his prosecution and defence teams) . . . what he actually saw was the man Jespersen, on that same sofa. There followed convincing evidence, confirmed by both State and Defence psychiatrists' expert opinions, of a second profound shock, the outrage of Jespersen's callous assumption that what happened the previous night before the accused's eyes was trivial, to be passed off over a drink between men.—

Like the arm on the shoulder, between Prosecutor and Defence Counsel in the corridors, passing over the scene in court where the one has been condemning a man and the other defending him. But Harald knows he should be the last one to be disillusioned by professional ethics; disillusion once begun, these days, here in this place, has ended up with his questioning his own.

—It does not require any preparation of premeditation for a conscious and rational determination to take revenge to be suddenly aroused at such a moment. The means of revenge in such circumstances is most likely to be some form of physical attack, with bare hands or whatever may serve as a weapon. It is unfortunate that a deadly weapon, a gun, was casually accepted as part of the household in that living-room and that it was lying on the table.—

How to follow the twists and turns, the swift about-face of what the man's saying as he retreats and advances, down over his text, up to take them into his confidence again; there is the desperation of half-grasping a direction his mind is taking, only to have it snatched away as if attention has been disastrously lost for precious seconds—what did that mean, what was the order of words that are the clues to be followed to a verdict forming? Each loses the way and is impatient with anxiety to know if the other has caught what is missing, and yet cannot risk to interrupt attention by whispering the question.

—But the accused could have chosen bare hands; instead he chose to pick up the gun and shoot Jespersen in the head. He has said in evidence 'The noise stopped.' What he didn't want to hear from Jespersen was silenced in the ultimate revenge, the taking of another's life.—

Not a liar, but a murderer.

Claudia sees that her whole life was moving towards this moment. All the ambitions she had so naïvely decided she was going to fulfil, when she was a girl, all the intentions of dedication to healing she has had in her adulthood—they were to come to this. The end is unimaginable; if we knew it from the start we would never set out.

—The District Surgeon's report is that the shot was accurately directed to a vital part, the forehead, consistent with deliberate action. Whether this means a certain series of actions had to be *consciously* taken to aim and fire it, as the State submits, or whether, as the Defence submits, to the hand of anyone who is familiar with a gun the necessary preparation to fire comes automatically, without conscious volition, is now the crucial matter on which the question of criminal capacity, as the State submits, or temporary non-pathological criminal incapacity, as the Defence argues, must be considered, having regard to the expert evidence and all the facts of the case, including not only the nature of the accused's actions during the period immediately relevant to the crime, but also the circumstances that preceded it in the personal history of the accused.—

The sonorous maze of clauses dazes. Even the uttermost limit of attention which is prayer lands in dead ends, turns upon premises which it seems to have just left. During passages like this the ranks of spectators rustle. All the pros and cons are no business of theirs, they wait for the narrative to recommence, a judgment is the remnant of the oral tradition round the fire; they're there to be told an exciting story.

Now it's taken up again, good, it's about the young man they've been able to study, face, gestures (what the judge called his 'manner') on the witness stand. It's about a murderer.

—Both State and Defence psychiatrists find that the accused's intellect is within high limits, his judgment sound. He is a young professional man of good family, apparently with a promising career ahead of him. There is no basis on which to question the Defence's submission that everything in the accused's behaviour as an adult has been contrary to the performance of any violent act. The evidence of a member of the common household, Nkululeko Dladla, states of the accused 'It is not in his nature to kill.'—

And there he is, that Dladla, sitting with the murderer's parents, right here. People turning to look at him: it is as if he himself has spoken, a hefty black man who wears like campaign medals the insignia of the gay, his tryst rings and necklaces. Harald and Claudia are moved by the judge's quotation of Khulu and are graced to be identified in the focus of attention that has reached him; under it Khulu is rubbing his fist back and forth across his jaw-line as he often does, they've noticed, when he wants to emphasize something he has said in his calm way.

Ah but listen to this, Harald and Claudia are saying simultaneously, without words, to one another, as the judge's narrative takes another unexpected turn, listen to this!

—Indeed, demonstrably, it has been in his nature to succour. The accused met Natalie when she had made a suicide attempt, and, on her own admittance, brought her back to life. After they commenced to live together as lovers, he saved her again from suicide. Although he was passionately in love with her, that the relationship was not a happy one is confirmed not only by Natalie herself, but by Dladla. It seems she was not grateful to the accused for saving her life. Asked why the relationship she and the accused had chosen was not happy, she replied in evidence 'He owned my life because he took me to a hospital.' Her attitude towards him as revealed under cross examination by the Defence was resentful, giving credence to Dladla's statement that although the accused 'was patient with her . . . like a sick person . . . she gave him hell.' She taunted him before other members of the common household. The indifference, if not defiance, with which she told the court that the child she is expecting might be either the deceased's or the accused's appears to be a particularly malicious example of taunting the man who loves her and is on trial for a *crime passionnel* of which her action is half, if not the whole cause.—

A judge knows everything. He's the vicar of the god of justice, as the priest is the vicar of God, he's privy to the confessional of the court, where witnesses and experts and the accused tell what Harald and Claudia would never have learnt. This knowledge, it's the basis of justice, isn't it? To know all is to forgive all?—no, that's fallacious. The man's dead, shot in the head. He's here under the ground of the city where this court is the seat of justice. But to know all: the judge is not going to follow, is he, any pressure for society's angry retribution, society being represented by the State; he's concerned with the fate of the individual as well. Motsamai must be thinking—what? Hope: it can't be repressed. Duncan; but it's somehow an intrusion to wonder what he's thinking, feeling. As if the sacrificial victim is anointed in his extremis, and removed from the contagion of human contact which he pursued to its awesome finality, the taking of another's life. But hope. Can it reach their son, from them.

—Unfortunately, it is not within the competence of this court to refer a witness for psychiatric examination.— And now the judge has allowed himself the indulgence of sarcasm, again an aside for those who may appreciate it.

Somebody stifles a rough laugh. It is out of order but probably what the judge expected he might get from the public.

—Therefore it is difficult to assess what the Defence submits, that the *extent* of stress this young woman was capable of imposing on her patient and devoted lover was great enough to culminate in his committing a crime in a state of criminal incapacity. There is evidence that Natalie had had other passing sexual adventures during the period in which she lived with the accused as his lover, and he had forgiven or at least tolerated these. Why then if he were not to have been reduced by her, finally, to a state where he was not responsible for his actions, would he not have forgiven, tolerated her betrayal once again?

We must turn now to the special circumstances of *this* particular sexual adventure. The court has learned from the accused himself that what he came upon that night after the party not only was his lover, Natalie, engaged in sexual intercourse with another man, that man was Carl Jespersen, a homosexual who had himself taken the accused as a lover and then discarded him, and who had repeatedly declared himself revulsed by women's sexuality. The accused has not confided to the court what his emotions are towards his present and former lovers, what interpretation he puts on a role in the spectacle apparently inconceivable for him to believe Jespersen would ever force himself to perform. It is the Defence psychiatrist's opinion that 'When he (the accused) saw her in the sexual act with his former male lover, he felt himself emasculated by them both.'—

Silence is a great hand spread over the court.

All at once the people on the public benches are no longer strangers, their prurience is stifled as the laugh was, their presence is protective around the parents of this man.

—The court can accept that it was 'not in his nature to kill'.

But what the accused saw in that act, and what he encountered in the deceased's attitude next evening were surely not in the nature of human relationships in even the freest of sexual mores. Given these exceptional circumstances of what might otherwise have been nothing more than another regrettable incident in a relationship fraught with problems, the State psychiatrist submits that if the accused were to have acted in a state of diminished capacity, unable to appreciate the wrongfulness of his behaviour, he would have attacked the deceased then and there, on the night when he discovered the couple. The psychiatrist's opinion is that the accused went to the house next evening with the conscious intention of vengeful jealousy built up during a day of solitary premeditation in the cottage. Asked whether she meant the accused intended to kill Jespersen, the psychiatrist's reply was that she was not able to say to what extreme the accused's intention might carry him.

This brings to the court's attention the question of the gun kept at hand in the house: did the accused have in mind, in conscious intention, the availability of the gun, which he admits having seen being produced in the living-room the previous night?—

The judge looks up conversationally, but his audience is transfixed.

—The psychiatrist called by the Defence found the accused to have been precipitated into a state of dissociation from what he was doing when he was confronted with the sight of Jespersen on the evening of 19th January. He submits that when the deceased said 'Why don't you pour yourself a drink' this attitude constituted a second blow like the one received the previous night. His professional opinion was that 'A tremendous emotional blow is as forceful as any external blow to the head.' Further, he states: 'With the impact of these last words he (the accused) recalls Jespersen saying, he would have entered a state of automatism in which inhibitions disintegrated . . . cumulative provocation reaching its climax in the subject's total loss of control.'

This raised again the question of the nature and extent of cumulative provocation acceptable as the extreme stress submitted by the Defence as justification for a temporary non-pathological criminal incapacity. The psychiatrist testified that—I quote—the accused 'is a man with a bisexual nature. That in itself is a source of personality conflict. He had suffered emotional distress when he followed his homoerotic instincts and had a love affair which his partner, Jespersen, did not take seriously and broke off at whim. He overcame the unhappiness of the rejection and turned to the other and probably dominant side of his nature, a heterosexual alliance for which, again, he took on serious responsibility. Even more so, since the alliance was with an obviously neurotic personality with complex self-destructive tendencies for which, when crossed in what she saw as her right to pursue them, she punished him with denigration and mental aggression.' The conclusion of this assessment, which I have already quoted earlier, was that when the accused saw her in the sexual act with his former lover, he felt himself emasculated by both.—

Claudia feels Khulu lift and let fall his arms. At her other side, Harald's profile is Duncan's, the order of resemblance reversed; confusion engulfs her. She is confronted with the face of a patient whom she referred for surgery to take place today; it's a fragment of the medical record that is her life, blown across her mind. *My assessors and I*, what is the voice saying—

—My assessors and I, of course, have to examine the evidence of psychiatrists carefully and give it due weight. However, as the highest court of the land has said, their science is not an absolute but an empirical one. Psychiatrists rely on what they have been told by the accused, often without critically analyzing these statements to determine whether they may not be proffered as self-serving. My assessors and I are equally capable of interpreting the evidence as a whole, led before us, as to whether or not there was criminal responsibility. Albeit that the Defence psychiatrist is of the opinion that there was no criminal responsibility, and even though the State psychiatrist, if somewhat reluctantly, has made some concessions in terms of our law, we are entitled to come to our own conclusions. We find as a fact that the accused's personal history of prolonged emotional stress is genuine; but is this enough?—

So confidently in control of their life, Claudia's and his own. First they were ceded into the hands of Motsamai; now in the power of this man who asks, but is this enough? The power's omnipotent. Only Duncan could answer.

—We have identified the decisive aspects of the case.

One: did premeditation of revenge occupy the accused during the day he spent alone in the cottage, and as a consequence did he go to the house intending to seek out Jespersen and cause him bodily harm?

Two: whether or not harmful intention was premeditated, when the accused picked up the gun and shot Jespersen, was he in a state of automatism in which inhibitions disintegrated and there was total loss of control?

On the matter of Question One, my learned assessor, Mr Abrahamse, a member of the Bar, and I are of the opinion that there was no premeditation of vengeful bodily harm, this based on the absence of dissimulation in the accused's evidence and the fact that, firstly, it is accepted that he had no weapon of any kind with him when he left the cottage; secondly, although the house gun was not kept locked away in security, merely in a drawer in a bedroom, it is reasonable to suppose that when the room had been tidied up after the party it would not have been left lying on the table. My learned assessor, Mr Conroy, an experienced senior magistrate, was of the minority opinion that there was premeditation, this based on the reasonable assumption that solitary self-incarceration in the cottage strongly implied this.

In the matter of Question Two, the court has devoted much careful deliberation to the contrary elements revealed between the only witness to the *crime itself* available—that of the accused himself, and the fact of the body of the victim—and the various interpretations of his act as presented to the court. The accused has testified that he did not see the gun when he entered the living-room, and he could not say at what point he saw it. Yet he admits that he could and did pick it up. He says that he 'didn't make any decision'; but, nevertheless, he fired it.—

The lifted gaze accuses them, the mother and father and friend of the murderer, although the judge probably doesn't even know where they are among the faces; they take that gaze upon themselves.

—There is some doubt as to whether or not he knew it was loaded. If he did not know—although it is reasonable to suppose he did, since at the party he could have seen this demonstrated—and he had to verify whether or not it was loaded by opening the chamber, the deceased surely would have had sufficient warning of the accused's intent and could have made a move, jumped up to defend himself. The validity of the submission that one may verify that a gun is loaded or not, whether the safety catch is on or not, and then take aim accurately at a victim's head, if one is not an experienced marksman and is in a state of inability to engage in purposeful conduct, which is one of the definitions of lack of criminal capacity, therefore also remains in some doubt. The accused has admitted that the gun, which he knew how to use, was nevertheless 'the only one I'd ever touched'. Usage which is not habitual generally requires conscious attention in order to be performed, however simple the process may be.—

The protection closed in around them has been withdrawn; the company have become spectators again, impatiently bored with all this legal yes and no and maybe and nevertheless. The import carried in the judge's next statement, carefully delivered without any of the histrionic ring that has sounded an alert in some of his other pronouncements, satisfies no expectations.

—Therefore it is the opinion of the assessors and myself that, although the crime was committed under extreme stress, it was a conscious act for which the accused bears criminal responsibility.—

Even Harald and Claudia, who have been balancing, in that intense concentration of theirs, the yes and no of convoluted discourse— O, if one could be sufficiently removed, safe enough from it to be bored—a moment of bewilderment passes between them before they translate the dry statement of reasoned opinion into the fallen hammer of verdict. Why go on, why is he going on, he's already picked up *his* weapon to hand and struck with it, full in the breast. Criminal responsibility. Our son is not mad. Duncan do you hear, did you take it in?

But the man is going on. He taunts, he can't leave alone what he has said, he has to do it again. Dangle hope.

—The court takes into full consideration certain mitigating factors, albeit that the accused has shown no remorse for his crime. Firstly, he did not carry any weapon when he went to the house. Secondly, he could not have known that the deceased would be lying on the very sofa where the sexual act had taken place before his eyes the previous night. Thirdly, the gun *happened to be there*, on the table. If it had not been there, the accused might have abused the deceased verbally, perhaps even punched him in the usual revenge of dishonoured lovers of one kind . . . or both.—

He seems now to abandon his text, to accuse the assembly and himself, the streets and suburbs and squatter camps outside the courts and the corridors, the mob of which he sees all as part, close up against the breached palace of justice. —But that is the tragedy of our present time, a tragedy repeated daily, nightly, in this city, in our country. Part of the furnishings in homes, carried in pockets along with car keys, even in the school-bags of children, constantly ready to hand in situations which lead to tragedy, the guns *happen to be there*.—

Khulu is jerking his head vehemently against self-restraint, but for Harald, the judiciary has had its little homily, yes. Does this have any bearing on what is going to be done with my son who, like everyone else, breathed violence along with cigarette smoke?

The judge takes command of himself.

—The gun was there. The accused had the volition to use it to deadly purpose.

The unanimous verdict of the court is that Duncan Peter Lindgard is found guilty, with extenuating circumstances, of the murder of Carl Jespersen.

I propose to adjourn the matter of sentence until ten o'clock tomorrow morning.—

The people have seen justice done. They are shamed, now, to be curious observers of the couple to whom something terrible has happened; they stand back, nudge each other out of the way to let Harald and Claudia and that black gay, that *moffie*—the witness, pass. Claudia's eyes meet those of a stranger; he lowers his gaze.

An emotional shock has the force of a blow on the head. But

this verdict is not a shock; it is the delivery of dread that has been held—only just—at bay for many weeks and has been drawing closer and closer for the days in this place, closer than the surrounding strangers; waiting to be brought down upon them, Harald and Claudia. In the movement of police, lawyers, clerks, gathering the documentation by which justice has been arrived, it is difficult to find Duncan. He's not there? Duncan was never in this place, never. None of this could have happened to their son.

At ten o'clock in the morning the court rises for the judge's entry. Papers glide one under the other; the sunlight from the eastern windows shines through the membrane of his prominent ears. He is an ikon to displace those to whom Harald has directed prayer in the past.

Apparently it is standard procedure for the Prosecutor and the Defence Counsel to joust briefly on the issue of sentence, as if it were not already determined on the papers under the judge's hands lying half-open like mouths ready to speak what is held behind his lips locked at the corners. The Prosecutor earnestly reiterates what he has elicited from the accused in his cross examination; there can be no question of ambiguity when the facts of the case come out of the accused's indictment of himself. —You remarked in judgment, Your Lordship, that he showed no remorse; now, further, a man who shows no remorse is also showing that whether or not he performed the act of murder consciously, it was the carrying out of an act that *he would have wished to have come about*. He has no regrets because the death of the man who spurned him as a lover and then was his woman's lover is what he wanted and it *is accomplished.* The accused who does not defend himself is the individual who therefore accepts that his crime is his crime, there is no mitigation to be claimed for it. To expect mitigation of sentence further than the concession of extenuating circumstances the court has already granted, is to bring into question what example, what message, our courts of law would send to society with such mitigation. Your Lordship has referred to the climate of violence in our country as a cause of great concern. A crime arising out of the cohabitation of people like the accused and his fellow occupants, his mates, in a house where none of the acceptable standards of order, whether in sexual relations or the proper care of a weapon, was maintained—if such a crime is to be regarded leniently, lightly, what kind of dangerous tolerance will this indicate of what is threatening the security and decency in human relations on which our new dispensation in this country is based? Yes, the gun was there; the crime of vengeful jealousy with which it was committed is by no means *excused by*, but belongs along with the hijacks, rapes, robberies that arise out of the misuse of freedom by making your own rules. That's where it all begins—defying all moral standards and claiming total permissiveness, as the accused and his friends have done, and which led to *permit* the murder of one of them, one of the *bed-mates*, by another—the accused. I don't have to remind the court that justice must be done to society as well as to the individual accused when sentence is passed commensurate with the damage he has done in taking the life of an individual, *and* to society—he, a highly privileged young man, a professional to whom society has given all advantages—by taking part in the moral free-for-all that abuses and threatens that society.—

Hamilton Motsamai is smiling as he rises. There's a slight inclination of the body that might be a bow in the direction of the Prosecutor. —M'Lord, the accused has not been brought before some commission on public morals, but before your court on a charge of murder.

With your permission, there is no charge preferred against him as the representative of a section of society.

He cannot be brought to account for encouragement of robberies, hijackings and rape so regrettably common in this time of transition from long eras of repression during which state brutality taught violence to our people generations before the options of freedom in solving life's problems were opened to them. I ask M'Lord's indulgence for this last digression . . .

The climate of violence bears some serious responsibility for the act the accused committed, yes; because of this climate, the gun was there. The gun was lying around in the living-room, like a house cat; on a table, like an ashtray. But the accused bears no responsibility whatever for the *prevalence* of violence; the court has accepted undeniable evidence that he had never before displayed any violent tendencies whatever, and heaven knows there were occasions when life with that young woman might have expected it. He was, indeed, a citizen who—to appropriate a term from my Learned Friend—upheld 'acceptable standards' of social order. His conduct condoned neither hijacking, robbery nor rape.

We are left with the conclusion that my Learned Friend is himself making a moral judgment on sexual preference, sexual activity, specifically homosexual activity when he speaks of the accused's co-occupancy of 'a house where none of the acceptable standards of order' was maintained. He thus classifies sexual relations along with the lack of proper care of a dangerous, a lethal weapon as equal examples of transgression of such acceptable standards.

M'Lord, the accused has not appeared before you on a charge of homosexual activity with a consenting adult; neither could this be a charge, under the new Constitution, where such relations are recognized as the right of individual choice. Homosexual relationships, such as existed in the common household, are commensurate with 'acceptable standards' in our country.

The court has made a majority decision that the murder to

which the accused has admitted was not premeditated. While regarding with its privilege of learned scepticism the conflicting testimonies of the psychiatrists, the court has come to its own opinion that, nevertheless, the crime was committed in a state of criminal responsibility and declared this decision in judgment. Yet there remains that in the course of the trial there has been much debate on this vital issue, and debate, it must be admitted, implies that a certain degree of doubt, a question mark, hangs over it. This degree of doubt merits being taken seriously as augmenting the consideration of extenuating circumstances granted in the judgment.

Ah-hêh . . . Finally—when calling for a sentence commensurate with the wrong-doing of the individual, the State needs to keep in mind the philosophy of punishment as rehabilitation of an individual, not as condemnation of the putative representative of society's present ills whose punishment therefore must be harsh and heavy enough to deal with collective guilt. Our justice has suspended the death sentence; we must not seek to install in its place prejudices that inflict upon any accused punishment in addition to, in excess of that commensurate with the crime he has committed, and the circumstances in which it was committed. The mores of our society are articulated in our Constitution, and our Constitution is the highest law of the land. My Learned Friend for the State speaks with the voice of the past.—

Now there begins some preamble from the judge that will not be remembered with any accuracy because all sense is deafened in strain towards what was going to come from him: the last word.

—I have listened carefully to Counsel both for State and Defence. It should have been clear to both Counsel that the proper sentence in this case to be imposed by this court is not dependent upon the convicted person's social or sexual morals. My function is to impose a sentence which is just both to the victim and the accused. A life has been lost. And as expression of my displeasure at the manner in which the gun in question was held without consideration of safe-keeping, I declare this gun forfeited to the State.

Although there are unusual and exceptional circumstances in this case the sentence must have a deterrent effect. The value of human life is primarily enshrined in our Constitution. The question of sentence is a very difficult one; it must not only act as a deterrent but there must also be a measure of mercy. After very careful consideration I sentence you, Duncan Peter Lindgard, to seven years imprisonment.

The court will adjourn.—

The last word. Handed down to the son, to his parents, to the assembled representatives of those other judges, the people of the city.

Over.

A decompression, a collapse of the nerves, a deep breath expelled—like the one that left Harald's spirit when the messenger brought news *something terrible has happened*: but this coming full circle, as it were, expelling the breath of relief. Over.

Even the period with him, Duncan, down in that place below the court afterwards, when all the others who had been around them and who had heard out the judgment, the sentence pronounced, seven years, had trooped out of the court, filed past them respectfully, Verster the messenger pausing a moment as if to speak, not speaking, another—a woman—leaning swiftly to say, Thank God (someone aware it might have been twelve years)— even while with their son, there was this strange remission. The three exchanged shyly and gently the banalities of concern for one another, Are you all right mother, dad why don't you sit down. Motsamai was there—in the persona of Hamilton again, shepherding the parents, how could they have done without him this one last time. On the way along corridors, he had undertoned gravely in the manner of delivery with which habitually he

approached, surged to express, and overcame dangerous subjects—
I must tell you we are very, very fortunate. You can't imagine. It
is the most lenient sentence possible. In my entire experience. The
minimum given in a case such as Duncan's. Seven years. We
couldn't have got away with less; it was my ambitious aim, but
then one never knows, even with the right judge, about the assessors. Those fellows, sometimes! Ah-hêh. Man! If they concur
on vital aspects in opposition to the judge! He has to take due
cognizance . . . Well, here were lambs, little sheep followed him,
hardly a bleat, nê.— Now it was an effort for him to keep his
mood down to their subdued level although he was familiar with
the way individuals stunned by the ordeal of a trial mistake their
state for a kind of peace that one doesn't want to disturb. It is the
mood in which he has seen other murderers vow a religious conversion. —Duncan won't serve the full term. Definitely not. Good
behaviour, studies and so on—I suppose you could still take some
other degree in your line of profession, Duncan, of course you can.
He'll be out by the time he's—how old are you now, again, Duncan, twenty-seven?—out by the time he's thirty-two. That's a
young man still, isn't it? He'll put it behind him.—

Hamilton also has plans. For them there was only the relief,
Duncan is no longer the target standing set apart in the dock,
strangers in intrusion of the most private event of their lives no
longer press around them; they have no awareness further than
this, in the twenty minutes, half-hour perhaps, with him, no sense
of its limit and what waits beyond it.

Counsel knows the devastating emotions relatives and the
newly-convicted are subject to when they meet for the first time,
which is a new time, after it is all over. Hamilton has to control
his empathy, which exists along with his professional satisfaction
in an extremely dubious case well defended by one of the best
advocates available. He is there to support, to help them accept
in themselves, between themselves and himself, the natural expression of emotions. Among his people (he would term it, in our
culture) a mother would be wailing. And how. Why not. But these

poor people—that little bitch was right in this instance—middle-class whites whose codes of behaviour they are sure are enlightened and free, are *the* ones that can contain everything in life and so should, in respect of everybody! Their son, poor boy, got himself into a mess that wasn't covered. And they themselves don't know what it is to respond to what is happening to them now. They show no emotion, just a distanced kindness towards one another.

No wailing from this mother. It is only—unexpectedly—the father who suddenly gets up from the chair he has been considerately offered and takes his son by the shoulders. A curious ugly sound between a cough and a cry, as if he were gagging comes from him. His wife the doctor seems able to make no move. Hamilton lets him alone in this, his moment. Only when he's turned away, his face in a dry rictus, does Hamilton go over and put an arm around him.

Harald had looked at Duncan in his calculatedly casual-fitting jacket and baggy grey trousers, the convention of unconventionality that had not prejudiced a worldly judge, and realized this was the last time he would be wearing these. Next time (and time is seven years) it would be prison clothes.

Over.

It's beginning.

Khulu was waiting for them on the steps of the courts. He walked with them in silence towards the parking lot. They tramp like prisoners, every footstep grinds. Motsamai's—Hamilton's task was successfully concluded now, he would be the go-between of Duncan and the prison authorities, but there would be little need for him to seek out or receive the parents, a successful Senior Counsel is a busy man. They stood a moment, delivered to their car. Claudia spoke for them both, to Khulu—Let's not lose sight of each other.

A prison is darkness. Inside. Inside self. It's a night that never ends, even under the strip light's bristling glare from the cell ceiling. Darkness even while, through the barred window reached by standing on the bed: the city trembling with light. That's anticipation. That's what's gone. There is nothing calling, nothing you are waiting for.

I am a rag on a barbed wire fence. You should have left me there.

A letter from Natalie?
I am a rag
on a barbed wire fence
You
should have left me there
No—no such thing as a letter from her; something she once wrote. One of the scraps she would leave for him to find anywhere at all, on the dashboard shelf of the car, beside the tub in the bathroom. Her affectation; her communication.

She could have been a writer. Her candle flame. Could have been the writer, the architect, the 'creative' couple. The family foursome, how satisfactory: along with the doctor and the provider of housing loans for the homeless. *Affordable*—there's that word coined for our time, for what you can get out of it without going too far for safety, good old Khulu's way to acceptance: he's afford- able by white males, in their beds.

She could have been a writer. To have put her to work in an advertising agency, inventing jingling fashionable lies to make peo- ple buy things they must be persuaded, brain-washed to need, want—this was the betrayal of that possibility. She showed con- tempt for my choice by doing something outrageous instead of using words against me because I'd debased *words*, for her, finally. I'd shut her up.

It wasn't her, it was him I shut up finally.

Always trying to win her round by bolstering her confidence in herself (that was it) imagining that by praising, always telling her how intelligent she is—

She laughed: How do you measure your dog's intelligence? By how it obeys commands!

The city's body-smell of urine and street-stall flowers. Not yet winter. Not even autumn quite passed, up at the window.

Jagged end.

What's that. Not something of hers, again. No.

Jagged end of a continent.

L'Agulhas.

It was with Carl, there. The sea shimmering into the shallows as the tide rose; rocks (L'Agulhas, 'the needles' in Portuguese, he explains, the Northerner who amuses himself by teaching the Southerner what he ought to know about his own country). The rocks bloodied in lichen. It was exciting, the two of them with the weight and distance of the continent behind them, sitting on the edge of existence there. They are only just out of reach of the heaving anger of the two oceans as the powers of opposing currents clash, Indian and Atlantic. With her—oh it was another place, the Indian alone from which she was dragged back to breathe. At the Atlantic it was with him. Where the two oceans meet, it's fatal. With Carl, come to the end of it all. When that happened someone picked up the gun and shot him in the head.

Jagged end.

Those who want an eye for an eye, a murderer for a murderer; they won't put it behind him. Harald does not know whether in this conviction, of which Claudia is probably and mercifully ignorant, he should offer: Perhaps he could go and practise in another country.

Out of something terrible something new, to be lived with in a different way, surely, than life was before? This is the country for themselves, here, now. For Harald a new relation with his God, the God of the suffering he could not have had access to, before. Claudia—she came out with something that plunged him into the disorientation within her, which he had not realized.

Perhaps we should try for a child.

That she should allow herself to turn to this illusion, a doctor, forty-seven years old . . . what hope could there be of conception, another Duncan, in her body.

I'm not menopausal yet.

He was tumescent with her pain, he made love to her anyway, for the impossibility. It was the first time since the messenger entered the townhouse and it was unlike any love-making they had experienced ever before in their life together, a ritual neither believed in, performed in bereaved passion.

The first months moved past them. Then old routines began to draw them along, in a return: the old contacts of every day, the context of responsibilities, faces, documents, decisions affecting others, whether to prescribe this or that antidote for someone else's kind of pain, whether the rise in bank rates could be contained without raising the monthly payments on housing loans, decisions in which a man dead on a sofa, a trial, seven or five years, had no relevance. Nothing else for it; nothing else for them. Only, in place of the usual leisure activities, the visits, the drive out of town is to another city, where long-term sentences are served.

A business colleague invites Harald to lunch. The man has just recovered from double bypass surgery on a heart blocked by thickened blood, and he eats all the richest choices on the menu. It seems to have been some kind of demonstration; he says, smiling, for Harald: —You have to die.— It's a delicate way of referring to and offering consolation for disaster, all suffer it one way or another, we're all people in trouble.

Harald and Claudia are taken up again in their own circle, no reason to keep contact with that communal household, that cottage no doubt occupied by new tenants. Baker, in whose bedroom in the house the gun was supposed to be out of reach, hardly could be expected to face in that living-room the parents of his lover's murderer, even if they could have brought themselves to be there. And Claudia had never entered the cottage after the messenger had told what he had to tell. The personal belongings of the previous tenant have been removed to the townhouse by a professional firm. Apparently as a mark of consideration, fellow occupants of the townhouse complex have not complained to Harald and Claudia that the continued presence of the dog is against the rules.

They have lost touch with Khulu. Unfortunately. Just as you lose touch with the one who is shut away from the course of your life long determined, so the circumstances that surrounded the period of crisis in that one's life produced their own strange intimacies which do not belong with the necessity of taking up daily life as you know how to live it. They haven't seen Motsamai again. Khulu visits Duncan—Duncan says, or rather this comes out in passing, in the exchange that takes place on a tacit level which avoids certain references and unanswerable questions, between him and his parents when they visit. Exchange of personal news; for Duncan now has his kind of news, he has completed the plan he was working on, a detailed favourable report from fellow architects on the project has come back (virtue of Motsamai's buddy relations with the prison commandant). Next visit, he can tell that he has permission to start studying for an advanced diploma in town planning. And the following month it is that he is—yes—taking on care of his health by working-out in his cell night and morning. He makes them laugh a little at the idea of his makeshift gym.

He looks well.

If somehow different from the way they carry his image within them, as some people carry a photograph in a wallet as an identification of commitment; his face carved more boldly, roughly, and the tendons showing in the neck of that prison garment those of a man older than twenty-seven. It's the way, when he was at boarding school, there was a visage, an outline in the mind that was not quite that of the boy they visited at the school; took out for lunch, when there was occasion to talk to him seriously about something.

It occurs to Harald that whenever they leave the prison now it is as it was when they left him at school. The span of time ahead, unthinkable seven years or five years, is telescoped to something by which it can be understood.

He knows that there is the unanswered question in their regard on him every time they visit; needing a response. The judge stated it as a fact, not a question. 'He has shown no remorse.' How could they know, any of them, what they have a word for. How could they know what they are thinking, talking about. Harald and Claudia, my poor parents, do you want your little boy to come in tears to say I'm sorry? Will it all be mended, a window I smashed with a ball? Shall I be a civilized human being again, for the one, and will God forgive and cleanse me, for the other. Is that what they think it is, this thing, remorse.

He brought me a book when I was awaiting trial, I think it was when he was so angry, so horrified that *he* wanted to accuse, punish me, but there was something in it he didn't, doesn't, never can know. The passage about the one who did it and the one to whom it was done. 'It is absurd for the murderer to outlive the murdered. They two, alone together—as two beings are together in only one other human relationship, the one acting, the other suffering him—share a secret that binds them forever together. They belong to each other.'

Writers are dangerous people. How is it that a writer knows these things? Only that this time it is the three of us, alone together. In the 'human relationship'—love-making and all the rest—Carl acted, I suffered him, I acted, Natalie suffered me, and that night on the sofa they acted and I suffered them both. We belong to each other.

I've copied that quotation again and again, don't know how many times, in the middle of the night from memory I've written it on a scrap of paper the way she used to scribble a line for a poem, I've stopped in the middle of a section, when I was concentrating on my plan, and had to write it out somewhere. He's dead, and he and she and I share a secret that binds us forever together. You couldn't put it better than that; he's dead, I somehow took up the gun and shot him in the head. There's another passage in that book; about the one who does it. 'He has gratified his heart's deepest desire.' When I found them like that, my deepest desire—what was it? If only I knew what it was I wanted, of what I saw was their betrayal or consummation of us three, and if because I couldn't have whatever it was I wanted, my deepest desire was gratified when I shot my lover and her lover. He's dead, I'm alive, rejoicing with all of them—my parents, Motsamai—that there's no Death Penalty any more. The murderer has outlived the murdered. Try and tell this to my judges, the one in court and the ones in the townhouse. It cannot be told, only be lived, in this walled space made for it. What's outside, what I can see from the Tantalus window when I stand on the bed—out there, after seven years (five, Motsamai promises), will it be put behind me, will the one who is dead and I not belong to each other still. I should ask an old lag that; we didn't move in the circle of criminals, in the house and the cottage. So many things we didn't know, never should have needed to know. The three of us, Carl, dead, Natalie and I alive, Nastasya my victim and, as Khulu says, Natalie my torturer, wherever she is, in what I've done we're bound together, whether she ever knows it or not, whether or not what she has in her womb is another secret.

The CD player is stored at the townhouse with other things. No music in these nights between these days of my seven years. The narrow aperture of the window keeps surveillance while the Judas eye in the door is shut; what disciple of functional architecture thought up specification for that lozenge of a window which divides so satisfyingly into segments made by vertical bars. The night cut in five pieces.

No player yet there are passages I'm hearing over and over, the adagio movement from Beethoven's 'Tempest' and the allegretto of a Schubert impromptu. He and I used to go to concerts in that time, the L'Agulhas time. With him there was more than Brubeck and who was the other jazz man. The deceased had a collection of recordings, Penderecki and Stockhausen, too. Listening to music that is formed in your own head, is there without any agency of reproduction— how? how?—through the hours you begin to know what music is. It's one of the ways—only one of the ways—in which order can be selected, put together, out of the original chaos. With her, I listened to this Beethoven and Schubert for my ears alone, through headphones; it's a bit like that now. She didn't want to listen; I see it wasn't because she needed to be tutored in appreciation etc., by me. It was because she was in rebellion against the principle of order; in anything, everything, that's why she never finished the poems.

There has to be a way.

Of course, if I were to 'confess' all this to Motsamai he'd get busy with grounds of remorse and maybe even succeed—he's a wizard in his devotion to his clients—in getting an earlier remission than he's conned me to count on. But then all this that I live would be taken away from me; I couldn't endure, without it, this space made for it.

The Last Judgment of the Constitutional Court has declared the Death Penalty unconstitutional. The firm and gentle tone of the Judge President has the confidence of a man who while he is conveying the ruling arrived at after several months of weighing scrupulously the findings of a bench of independent thinkers, himself has been given grace. There is a serenity in justice.

If the decision had been for the State, once again, to have the right to take a life for a life, it would have been too late to decree that Duncan should be hanged one early morning in Pretoria. He was already secured by his sentence: seven years. Yet the news sets her visibly trembling; he takes her two hands to steady her; and himself. The ultimate sentence held off by a moratorium was the threat that it still existed; on the Statute Book, even Motsamai had said. And while it still existed it would always have been what, for their son's act one Friday night, could have been exacted. So it is release, relief, a curious trace, like happiness; how strange that it should be possible to feel anything like this. Duncan is still where he is.

Harald and Claudia decided to go away. On holiday. It is

awkward to admit this to Duncan, in the visitors' room. He says, About time you took a break! How long is it?

But let's avoid that; the last holiday was before, when there was a customary systole and diastole between work and reward. Many months have passed for him where he is and them outside.

To the Cape. —Didn't you once go to L'Agulhas? Would it appeal to us, you think?—

—It's the end of the continent—he says, in homage.

—Or maybe Hermanus. But we'd rather like to try somewhere new.—

Wherever it was that they did go, flew, took the car, the beckoning world was beautiful. He was in his cell and a wretched child covered his head with his arms as he slept in the streets of Cape Town beneath the eternal mountain that made you want to live, as it does, forever. What looked, from the perspective of a moving car, like the refuse dump of a city was a vast low surface of board, tin, plastic rags and people reduced to detritus under a sky gloriously feathered, a cosmic bird, cirrus gilded by light shining from billions of miles away. A splendid night shuddered thunder with lightning fleeing in all directions. The serene sea covered rotting ancient wrecks and present pollution alike with a sheen of lucent colour, and rested the breasts of gulls. You could have walked upon that water, no wonder Harald could believe it once happened.

Signals of life, from everything, in spite of everything. The plane's shadow a great butterfly passing over green, and crops in ear, and lilac desert. From a window, valley lights at night fluttering to attract, attract. Claudia began to have the feeling that she and Harald were waiting for some signal, the signal that would move life on, take them out of the regression in which they had taken refuge, going through the motions, their echoing voices occupying what was emptied of meaning. She tried to think of this in practical terms: perhaps they should leave the townhouse complex as it really was already, void of their life there. Perhaps they should move house.

Could any team of professionals with their packing cases and vans make such a move; and wouldn't it all, the stored possessions that were Duncan's from that cottage along with everything else, be delivered, unloaded, surround Harald and her in the next habitation?

Motsamai made sure that the firm sent Duncan sections of their projects to design. He never saw the completed set of plans for which he was drawing certain vertical, horizontal and lateral projections, aspects from the North and South, East and West. But he thought sometimes how his own work was already achieved: the structure of this cell was his accomplishment, designed to the specifications of his life.

Harald and Claudia did not move. At the beginning of summer there was a call on the answerphone when Harald, as so often, came home to the townhouse before Claudia. The voice was at once familiar: the bass African accent and casual delivery of Khulu. *How're you folks doing? I've been meaning to come round. But you know how time goes, anyway I hear about you from Duncan.*

Claudia did not want to return the call at that house. Harald understood: Baker might answer. He remembered the newspaper for which Khulu had said, in the talk he kept up when the three went to a café between sessions of the court, he did most of his reporting. Harald had his secretary call there several times but without success, and a message was left.

He/she. A summons on the security monitor, on a night when they were not expecting anyone. Claudia answered, this time. Khulu announced himself. When he reached their door, both were there to meet him, there was the keen sense of a pleasure deprived in not having sought him out months ago, themselves. His heavy arms went about each in turn. Animation filled the room, while

Harald fetched drinks, and Khulu called—Claudia, you got bread or something, some fruit, I've been out on a story, nothing in my stomach all day!—

Claudia had a young man for whom to put together a meal. She came back and forth with cold meat and cheese and chutney and bread, and Harald brought the fruit bowl. Khulu ate with in-attentive zest while talking about the changes in ownership of newspapers with the acquisition of a group by blacks. He was proud of this; and sceptical about the advancement of his career that Claudia suggested it would mean for him; Harald lifted a hand in the gesture that came from his experience in matters of financial power, the rivalries which take place up there in board rooms when seats are vacated by one set of backsides and taken up by another. There was laughter at this uninhibited expression of understanding that the mood brought by this visitor made easy.

But Khulu was also a messenger. When he had pushed aside the plate of banana skins and turned in the chair with the beer glass in hand, he made his delivery.

—Duncan wants you to do something about the child. If it's not his, it's Carl's. So Duncan—

Duncan has entered the room, the townhouse. The dog, sleeping beside Harald's chair, might even get up to greet the empty doorway.

No-one speaks, and then Khulu takes a mouthful of beer. He shifts the bowl of fruit to make room for the glass. —So Duncan wants.—

He/she.

—What is it we could do.—

Harald remembers well: —That girl won't have anyone claim the child! What she said in court. It's *hers*.—

—Duncan doesn't agree.—

—What is it he wants—blood tests, Motsamai to start all that? And to what purpose? Prove the child is his and take it from the mother? Where to? To whom? If he succeeded, who's going to take care of a child for seven years. Seven years old, five years perhaps, before he could.—

—I don't think Duncan means that.—

—Then I don't understand it at all. Where the whole idea comes from. Is he losing all sense of reality, shut away there. After all that's happened to him, he's gone through, to rake up this, drag another generation into it.—

—Harald, wait.—

—What can I say—I don't think he means to take the kid from her. No way! Blood tests and all that. The kind of thing the Sunday press puts on the front page. You know Duncan is a thinker, he's got his own idea about whatsit again, paternity.—

—Who knows whether the child is even born yet. Or whether there ever was a child. I've had patients with her kind of history who produce phantom pregnancies. Duncan may be distressing himself for nothing.—

—It's here, it's about a month old.—

Harald sits looking at Claudia until she says as if she already knows: —What is it?—

—A boy.—

—So what do you think Duncan means.— Harald tries to force himself to think of this as a proposition to be put upon the table between the fruit bowl and the glass bleary with beer dregs. —Money?—

—Not so much that, but yes, babies need things, I suppose. Some sort of back-up for her, make sure she can take proper care of it.—

—We don't even know where she is.—

—I know how to find her.—

Perhaps the girl is holed up somewhere with her baby, secret from the world, and she does not know that the men, Duncan and Khulu are after her; for Claudia, who has seen so many births, there was a moment of pure possession like that, for herself after giving birth, she had thought long forgotten. —Perhaps Duncan should leave her alone.—

The two men misunderstand Claudia; what they hear is embittered opposition to any money, back-up, contact, being provided for that girl and her doubtful progeny.

Khulu gently repeats the expression of Duncan's will. —I know where to find her.—

In the family.

This is a matter between them, the three in the townhouse. They part that night with the intimacy of court days restored.

Khulu Dladla has his own knowledge that this couple to whom the fact that he's black and gay doesn't preclude his being, to them, like a son—well, they're white, after all, and what they're appalled by is that they might be expected to prove themselves as parents to their own son by taking in the kid, themselves. As if—with his people—this would need a second's thought! Children belong, never mind any doubts about their origin, in the family.

There was no conception for a forty-seven-year-old. But there is a child.

It is provided for through the offices of Senior Counsel Hamilton Motsamai's chambers; the one condition Harald and Claudia took courage to insist, with Duncan, was that arrangements should be made by Hamilton, and not in personal contact with them. Duncan doesn't demur, let it be as they like, he smiles as if leaving his father, fellow reader, to choose books for him, and he doesn't offer any expression of gratitude, either. Everything is suddenly simple between them; why? Harald wonders whether he has been seeing her, Natalie/Nastasya has her visiting days at the prison? Or she's written letters, her poems. One can't ask. But he's been able to come to them, his parents, with anything at all, even this matter of the child. They're there for him.

Perhaps in time—even five years is long—they'll see the child; Hamilton is confident, as always: he'll get round her just as he led her to condemn herself out of her own mouth under cross examination, he'll arrange what he calls access. Get to know the small boy. Have him at the townhouse, watch him play with the dog.

And Duncan?

Duncan has been granted permission to work in the prison library as well as pursue his studies in his cell. It is not much of a library, in terms of the kind of books that he and Harald have a need to read; the works that are dangerous and indispensable, revealing to you what you are. It's not much used. The long-term prisoners who occupy cells adjoining his are mostly men for whom life has been action not contemplation; in violence, his and theirs, is the escape from self. When you kill the other you are trying to kill the self that plagues your existence. Then only the brute remains to live on, caged: most of them are terrible, filled with mumbling hate, dangling fists clutched to strike again, such hands can't take up these frail objects, binding and paper, that could offer them the only freedom there is, behind these walls.

Who on earth is it who decides what should and should not be suitable for criminals to read, presumably on the criterion that there shall be nothing to rouse the passions that have already raged and destroyed? Rehabilitation. Plenty of religious stuff; as if religion has never roused murderous passion, and is not doing so again, outside the walls. Self-improvement manuals that are seldom taken out: Teach Yourself Bookkeeping and Accountancy, systems for a life that knows no chaos. But among the paper-back stack of mysteries (why should it be considered of interest to inmates to read of fictitious killings when we've performed the real thing?)— among these broken open at the spine as if what was to be found in them was to be cracked like a coconut or prised like an oyster, there are some real books, God knows how they got there. Maybe when you're let out, done your time, as we say in here, it's the form to donate your books for someone who's surely going to come after. I sometimes find something for myself. There's a translation of the Odyssey with fishmoths that have given up the ghost between pages. I've never known this book, its exalted category along with the bible, more than at second-hand from quotations in other books; if Harald's read it he somehow didn't succeed in interesting me. The architecture of ancient Greece—yes of course, that was more my line as a student, and I have the usual stock of bits and pieces of mythology. Oedipus put out his eyes for his crime. That's about all. But now there's something that's for me, that's been waiting for me, in this place, in my time. Time to read and re-read it. 'With that he trained a stabbing arrow on Antinous . . . / just lifting a gorgeous golden loving-cup in his hands,/just tilting the two-handled goblet back to his lips,/about to drain the wine —and slaughter the last thing/on the suitor's mind: who could dream that one foe/in that crowd of feasters, however great his power,/could bring down death on him, and black doom?/But Odysseus aimed and shot Antinous square in the throat/and the point went stabbing clean through the soft neck and out—/and off to the side he pitched, the cup dropped from his grasp/as the shaft sank home.' And there is Odysseus shouting at the other men around Penelope 'You dogs! . . . /so cocksure that you . . . wooed my wife/behind my back while I was still alive!'

The moment when you put your hand out to do it—the man in the madhouse was right, I don't remember that moment but I reconstruct it, I've had to; I've found out that you think it's a *discovery*, it's something that's come to you that has never been known before. But it's always been there, it's been discovered again and again, forever. Again and again, what Odysseus did, and what Homer, whoever he was, knew. Violence is a repetition we don't seem able to break; oh look at them, my brothers—*Bra*, they have the right to claim me, we crowd of feasters on our own carrion in this place made secure for us alone—I look at them when we're in the yard for our exercise, and they tramp and they lope round and round, round and round. I haven't come to the end of the book, I don't know how Odysseus reconstructed what he did, what way he found for himself. Put out your eyes. Turn the gun on your own head.

Or throw away the gun in the garden. That was a choice made. Can you break the repetition just by not perpetrating violence on yourself. I have this life, in here. I didn't give it for his. I'll even get out of here with it, some year or other. The murderer has not been murdered. My luck, this was abolished in my time. But I have to find a way. Carl's death and Natalie's child, I think of one, then the other, then the one, then the other. They become one, for me. It does not matter whether or not anyone else will understand: Carl, Natalie/Nastasya and me, the three of us. I've had to find a way to bring death and life together.